THE SEELIE KING'S WAR

Books by
JANE YOLEN

Books by
ADAM STEMPLE

Singer of Souls
Steward of Song

Books by JANE YOLEN and ADAM STEMPLE

Pay the Piper: A Rock 'n' Roll Fairy Tale
Troll Bridge: A Rock 'n' Roll Fairy Tale
B.U.G. (Big Ugly Guy)

The Seelie Wars
The Hostage Prince
The Last Changeling
The Seelie King's War

THE
SEELIE KING'S WAR

THE SEELIE WARS: BOOK III

Jane Yolen & Adam Stemple

VIKING

VIKING
An imprint of Penguin Random House LLC
375 Hudson Street
New York, New York 10014

First published in the United States of America by Viking,
an imprint of Penguin Random House LLC, 2016

LIBRARY OF CONGRESS CATALOGING-IN-PUBLICATION DATA
Names: Yolen, Jane, author. | Stemple, Adam, author.
Title: The Seelie king's war / Jane Yolen and Adam Stemple.
Description: New York, New York : Viking, an imprint of Penguin Random
House LLC, 2016. | Series: The Seelie Wars ; book 3 | Summary: "Aspen (the
hostage prince) and Snail (the midwife's apprentice) must gather an army
to face the Unseelie forces that want to destroy Aspen's home country"
—Provided by publisher.
Identifiers: LCCN 2015040304 | ISBN 9780670014361 (hardcover : alk. paper)
Subjects: | CYAC: Fantasy. | Princes—Fiction. | War—Fiction.
Classification: LCC PZ7.Y78 Sci 2016 | DDC [Fic]—dc23 LC record available at
http://lccn.loc.gov/2015040304

Printed in USA

1   3   5   7   9   10   8   6   4   2

Designed by Eileen Y. Savage
Set in Galliard

For the real Maggie Light.

—J.Y.

For Tom and the Lady Jody,
landed gentry of the highest quality.

—A.S.

N

King Obs's Keep

Wester
Tower

Great Midden
Heap

Water
Gate

UNSEELIE
CASTLE

Unseelie
Lands

Shifting Lands

The
SHIFTING LANDS
include the following:

The Speaking Plains
❖
Birch Braes
❖
The Wild Woods
❖
Ea's Falls
❖
The Crooked Steppes
❖
Esker Hills
❖
The Hunting Grounds
❖
Lake Country

CONTENTS

THE
SEELIE KING'S WAR

ASPEN, THE NEW SEELIE KING

*K*ing Ailenbran Astaeri, Bright Celestial, Ruire of the Tir na nOg, and Lord of the Seelie kingdom, who for a brief time had been known as Karl the minstrel, and who still thought of himself as Prince Aspen, looked out the throne room window through the shifting panes of glass that showed both near views and far. He looked at the green fields of Faerie, the golden fields of the farmland full of wheat, the scrub fields of the mountainsides where only wild flowers flourished on the disturbed ground—poppies and willow herb and wild onion. He watched for a time and tried not to think about what they would look like in a fortnight or two.

He failed.

The crops will be trampled flat by Unseelie feet, the roads clogged with siege engines and soldiers. The smoke of burning buildings and bowers will darken the sky, and the night creatures will march in the day.

Aspen shuddered and chewed at the already savaged

thumbnail on his left hand. *Karl the minstrel would find it hard to play the lute with that finger*, he thought bitterly. Not that he'd been much of a minstrel. And he certainly wasn't going to have time to be much of a king. A king only because his father and brothers had died in the first days of the Seelie Wars.

A war I started, he thought miserably, *because I was tricked into it. Because I was stupid, cowardly, and much too easily guiled by that scheming, sharp-beaked drow, Old Jack Daw.*

He scrunched his eyes shut but couldn't stop his self-recriminations.

A war, he thought bitterly, *which will surely be called the Seelie King's War, and not without reason. After all, as Hostage Prince, I ran off—no matter that I had been tricked into it. So the Unseelie king had every right to invade this land. My father's land.*

"Ahhhh!" Aspen screamed, and pushed himself away from the window. It was suddenly very quiet, and Aspen remembered he wasn't alone.

Just moments ago, the throne room had been filled with the soft hiss of counselors' whispered conversations, the *scritch-scratch* of scribes' quills, the swish of the servants' and maids' footsteps as they scurried in and out of the large room on slippered feet. But now everyone had stopped what they'd been doing and stood staring at their monarch.

"Erm . . ." Aspen hesitated. *What would a real king do in this situation?* He tried to ignore the nagging thought that a real king wouldn't find himself stuttering and blushing in front of a roomful of his subjects.

He also probably would not have spent his first week of rule asking everyone he met the three unanswerable questions he'd been ensorcelled with:

What is the Sticksman?

How does one become the Sticksman?

How does the Sticksman come not to be once more?

Luckily, by now Aspen had interrogated everyone who worked in or around the castle, so he could hold normal conversations.

So what would a real king do?

And then it came to him. *A real king would bark orders and make proclamations.* He forced what he hoped was a confident smirk onto his face. *I can do that.*

"Fetch Snail!" he shouted at his steward, Balnar, an elf so old that he had not enough magic left to keep his hair from going steely grey. Aspen tried to make his order sound kingly and proud. By the way Balnar bowed smartly and rushed from the room, Aspen felt as if he'd accomplished at least that much.

But then he thought about how what he said could be interpreted and pictured the steward and some of the few uninjured soldiers at the palace rousting Snail out of bed and dragging her bodily to the throne room. . . .

"Wait!" he called after the steward, his voice cracking and sounding most unkingly. "Stop him!" he yelled at the counselors. They jumped to their feet and scurried after the steward. The scribes were halfway out of their seats as well, looking confused. Aspen realized that even he was several steps toward the door when Balnar returned.

Straightening up and tugging down the hem of his golden tunic, Aspen took a deep breath. "Go to the Lady Snail's chambers and ask her politely if she would join me."

"Your Grace," the steward said, and this time he left the room at a more stately pace.

Aspen glared at the rest of the room, and the counselors, scribes, and servants swiftly returned to their tasks. Then he chewed at his thumbnail some more and hoped Snail arrived before he got down to the bone.

◆ ◆ ◆

WHEN SNAIL FINALLY entered the room, her mismatched eyes conveyed concern and anger in equal parts. She had probably been up half the night tending to her patients, the ones who could—possibly—be saved. Aspen could tell she'd been woken. Her red hair was more flyaway than usual, and she'd obviously had no time to pull it back. She did not bother asking him what was wrong. She knew. Everyone knew: an Unseelie army was marching toward the castle, and they had no hope of stopping it.

"Out," she said, and Aspen almost headed for the door himself before he realized she was speaking to the rest of the room.

They hesitated. Snail had no title, no official standing. She was not even fey but a changeling, a human child stolen from her parents shortly after birth and brought to Faerie to work as a drudge or servant in the Unseelie Court. But she was also Aspen's only friend and best counselor. He had made it very clear from the beginning that her words were as close to law as his.

The room cleared. Quickly. Only Balnar had the gall to frown. But it was the same frown he used for any breach in decorum, and he'd shot Aspen the same look at last night's dinner when Aspen had used the wrong utensil to spear a rutabaga.

As hostage in the Unseelie Court from the time he was seven, Aspen had often picked up root vegetables from a plate with his fingers. Not that too many vegetables were served in the Unseelie Court. Carnivorous lot, they were.

Once Balnar left, Aspen turned to Snail. "Good of you to come."

She gave a shallow and ironic curtsey. "Did I have a choice?"

"Always," he said seriously.

Snail's face colored for the briefest of seconds before she shook it off. "Why did you call for me? Has something changed?" She didn't sound hopeful.

"No." Aspen sighed. "We still face certain death in a few days."

She hopped up onto the giant throne that dominated the room and perched birdlike on the arm.

Like everything else in Astaeri Palace, the throne was gilded, gaudy, and garish. Rubies sat side by side with diamonds and jade, silver filigree fighting with gold gilding. Even the throne's cushioned seat was decorated with pearls. *Though*—Aspen thought miserably—*all the jewels will be picked out in a couple of days by Unseelie monsters gathering treasures.*

As a child, Aspen had thought the throne magnificent. But since escaping the Unseelie Court with Snail, he seemed to see things more through her eyes than his own. Instead of a bejeweled, golden throne from which the bright and beautiful monarchs of Faerie dispensed justice, he now saw an oversized and wildly uncomfortable chair from which he was supposed to rule over a kingdom whose whole history was one of betrayal, slavery, and death.

Snail leaned over and patted the cushion. "Have a seat."

Aspen shook his head. "I do not want to. And I do not deserve to. I am no king and this is no kingdom." He frowned. "Or rather, even if it was once, it will not be in a few days."

"No!" Snail barked at him. "We've come too far to give up now. We just need a little help."

Aspen could not stop himself; he smiled at her.

"Don't smile at me," she said. "I most mistrust you when you smile."

Aspen sat down on the windowsill, still avoiding the throne. The smile, so quickly come, was now gone. "There is no help. There is only you and me." He looked out the window again, focusing on the pane that showed the grass in the palace garden. He wondered idly how long it would remain green. "You and me."

Suddenly Aspen's head snapped up, and he turned back to Snail. "You!"

"Me?"

"Yes!" Aspen hopped off the sill and went back to the dais that held the throne. "You. *You* are human."

Snail's mouth turned down. "What's your point, fey?" she growled.

How quickly her temper turns, he thought. For some reason this made him smile again. *If she thinks she's angry now, wait till she hears what I want her to do. What I need her to do.*

"That is where we get our help," he said.

"I don't under—" She stopped cold, and he saw the understanding hit her, widening her mismatched eyes. "No."

"Yes!" Aspen said, and grabbed her hand. "You have to."

Snatching her hand away, Snail almost looked frightened, though he was not sure she ever felt that particular emotion. Snail always seemed to channel fear into anger and energy.

"I . . . I can't. I don't know where to find him, anyway. And even if I did find him, he wouldn't come." Snail's words tumbled out as if they were stones over a waterfall.

"Why would he want to help you? What does it matter to him which oppressor king wins?"

"Because I can offer him something that Old Jack Daw won't."

"What's that?" Snail asked.

"Freedom," he said.

"For everyone?"

"Every. Last. One. Plus a piece of land, so they feel vested in it. And for those who choose not to stay after the war, a parting gift of gold to help them on their way to wherever they wish to go."

"Even if it means returning to the world of humans. Where your people stole them from in the first place?"

"Even then," he said, though he knew as well as she did what dangers lay there. He hoped that wasn't the route she decided to take.

Snail pushed herself slowly off the throne. Took a step toward the edge of the dais, then stepped back.

Aspen didn't dare speak. He barely breathed. *This is the only way. I am sure of it.*

She glared at him in that sharp, bossy way she had before asking, "Why should he trust you?"

He was ready for that. "Because *you* do."

"And why should *I* trust you?"

He wasn't ready for that. *How can she ask me that? After all we've been through? How many times have I saved her life?*

How many times has she saved mine? He almost blurted all this out, but then he saw the look on her face and realized that she *did* trust him. But she needed something solid to bring to the old man. In one smooth movement, Aspen swept his sword from the scabbard at his side and knelt before her. He held it with his palms upward, offering it to her. It glowed with a golden light.

"Snail, this is the sword of my father and his father and all our fathers back to before the worlds were separated, before the courts split, when mortal and fey lived as one under an endless sun. It carries a piece of that sun within it and only glows for the trueborn ruler of Faerie." He looked up at her and hoped she could sense the power in his words and realize he spoke not just truth but geas, the truth become magic, become prophecy. The words his mother had taught him when she handed him the sword. "If my words prove false, let this sword break in twain and no Astaeri rule for a hundred thousand years."

Snail's eyes were bright as she nodded. "All right."

Aspen stood, smiling, and sheathed the sword. "Balnar!" he shouted, and the old elf entered the throne room instantly, bowing low, a perfect and proper six paces away from his liege. Aspen was certain Balnar had overheard every word he and Snail had just said to each other. He was also certain Balnar would never speak of it to another soul.

"Your Grace?"

"Fetch General Limnith and tell her to ready her seven best soldiers to travel." He turned to Snail. "Sorry it is so few, but—"

"But it's near a fifth of what's left of your standing army," she said.

She was joking, but it was close enough to the truth that Aspen could not bring himself to laugh.

"Shall I tell her why, Your Grace?" Balnar asked.

"You may, but only speak of it to the general. They are to guard Snail as she goes to raise an army."

Snail leapt off the dais, landing before Balnar. She lifted her chin to look way up at him. Aspen could see the old steward trying desperately not to look down his nose at her.

"A human army," she said, daring Balnar to comment, but all he said was "Your Grace" to Aspen, and "My lady" to Snail, then he bowed low and left the room. Snail watched him go, and then turned to Aspen.

"Tell the professor I said hello," Aspen said.

"I don't think I will."

"Stay safe."

"I don't think I can."

Aspen nodded. "Bring me an army, Snail."

Snail set her mouth firmly and gave a short nod. "I'll try." Then she walked stiffly out of the room.

Aspen wondered if he would ever see her again. He turned and looked out the window, this time through the pane filled with waving grains of wheat. He pictured the fields filling with Unseelie soldiers—trolls and boggarts, Red Caps, dire werewolves, jostling drows trampling the gold. But this time he was trying to figure out how to hold the castle walls for even an extra hour.

Snail would need every bit of time he could give her.

I will buy that hour with my life if need be. For Faerie, he thought.

And for Snail.

SNAIL ON THE ROAD

Snail hadn't time to change or pull her hair back into a horsetail. Luckily she'd taken a bath before falling asleep, mostly to wash off the blood and flesh, pus and puke that had adhered to her skin. As a midwife's apprentice, she'd learned a lot about cleanliness. But as a battlefield doctor . . . well, things weren't quite that simple.

And that so-called sleep of hers had been much delayed because of the numbers of wounded she'd been tending at the Astaeri chapel, where carvings of winged feylings watched hollow-eyed over the wounded and dying. Then what sleep she finally fell into had been cut brutally short by the steward's wake-up call.

That nipped-nose busybody, toffier than a toff was what she thought of him, rarely addressing him by name. *Balnar. Whatever that name means. Probably,* she thought, *it translates into knee bender. Or bottom polisher.*

When he woke her, she told him some of what she was thinking. If it bothered him, he'd made no reply. Either he was too well schooled to show his annoyance or those words didn't translate easily into High Court Seelie.

She'd wanted to tell Aspen off as well, but doing so in the throne room, especially when he looked so miserable, made the words feel like an infant's whine-stopper in her mouth.

And then Aspen had suddenly grinned at her, and all she wanted to do was bop him on the nose. But kings—even sort-of-friendly kings who have rescued you as often as you've rescued them—don't take lightly to being bopped. On the nose or anywhere else.

So she'd glared at him. It wasn't as if she hadn't glared at him before.

Aspen.

Her old companion.

Her *only* friend.

She never called him by his king name—which was unsayable, syllable after syllable tumbling out. She'd tried to pronounce it as they'd flown from the last battlefield to the castle on that flying rug creature, the bowser.

Aspen had watched as she'd struggled with it.

"Just keep calling me Aspen," he'd said at last. "Or Prince. Or Hey You! I'm not really . . . any different now."

"Except for that gold thing," she'd told him, meaning the golden aura of the Seelie king, which seemed to come and go without his knowing it, or at least without his acknowledging it, except for a swift grimace every now and then as if the gold actually hurt.

❧ ❧ ❧

As Snail raced down the stairs, trailed by seven soldiers who were the new king's gift to her on this impossible task—bodyguards or watchdogs, she didn't know which—she said that long, silly name aloud. "King Ailenbran Astaeri, Bright Celestial, Ruire of the Tir na nOg, and Lord of the Seelie kingdom."

It was a mouthful. She *knew* Aspen. Trusted him. Even liked him. But she didn't really know this Ailenbran person.

"Yes, your ladyship?" asked the soldier closest to her, a tall elf with her hair shorn to the roots. Only the red buttons on her shoulders proclaimed her sex, clan allegiance, and rank, though not her name. She was female. Of the House of the Poppy. She seemed to be the one in charge. "Do you need to speak again to His Majesty?"

"No, just . . . just trying out his name."

"It's hard for strangers," the woman said.

But Snail wasn't a stranger, not to Aspen, the Hostage Prince. Not to the poor captive prince in the Unseelie Court who had been tricked into breaking the truce. Not to Karl the minstrel—Aspen's runaway name—with whom she'd battled ogres, trolls, drows, carnivorous mermen, never abandoning one another. It was only this new King Ailenbran who was strange.

But I haven't changed, she thought. *Not at all. Well, not often, anyway.*

"My lady . . . ?" the elf guard asked.

Snail realized the silent conversation she was having with herself must have shown on her face.

"Just practicing," she said. She didn't say for what, and the guard didn't ask.

But she grunted and looked Snail up and down.

Snail knew her type. Hard to the core, no room for compromise, quick to make decisions, quicker to choose sides. She'd met quite a number of them in the three days of saving what Seelie soldiers she could, bringing them back to the Seelie fortress on the flying bowser, some of them raving with fever, some of them weeping their losses.

That was when she'd learned the names and totems of the Seelie clans. She'd felt it was the least she could do for those in her charge. The best she had was long spent in her own private battle against rent flesh, broken bones, and gushing blood. And burying the ones who didn't make it, the majority of her patients. When the last who could be saved had been delivered to the castle, and she'd looked around for the bowser to thank him for his hard work, he'd disappeared.

"Gone off," a palace guard had told her. "Just flapped itself up into the air, spun over the place twice, and disappeared." Wearily, he pointed to the south. "That way."

Remembering all this, Snail turned to the Poppy soldier. "Tell me your name, warrior," she said carefully. They preferred the term *warrior* to *soldier*. Snail felt strongly that if she was to die on this commission from the king, she should honor the names of those who would die with her.

"Alith, m'lady," said the elven guard without the slightest hint of sniffery.

"My name is Snail," Snail returned. "At least, that's what my stepmother called me, and what the king prefers, and is as close to a real name as I have. I had another, but it didn't stick." *Sofie*, she thought, but didn't say it aloud. She nodded at Alith. "And I'm no real lady, you know, just a battle pal of the king's."

One of the soldiers, his buttons blue and green, like Snail's eyes, snickered behind them and whispered loud enough to be heard: "*Battle pal*, that what they call it now?"

Snail made no move to silence him, but Alith turned and glared.

"One more such outburst, *soldier*," Alith told him, the term diminishing him in public, "and you will be sent home in disgrace." Her face was stern enough to be made out of wood. "The king has sent the *doctor*"—she emphasized Snail's position—"on a mission so secret, neither you nor I know aught about it but to obey m'lady's every command. And you *will* obey, or I shall battlefield you, and no one will bring me to account for it. I am of the House of the Poppy, the house where General Limnith resides. I am daughter of her first family and hold the records of the house in both archery and the sword. You are an upstart of an upstart house, here only because your betters died so recently in battle, they have not yet even been praised and sung into the earth."

At that moment, Snail knew that Alith would get her where she needed to go or die for her.

Or both.

❖ ❖ ❖

AT THE BOTTOM of the castle steps, a pair of equerries held the reins of seven horses, two rangy roans, three blacks, two greys.

Horses! Snail thought. *Why does it have to be horses?* The bowser had been bad enough, but she'd managed all right because he'd liked her. Understood her. But the closest she'd ever gotten to a horse was to the unicorns who pulled Odds's wagons, and they were skittish beasts with minds tuned only to grass, grain, and water.

She knew that on the bowser, flying high over the heads of the Unseelie folk, she'd be able to watch their maneuvers, spy them long before they were even aware she wasn't just a strange bird overhead.

But horses . . .

"These are our fastest steeds," Alith was saying. She took the reins of one of the roans, about one-third the size of a unicorn. "This one is gentle, and she will listen to your hands."

"My *hands?*"

"On the reins, m'lady." She handed the reins to Snail,

who eyed the horse with a certain amount of distaste. The mare eyed her back in much the same way.

Alith came close, almost whispering in Snail's ear. "You . . . er . . . *have* ridden before, m'lady? Yes?"

Snail hissed back, "I was a midwife's apprentice before. . . . We didn't have a lot of horses. But I helped drive a team of unicorns in the war." She didn't add that this meant she'd mostly sat talking to Dagmarra the dwarf who did the actual driving, holding on to a rein only when asked to, which was practically never.

"Well, speak to the mare as you do to a laboring woman, with kindness intermixed with authority. She just wants to please you, bred for it, though it may take her a while to figure that out."

That made as much sense to Snail as anything could. She leaned in and said to the little horse, "I will guide you if you will guide me, horse." But even she could hear the uncertainty in her voice.

The mare shook her head.

"Her name is Goodspeed," said Alith. "Blow softy into her nostrils first. Your breath will become her breath."

"Listen, Goodspeed," said Snail, sending a breath into the horse's soft nostrils, one side and then the other, "I'm as new to you as you to me. So we will learn together. But . . ." And then she spoke the last four words with the authority of a midwife, battle doctor, and gravedigger. "But go we must."

"And," Alith said, "with good speed."

"With good speed," Snail repeated, just as the equerry moved close to help her mount.

❖ ❖ ❖

THEY RODE SOUTH, which was where the king's foresters had informed the general that Professor Odds and the changeling hordes had been heading. The foresters knew, because if any king's deer was killed—a deed punishable by death—it lit up a sorcerer's map in the Royal Forester's Hall. But King Ailenbran had granted the changeling army dispensation to hunt his deer, though they may not have known it, so they were safe from prosecution. Snail had been so proud of Aspen then, though hadn't told him so. Now she wished she had.

As they rode on, Snail leaned over her horse's neck often to tell her what a good, swift companion she was. At each word, the little roan seemed to move faster.

"Thank you, Alith," Snail whispered under her breath.

Snail supposed that they were making good time, but the paths through the woods seemed endless, and endlessly similar. The trees were unmoving bark-clad sentinels they had to maneuver around. Some had even fallen down and blocked paths, which meant two of the soldiers—a different pair each time—had to dismount and haul the offending greenery to one side.

They also had to rest the horses at frequent intervals.

At one such rest, Alith had explained, "The horses cannot keep going without a stop. They will if you ask them to. They will burst their hearts for you. But then they will be dead, and you will have no way to move quickly."

The bowser needed no such stops, Snail thought. *He simply flew us where we wanted to go, then lay on the ground, spread out like the rug he so closely resembled, and slept until called upon again.* She suddenly remembered one time when she'd been so exhausted she could hardly stand, dropping down in the meadow grass right next to him. While she was sleeping, he'd wrapped himself around her, and she'd slept to the bowser's snores like the rumble of thunder before heavy rains. She doubted a horse could do that. Goodspeed or not.

AHEAD, THE TREES seemed to thin out, and the moon was already high above the tips of the tallest firs.

Alith held up a hand. "We camp here."

The excuse she offered Snail was that the horses needed the stop, but Snail suspected Alith knew that she either had to get off Goodspeed or drop off. Her thighs felt loose and wobbly. And her back felt as if someone had stuck old Chef Bonetooth's sharpest cleaver into the lower part of her spine.

"We all need sleep," Alith added.

Snail doubted that. No one else looked in the least bit tired.

"How long, sir?" asked one of the men, a hawk-nosed fey with a row of crooked teeth who looked far older than the others. An army commander, it seemed, was always a "sir," never a "ma'am."

"We'll take an hour-long watch each, Snaggle," Alith told him.

Snaggle, Snail thought, almost giddy with exhaustion. *How appropriate.*

"We leave at first light." Alith turned to Snail. "A few hours only, m'lady." It was both a warning and an apology.

Snail nodded. "Understood."

She dropped off of Goodspeed immediately, then dropped into slumber almost as fast.

ASPEN'S MEETINGS

With Snail gone, Aspen threw himself into devising a clever scheme sure to save the castle from the approaching horde. At least, that was his plan.

First he talked to his generals again, General Limnith of the Home Guard and long-retired general Frogmouth PondHopper. They met in a small, private chamber off the throne room.

Balnar shuffled around, moving thick tapestries aside so sunlight could shine through the mundane glass, speaking little but absorbing a great deal.

General Limnith stood straight and tall and severely beautiful as she reported to Aspen the impossibility of their situation.

"We could not defend these walls against a one-armed boggart with a wooden eye and a dodgy hip."

It was the same thing she had said to him after the last of the battle refugees had been flown in. Aspen thought the general's remark odd, given that she herself limped and wore a patch over an eye lost in the last Seelie War.

The bowser had been magnificent in its flights, never hesitating nor complaining, nor—as far as others could see—flagging.

But to Aspen, the animated rug had looked worn, dusty, grey. He would have ordered the bowser cleaned and brushed when the last Seelie folk had been brought into the castle, but when he looked around, the thing could not be found.

"East," a guard had said, pointing southeast, toward the coast.

At the time, Aspen had been angry at the bowser's flight from them. But afterward he realized how little he understood about made things. Did they have a natural wear-out the way magic things did? Or did they go on forever? He decided just to be grateful for all that the bowser had done.

"Even if your lady Snail finds this professor of yours," the general went on, "even if she convinces him to bring his people to the castle, *and* they get here on time, a mess of mud-men manning the ramparts will be about as much use as a boar at a birthing."

Aspen wondered if the "boar at a birthing" metaphor was a jab at Snail's former occupation but quickly decided the general did not mean anything by it.

"And, yes," Limnith added, flicking her long silver braid

for emphasis, "I think sending a midwife's apprentice to raise an army is an exceptionally poor way of running a war, though a very good way to lose it."

Or I could be wrong, Aspen thought.

He was about to reprimand her when PondHopper snapped at a passing fly.

General PondHopper had been ancient before Aspen's father had been born, though terrifically loyal, as all of the Toad Clan were. Balnar had reminded Aspen of this just the day before.

"Pond!" barked Limnith, which startled the old frog prince into closing his mouth and saluting.

She turned back to Aspen. "Majesty, my apologies. That is the problem with bringing these old *amphis* out of retirement."

"We had no choice," Aspen told her quickly. "As we have no choice in sending a *midwife–field surgeon*"—he made the distinction quite clear—"off on a mission of great moment."

The general wasn't slow. She understood his emphasis, realized her mistake, and nodded solemnly. Then she saluted briskly before taking PondHopper's withered right arm in hers, marching them both out the door before Aspen could dismiss them.

Well, he thought, sighing, *that went about as well as could be expected.*

As soon as the generals left, Balnar—always anticipating his king's next move—ushered in a trio of invited Seelie architects. Aspen had wondered if there might have been something in the palace's structure that he and the generals had overlooked in thinking about defenses. These architects were from the greatest schools, scholars of the art, some even descendants of the palace designers. Having been raised primarily in the Unseelie Court, Aspen had been a bit surprised to learn that Seelie architects all lived long enough to have heirs. Unseelie architects invariably died along with their secrets shortly after building whatever castle, keep, or cairn they'd been commissioned for. But then most Unseelie architects were changelings, stolen from the world of men and raised to build, never knowing what their fate would be.

And in truth, he thought, *we Seelie are no better.* The architects of Astaeri Palace may have been elvish, but the labor was all slave. It was well known that just the making of the moat for Astaeri Palace had cost the lives of more than a thousand slaves, thousands of years ago, in the time of his great-great-grandfather. To raise the building itself, he supposed, the number had likely been too high to count.

He asked the architects his three Sticksman questions, which they gaped at, and then pressed them for information on the palace.

They blathered on for an hour before the balding dwarfling, highest ranking of the three, admitted, "There are no secret doors, hidden passageways, or collapsible walls, sire."

The second, an elflord who'd probably been so low in his family ranking, he'd taken neither to the army nor bardry, added, "No trapped corridors, nor any other architectural oddity that would allow us to win the day." He seemed almost happy to report this to Aspen, who was—his sneer said clearly—too young and too much the Hostage Prince to claim his allegiance.

He may be right, Aspen thought, *but I'm all he's got. All any of them have got!*

"And no time to build any," added the third-ranker. His straggling beard waggled with each syllable he spoke, like a bad actor in a second-rate troupe.

Aspen dismissed them, and called in Mishrath, the last wizard in the realm. Too close to death to survive traveling with the army, he was ironically the only wizard still alive after the great battle where the king—Aspen's father—had died. Mishrath's study—School of Illusion—had fallen out of favor in recent centuries, so it hadn't been thought he'd be terribly useful in a battle, anyway.

Like most old wizards, Mishrath was a wizened creature, eaten up from the inside by the magic he used. He was so wrinkled, shrunken, and stooped, Aspen couldn't even tell what clan he was from, though if anything, he seemed tortoise-like. That was odd, because there were no tortoise clans in the Seelie kingdom. The last of them had died off centuries earlier, due to change in the weather and the scarcity of ponds, or so his mother had told him when she had given him a crash course in Seelie history since his return. The frog clan, it seemed, might be next.

"Mishrath reporting, Your Majesty," the old wizard wheezed, his voice as wizened as he. Standing no higher than Aspen's waist, he wore robes that had likely once been the black of his order before time and misuse turned them grey. His hat, likewise grey, now slumped from proud and pointy to a simple heap of cloth mounted on top of a wrinkled mass of grey skin. Two milky white eyes bugged out of those folds of skin and fixed Aspen in a myopic gaze. "And what would you have of me?"

"Your wisdom and your service," Aspen answered. "But first I must ask you three questions—"

"Ah, yes," Mishrath broke in, something Aspen doubted he ever would have done talking to the late king, "I have heard of your three questions." He held up three fingers. They were all the fingers he had on his hand. "What is the Sticksman?" he asked, then answered himself. "A creature both of and not of the Unseelie Court." He ticked one finger off, coughed lightly into the crook of his arm, and went on. "How does one become the Sticksman? It is not known of a certainty, but there are whispers of hints of stories of tales that might lead a wise man to the answer."

"What?" Aspen was startled. He had asked his questions of dozens upon dozens of folk, and this was more than anyone else seemed to know, though the old wizard's answers—like prophesies—made little sense and probably would only be understood in retrospect, after they were fulfilled. But Aspen could feel the quest's magic urging him to find out more. "Where do I seek these hints? From whom—"

Mishrath ticked off a second finger and went on as if Aspen hadn't spoken. "How does the Sticksman come not to be once more? That is the most important riddle of the three and the only one that truly wants answering." He closed his last finger down into a fist and stared at it for a second as if the answer lay tight between his knuckles. This time he coughed into the fist, louder than before, then shrugged. "And of the third question, I have no knowledge at all."

Aspen felt the surge of hope die. "Oh. Well, I—"

"But that does not mean there is *not* any knowledge."

"Oh! Then—"

Mishrath interrupted him again, and Aspen thought, *I am not sure he needs* me *here for this conversation.*

"Do you know why the Wizard's Tower was built so high?" the old wizard asked.

Aspen shook his head, though he knew the wizard did not notice.

Mishrath pointed down at his feet. "It is so no one ever thinks to look underneath."

Then he turned and shuffled halfway to the door, before looking over his hunched shoulder. "Oh, and as to the

Unseelie invasion there is nothing I can do. We are all dead. Farewell, Your Grace." Then he shuffled the rest of the way out, coughing all the while, and Aspen was left alone.

Gape-mouthed, Aspen watched him go. He knew there were other people he should talk to: diplomats, tradesmen, hunters, weapon-smiths, laborers. . . . But the Sticksman's quest was hard upon him now, and all he could think about was discovering what lay underneath the Wizard's Tower.

"Well," he said aloud, "Mishrath said we were all dead, anyway. May as well keep this last promise before I die."

He spoke to an empty room, though he was sure, behind some curtain or in some hidden niche, Balnar, waiting, heard him. *That is*, Aspen thought, *both disturbing and comforting.*

Leaving the small side chamber, Aspen walked back out through the throne room, waving aside an assortment of clerks and courtiers, and Balnar, who suddenly materialized at his side.

Bowing, Balnar asked, "May I inquire, Majesty, where you are going?"

"Secrets, Balnar. I am off to discover secrets."

He hoped they would be worth the time he was spending. He had so little of it left.

4

SNAIL'S MISSION

The sun had not yet risen when Alith woke Snail, plucking at her shoulder. *She* looked perfectly rested, though Snail guessed the warrior had probably gotten little to no sleep at all.

Standing carefully, Snail felt every muscle and bone, each with a different ache, some as sharp as a sewing needle, some spread out like a bruise. She looked around at the soldiers, who seemed to rise from the ground and gather around the campfire with fluid movements. Even the oldest ones seemed unhurt from the previous day's ride, or the sleep on the damp ground.

She was about to mention her aches and bruises to Alith when the commander gave a huge snort, like an angry drow, and said in a fierce, breathy whisper, "I shall kill him!"

Not the time for complaining, then, Snail thought.

Evidently, sometime in the night, the trooper who'd been dressed down so thoroughly by Alith had bolted. Snail wasn't sure whether they were better off with or without him. She only hoped he'd gone home and not to offer information about them to the Unseelie generals. *Best keep that to myself*, she thought.

However, Alith had come to the same conclusion on her own. She cursed the man, his household, his clan with a ferocity that was truly impressive. "May his name never be noticed. May his clan be lost to him forever. May his limbs wither, his nails fall out, his fore end drop off and his hind end slope away. May his nose . . ."

With each new curse, Alith threw ashes into the cooling cookfire, and the fire flared, first green, then blue.

Even in the Unseelie Court, Snail had never heard such ferocious and long-lasting cursing. But she certainly knew dark magic when she heard it, and she shivered from the force of its power.

Stepping carefully away from Alith, who never even noticed her move, Snail joined the soldiers, one of whom passed her a cup of jav and a piece of greying journeycake. As the food and hot drink went down, Snail felt her brain begin to function again, even though she still worried about climbing back into the saddle.

When Goodspeed was brought to her, she put her hands once again on each side of the horse's head, blowing gently into its nostrils, whispering, "I hope you have no aches or bruises from me. I forgive you mine."

Seemingly impervious to any aches herself, Alith ended her curses and moved easily into her own saddle, calling at the same time, "Mount up!" to the men.

"I wish these horses could fly," Snail muttered as she clambered clumsily up on Goodspeed with the help of old Snaggle. Then, gritting her teeth, she nudged the horse with her heels.

THEY FOUND THE cursed runaway several miles farther on to the east, hanging from a larch tree by his hair, his arms and legs sprouting red-fletched arrows as if he were some strange, feathered beast.

Not one of the little troop seemed surprised.

"That Groan—he always was a bad 'un," said Snaggle. "Me and the boys had to straighten him out more than once."

Snail didn't inquire about what *straightening out* meant. Though she did wonder idly if Alith had followed Groan earlier and killed him to stop him selling them to the Unseelie army. She wondered if the commander's cursing had just been a show to keep the rest of the soldiers in line. Or if Snaggle and the boys had shot those arrows as part of a plan to set the runaway straight. Or if his death was due to the Border Lords. Or the humans. Or . . .

"Where's his bloody horse?" someone asked.

"We've no time to look for it now, Pad," Alith said. "Probably taken by whoever killed him. But, on the way back, maybe we can find—"

"If the trail's not too old then," Snaggle grumbled.

"Not that it could be older than you," Pad snapped.

It broke the tension, and a small chittering that Snail realized was laughter ran through the troop, though Alith didn't join in.

None of them seemed to question who the runaway's executioner had been. It was as if they already knew—perhaps by the way he'd been killed or by some clue in the arrows. Of course, Snail didn't know one arrow from another, or one method of execution from another. Or if she was the cause of Groan's death.

She could have asked but kept silent.

Actually, she didn't want to know.

※ ※ ※

AT LEAST THE troop took time to bury him, cutting off his clan badge to bring back to his people, something Snail knew none of the Unseelie folk would have done. Even the Border Lords—who liked to boast of their closeness to one another—would never do any such thing, of that Snail was sure. She'd seen how they'd acted when she and Aspen had crossed the river between the two kingdoms. The Border Lords hadn't even tried to rescue their comrades from the carnivorous mermen or search for their bones. She shuddered at the memory.

While the rest of the troop finished the burial, Alith sent Snaggle with a younger soldier—Snap—up ahead.

"Eyes and ears only," she warned them. "No heroics. Just count the enemy, note how and where they are situated. Come back with a report."

After the two had gone, Snail and the others pulled back until they were hidden again in the woods. Alith alone moved forward to the edge of the trees to keep watch for the scouts' return.

Easing herself off the horse without any help, Snail sighed with relief, though not loud enough to be heard.

"Doing well, m'lady," said another of the soldiers. Mums was her name, about Alith's age. She'd none of the commander's grace, or beauty, but had a grin that seemed to wreath her mouth. "Well, that is, for someone unused to riding." Her grin softened the critique.

"Does it show?" Snail grinned back.

"Only when you get up or down," said Mums.

Snail humphed. *Not so bad, then.*

"Or when you're riding." Mums grinned even more broadly at that, and Snail realized she'd not been criticizing but making a joke. Or at least mostly a joke.

The sun had passed above the trees and was well toward the horizon when the scouts returned. They trotted along the road as if careless of who or what might see them. Their coats with the clan insignia had been hidden in their packs, along with their bows and arrows. They wore weather-beaten straw hats slumped on their heads. To the casual eye, they could have been two old farmers out for a ride or returning from a harvest, except for the way they sat in their saddles, straight-backed and with a feral alertness to everything around them.

"Mount up," Alith commanded, and everyone was up and ready by the time Snap and Snaggle reached them. That included Snail, whose mounting ability still consisted of scrambling, wiggling her bottom, and trying not to kick Goodspeed too badly on the way up.

"You took your time," Alith said dryly to the scouts. They obviously hadn't. Their horses were bathed in sweat and houghing.

"'Twas a nice day for a leisurely ride," Snap said.

"Report, then."

Snap was first. "Quiet until over the second hill, and then—"

Snaggle interrupted, "Way down below, a big encamp-ment. About two thousand folk, but that includes women, children. In the center, a gaggle of greenish wagons, three, maybe four."

"Which is it?" Alith said quickly.

Snap and Snaggle glanced at one another.

"Four," Snail said, "all connected by arched roofs about eight feet high. Twelve large wooden wheels, six on each side. It makes the cart look top-heavy, like a moving mill, but it's an amazing contraption. Breaks down into a stage for performances."

"How does she . . . ?" Snap whispered to Snaggle.

"*Who* is she," Snaggle countered, "to know all that? A spy . . . ?"

What he said confirmed what Snail had already guessed: only Alith knew the whole of their mission.

Alith nodded, looking at Snail. "The professor's, I presume."

"Yes." Snail spoke directly to her.

"Then we ride."

Alith was about to give the order when Snap said, "Sir!"

She turned. "Yes, soldier?"

"The wagon's in the middle of those two thousand changelings, many of them armed."

"Not the children," Snail said.

"Armed with what?" Alith asked at the same moment.

"With whatever they scavenged from our dead and the Unseelie, I'd guess," said Snaggle directly to Alith. "Them changelings don't usually go armed except with—well— turning forks or scythes or horseshoes."

"You'd *guess*?" Alith glared at him. "I don't send scouts out to guess."

Snail interrupted the dressing down she feared was about to begin. "It's what *we* changelings do," she said in a steady voice. "We scavenge, adapt, change, make better. We invent, reinvent . . ." As she spoke, she understood for the first time what she really was. "And the professor is the greatest of us all. It's why King Ailenbran wants me to speak with him."

"Sorry, m'lady. No offense meant." Snaggle turned back to Alith. "There's more."

"Spit it out."

"Spiders big as trolls. Bigger. All around the perimeter."

"Nonsense. Spiders don't grow that big. That would take magic. Changelings do *not* have magic."

"He's right," Snail said. "But those spiders are *made* things. Out of iron and—"

"Iron?" Alith shuddered.

"But they won't hurt me," Snail added quickly. "Or any of the humans. Iron only hurts the fey. Get me to that second hill, and I'll ride into the camp alone."

"No! I have my orders from the king," Alith said. "You will not go alone."

"Even the king can't command the spiders or get help from the professor without me," Snail said. "It's got to be done my way."

"We will get you over the second hill or around it," Alith agreed. "Whichever seems safest. After that, we shall see."

Which means, Snail realized, *that I'll have to* make *it* happen.

Meanwhile, Alith had turned to her troop. "We ride. Snap and Snaggle in front. Me next. Then m'lady. Then Mums, Fen, and Pad." She drew a deep breath, let it out. "Damn that mouthy, silly Groan. Seven's a better number than six."

The others grunted their agreement, even Snail.

Alith added, "We could have used him now. *And* his horse."

"For target practice," mumbled Snap, but no one thought that funny, and Alith gave him a look that could have curdled a mouthful of milk.

The warriors moved their horses into the lineup, and off they went, first walking, then trotting, along the open road.

A horse walking, Snail thought, *is bearable*. But what she thought about trotting was lost in a melody of pain. Only when they burst into a canter did she get some sense of what real riding could be like—wind in hair, blur of trees, a loose, rocking sensation. Unfortunately, even fey horses couldn't sustain a canter for long. Especially the exhausted mounts of Snap and Snaggle. Now Snail understood why Alith was so angry at Groan. *We could have swapped out horses and set a faster pace.* Without a spare, there would be less cantering and more walking. It left trot as their fastest, easiest gait.

Easiest for the horses.

Not—alas, as Snail already knew—for the riders.

5

ASPEN AND THE WIZARD GAMES

$\mathcal{S}$prouting from the earth on a hillock some fifty paces to the east of the main building, the Wizard's Tower was not precisely a part of Astaeri Palace. It was ostensibly attached, but only by an invisible bridge that presumably stretched from an arched opening in a fourth-floor wall in the eastern wing of the palace to the Eldritch Door on the second floor of the tower. To visit the tower was to put yourself entirely in the power of the wizards who resided there. Unless you could fly.

Aspen could not fly. At least not without the bowser. And the bowser was somewhere with Professor Odds and the changelings.

The humans. If he was to make a pact with them, he had to remember to call them what they called themselves. Using the term *changeling* would only remind them of their shared history, a history in which the Seelie people did not feature as heroes or even friends.

He stood at the arch that opened to the air, looking across

the invisible bridge to the Wizard's Tower and down to the rocky ground below and wondered. He wondered a little about why the door into the tower had a name but the portal out of the tower did not. But mostly he wondered why he could not fly.

Plenty of fey fly, he thought miserably. *Why not the king of the fey? I command armies and fire, and yet the smallest, silliest sprite has the advantage of me up here.*

He almost turned back around, but the thought of returning to the throne room to hear more bad news made him push forward.

Mayhap, I'll fall to my death and not have to watch my kingdom destroyed.

With this comforting thought, he stepped out into thin air.

And fell.

His life barely had time to even *begin* passing in front of his eyes before his foot hit something solid.

Very amusing, he thought with just a touch of anger. The wizards must have thought it a great jest to place the bridge just a little lower than expected. The sensation of falling with no chance of injury. *Just a reminder of how much I am in their power right now.*

He shuffled carefully through the air, trusting that the bridge's magic had not died along with most of the wizards. The ground sloped up and the invisible bridge down, so that by the time he was halfway across, the fall began to look survivable. By the time he reached the Eldritch Door, the rocks below had been cleared away, and if he fell, it would only be a short drop into soft grasses.

I get it: trust in us and we shall see you through. The wizards' subliminal message had the opposite effect on him. It made him trust the wizards less, not more. He approached the tower cautiously.

The door was made of a single block of stone, though it was marked into four sections as if it were wooden and paneled. In each section was a carved face, four faces in all. Each turned stone eyes on Aspen as he approached.

"Greetings, Your Grace," said the top left face, an elven warrior, pointed ears poking out of his helmet.

"And well met," said the top right face, a Green Man with leaves in his long hair and beard.

"What business do you have in the tower?" asked the bottom left face, its boggart's rat features pinched, squinched, and shifty.

The bottom right face had tentacles for eyes and a jagged slash where the mouth should go. It was hard to look at, yet hard to look away from, and it howled something unintelligible that made Aspen's brain want to slither out his ear and run back to the palace on its own.

"I—I have come for knowledge," he stuttered, forcing his gaze back to the elven warrior face. It was what one always answered when asked that question by wizards or their minions. Even if what you wanted was power or spells or the destruction of your enemies, you always answered "knowledge," or the wizards were likely to refuse. His tutor Jaunty had taught him that.

"Then enter," said the warrior, "and may you find what you seek."

"And yet leave some behind for those who follow," added the Green Man.

"Hrmph," said the boggart.

The bottom right face said nothing, but its tentacle eyes waved at him as the door swung slowly open. Aspen sidled through sideways, staying as far from the capering tentacles as possible.

The room he entered was octagonal and tiled in pale stone that reflected the natural light.

Natural light? he thought. *But there are no windows.*

From the outside, the Wizard's Tower was a window-less monolith. But here in the entryway, broad windows stretched to the ceiling twenty feet above, sunlight streaming through every one. All of them seemed to be showing the actual view from the tower.

Why not have regular windows if the magic windows just show what is outside anyway?

Aspen was certain there was another message here, but he failed to understand it.

That's the trouble with wizards, he thought. *Too cunning for their own good. No wonder no one trusts them. And the middle of a war is no time to be playing games.*

The room was empty except for a short elf in a black robe. He stood in the middle of the room and looked up as Aspen entered, his face shadowed beneath a voluminous hood, making it appear featureless.

Bowing low, the elf said, "Welcome to our humble tower, Your Grace." His voice was a pleasant baritone. "What is it you seek?"

"Knowledge," Aspen said again. But all the while he was thinking: *How many dark deeds are dressed up as a search for knowledge?* Though he actually *was* after knowledge today.

"A noble pursuit." The elf raised his right hand, and the giant windows faded away, replaced by seven spiral staircases. "Each staircase leads to knowledge of a different ancient realm." He began pointing to each in turn. "Faerie, Tir na nOg, the Land of Men, Trollheim—"

More games, Aspen thought. "I was told to search beneath the tower." He tried hard not to sound exasperated.

"Ah," the elf said. The windows reappeared, but now it was night outside and thin moonlight illuminated the hall. "The Catacombs of Lost Knowledge."

"Yes," Aspen agreed, "that sounds like the place." He hoped it was the right response.

The elf held his arms out to the sides, and his robe began to shiver. "It is not my place to advise or deter the seeker, only to warn: not all knowledge that was lost was misplaced. Often it was hidden. And only because it could not be destroyed." The black robe dropped to the floor, and the elf dropped with it, both dissolving into a black puddle. Aspen stepped forward and looked down into the puddle. Instead of his own reflection, he saw the elf's hooded face blurred by the rippling water.

"Good luck, Your Grace."

Then the face became a hole in the floor with a rope ladder hanging down into darkness.

Aspen sighed. *More games. More wasted time. If,* he thought, *we manage not to lose this war, I am going to ban all wizard games.*

"Why can there not just be a set of stairs?" he asked aloud, not expecting an answer. Then, shrugging, he looked closely at the hole. The darkness seemed almost solid.

But if it was games the wizards wanted, he would play them. After all, he was the king of Faerie and fire danced at his command.

He called a ball of fire to his hand and sent it down the hole. The orange flames illuminated a tunnel with walls the same tile as the floor, leading deep into the tower. The long rope ladder went down and down. He could not see a bottom. But what did that matter? He either died here or in battle a few days hence.

Calling the fire back, he set it to float by his head as a constant light, first making sure it was cold, not hot. Then he levered himself over the side of the hole.

The ladder was steady, so he started down. At first, the

going was easy. He started counting rungs and was to sixty when he sensed more than saw the tunnel open up into a room. The ladder was now hanging freely and swung slightly as he continued his descent.

"As long as it remains slightly," he whispered, the sound of his own voice a comfort. He wished again that he could fly. But no amount of wishing gave him wings.

I must be close now.

But it was another twenty rungs before his left foot touched down on floor instead of ladder. He made certain the floor was solid before letting go of the ladder. *Never trust a wizard*, he reminded himself.

His cold light showed him that the floor was tiled like the room far above, but in black, which didn't help alleviate the gloom. He reached for the fireball. Before he could set it floating about to show him the measurement of the room, torches sprang to life all around him.

By this new and brilliant light he could see that he stood in the middle of another octagonal room. Eight wooden doors led out of the eight walls, each with a torch on either side. In the middle of the room stood a short elf in a black-hooded robe.

Aspen sighed. *Even more games?*

"Welcome to the Catacombs of Lost Knowledge, Your Grace," the elf said in a pleasant baritone. "What is it you seek?"

"Knowledge," Aspen said, this time quite a bit more sharply. Then he added, "Um—are you the same . . . ?"

"Yes and no," the elf said. "I am an iteration of the same source."

As if that explains everything. Or anything.

"But he is the Welcomer," the elf went on, "and I—"

The elf pushed his hood back, and Aspen saw that it wasn't the shadows from the hood that had made the elf's face seem featureless. His face *was* featureless. It was smooth and flat, with only the slightest protuberance where a nose should have been. Instead of eyes, there was just more smooth skin. Below the nose-bump a thin line was just now opening up into a lipless mouth.

"I am the Archivist," the faceless elf finished. "An iteration of my maker."

"And who was your maker?"

"Is that the knowledge you seek?"

"No, but—"

"My maker made the tower to hold knowledge. And he made us to hold the tower." The Archivist waved a hand at his featureless face. "Put too much of yourself into your creation and you may lose yourself entirely."

"I do not understand."

The Archivist inclined his head. "All magic costs. You wield the regal flame, but can you cast it for days on end?"

"Of course not! It wears me out."

The Archivist nodded, said again, "All magic costs. The

cost of an iteration was a piece of my maker."

Aspen thought that maybe this maker could have spent just a little more of himself to give his creations eyes. *But what do I know about iterations anyway?* Then he realized something.

"I should ask you my three questions," he said to the Archivist. "But I do not *need* to. Why is that?"

"Were you entreated to ask these questions of every *creature* you meet?"

"Yes."

"I am not a creature. I am an iteration, so you need not ask me," the Archivist said. "But you can. So tell me what you seek, as I understand your time is not limitless."

Well, at last! Aspen thought of the Unseelie armies even now converging on his castle. "I have come seeking knowledge of the Sticksman. What he is and how he came to be and how he could cease being." He hoped that would be thought of as one long question.

The Archivist was silent for a moment. He might have been deep in thought, but it was impossible to tell from his lack of face. Finally he spoke. "That knowledge is old. Older than the tower. Older than the kingdom. Almost older than the Seven Realms."

"Does that mean you do not know it?"

The Archivist shook his head. "It only means we will have to travel to reach it."

"Travel? I have no time to travel."

"Interesting that you should say that. For that is exactly what we must travel through."

"What do you mean?" Aspen said. "What must we travel through?"

The Archivist gave him a lipless smile. "Time." He shot out a pale hand and grabbed Aspen by the shoulder. An icy blast of wind hit them in the face, and the Archivist's cloak billowed out behind him like a giant raven's wings. The torches guttered and died, and in the pitch black Aspen felt the floor disappear.

And then he fell. For a long, long time.

6

SNAIL'S MOUNTAINS

The ride to the first hill was easy on everything except Snail's bottom. She didn't complain. There was no use in doing so. But in her head, every third or fourth bump in the trot she thought, *Ow! Ow! Ow!* The cry was so loud in her head, she was sure everyone heard it, but of course, mind reading not being a Seelie gift, none of the troop was aware of her pain.

Snail thought Mums, riding right behind her, might have guessed from the stiffness of her posture, but if so, Mums never said a word about it.

That, Snail thought, *is the problem. No one says a word. Though it would be nice knowing that someone understands my pain.*

Instead, she endured in silence until they finally stopped to rest the horses and have a quick meal of journeycake and cold water fresh from a nearby stream. As they huddled together, their horses off grazing on the tall grasses beside the path, Snail saw Snaggle pointing.

She followed his finger, and just a few miles away, there was a mountain rising from the plains like a giant's fist.

It must be the first of the two hills, Snail thought. *Though it looks more a mountain to me.* She didn't know if it had a name, so she turned to ask one of the two warriors closest to her, Fen and Pad. In this light, she realized how much alike they were—large headed, short armed, with skin a slightly greenish tint, and hard, raised lumps as big as diamonds on their faces. They could have been brothers, or cousins.

Toad Clan, she thought. "Can you tell me . . ." she began.

"Little Sister," said Pad, his voice loud enough to address the entire troop.

It took Snail a moment to realize he wasn't talking about her but saying the mountain's name.

"Looks big to me," Fen muttered.

"Until you see the other," Pad countered. "Bigger mountain, bigger valley."

They began taunting one another, as warriors will, about things big and small, some of which brought a blush to Snail's cheeks, so she turned away. Goodspeed seemed to sense her embarrassment and wandered a short distance away from the other horses to chew on grass that looked the same to Snail but must have tasted sweeter to her.

"Thank you, Goodspeed," she whispered into the mare's ear.

THEY RODE HALFWAY around the mountain, making sure to stick to the woods after Snap and Snaggle had gone ahead again to be certain it was safe. The tall fir trees lent them cover but also kept the forest floor clear of undergrowth. This meant it gave them a clear riding track but left nothing for the horses to graze upon.

There was no one—not fey nor human nor made creature—anywhere around Little Sister as far as the scouts could tell. And indeed the troop met no one along the way.

They came at last to a small meadow between two separate stands of trees—the firs that they had just ridden through and some old-growth forest.

"Father and the White Ladies," Mums whispered to Snail, nodding in the direction of the second stand of trees, where a tall oak bent over with age stood surrounded by delicate, blotchy white birches. Behind them the oaks grew thick as an army.

Snail nodded, though she'd never heard them called that before.

Here in the meadow the grass was knee-deep, much to the relief of the horses and their masters. Alith had the troop set up a sketchy camp. "Unpack only essentials," she warned. "We may need to leave at a moment's notice." Her face gave away nothing, not fear, not caution, not worry, not relief.

The troops were warned to be on whispers only; the horses hobbled, overseen by the Green Brothers, as Snail was beginning to think of Fen and Pad. After the horses had grazed for a while, then watered at the tiny south-flowing stream near the darker end of the meadow, long cloths like feed bags were tied around their faces.

"They are trained to quiet, m'lady," said Mums, "but also to the muzzle. It's better to be safe than sorry."

Snail nodded in agreement, though she couldn't think of a single moment in her life when she'd felt safe. She tried to go help with getting Goodspeed settled for the night, but once by the horses, she found herself in the way yet again. Fen and Pad—with the benefit of years of experience—had already dealt with all the mounts, even Goodspeed.

At this point, feeling useless, even helpless, Snail started to walk the perimeter of their little encampment. But angry looks from each one of the small troop sent her skittering back to the center, where a meal of sorts was being set out. They all clearly wanted her both out of the way and out of danger.

And danger to me, she finally understood, *is more danger to them. I'm no help at all but an aggravation.*

DINNER WAS MORE journeycake, plus a scraggly salad of gathered wild onions, horse mushrooms, fennel, dandelion leaves, and chickweed, all found either in the meadow itself or in the vicinity of a small stream that ran along the northern edge of the mountain's foot.

Even as they ate, Alith set the watch. Everyone but Snail was to have a turn.

"Why not let me stand an hour?" Snail said to Alith, trying hard not to sound like a beggar outside the castle walls. "You're already down one man, and it would give your people an hour more of sleep."

Alith's mouth twitched into a controlled smile, one you might give to an unreasonable child before you put her to bed. It made Snail long for Aspen.

"Your counting is flawed, m'lady," Alith said. "We'd have to set two to guard you during your watch." Even the limited smile was gone now, replaced by a hard stare. "Easier to keep an eye on you while you're on the ground and asleep."

So she'd made it clear. Snail might be the most important member of the troop, the reason they were here. But as such, she needed guarding, guiding, watching.

"Your job comes later, m'lady."

Snail understood the message behind what Alith said: if she were out on the front line, anyone might grab her—Unseelie, human, even a made creature. And if that happened, it would not only endanger every member of Alith's troop—it would endanger the entire mission. And the mission was all that stood between the Seelie Court and total devastation.

How could I have been so stupid, Snail wondered, *and for so long*? She nodded at Alith. "Of course, of course."

As soon as she'd finished her cold meal, she curled up where she was told, in the middle of the encampment, without a word more of complaint.

THE WIND HAD dropped, and Snail could hear the guards whispering. She listened for a while, eyes closed, pretending to sleep, but it was cold and they were camping without fires. This close to their destination, Alith didn't want to alert or spook anyone.

The guards spoke of the weather, the food, the conditions of their horses, anything but what really concerned them—the enemy, who might even then be creeping through the undergrowth toward them.

After a while Snail stopped listening, because she was really waiting for the moment when she could open her eyes again, unseen by anyone else.

Even pretending sleep, I can still keep watch, she thought. *And be ready should there be danger.*

Except, when she opened her eyes again, it was first daylight, a bright pearl of a morning. Everyone else was already up, and she was the last to get to her feet for another handful of cold journeycake and water. She couldn't believe that she'd slept the night away, and without dreams.

ALITH GATHERED THE soldiers around her in a circle, her face sterner than Snail had seen it so far, though not as angry as when she'd cursed the runaway Groan.

"There will be just four of us going ahead," Alith said. 'The rest of you will stay here, with Mums in charge."

"Begging your pardon, sir!" It was Snaggle. "She's not senior." He looked a bit miffed, and Snail guessed that he was the one who should have been chosen.

"No, she's not," Alith said smoothly, "but you and Snap will be coming with me. I need the most competent scouts and fast-thinkers. I will be guarding m'lady, but I need your swift arrows at the ready as well. Mums, Fen, and Pad have other skills we need here at our base camp. Swiftness, slyness, and brotherhood to make sure any message of disaster gets back to the palace. One of those three will be sure to bring it home."

The way she spoke, softly, distinctly, without rank or rancor, and the way the others listened without an interruption, not even a mew of protest, made Snail realize that they were all thinking that this was a valedictory speech, a farewell. Alith didn't expect them all—or indeed any of them—to make it through the next few days. But she wouldn't say such a thing aloud in case it turned into a fey curse that would bring disaster down upon them all.

As if, Snail mused, *disaster needs any help right now.*

"May I say a small amen?" It was Mums, the last of the

troop whom Snail would have expected to ask any such thing.

Alith nodded, and Mums began: "May the Light carry us on our journey, may the Light . . ."

Snail stopped listening, because suddenly she was thinking that no one in the Unseelie lands would have ever asked for help from the Light. Those two opposing forces, Light and Dark, were at war here. In the in-between sat the changelings, the humans. *Whom do* we *ask for help?* she wondered.

That was when she heard a round of muttered *As you will it* that went around their circle. Alith's whispered *As you will it* was the final punctuation before everyone returned to task.

While the men collected their scattered gear and rounded up the horses, Alith took Mums and Snail aside, putting her arms around them both so that it looked as if they were saying a simple goodbye. She began to speak rapidly with such quiet passion, only the three of them could hear.

"You are to send the Greens after us, once a hand's length of sun has passed. And then another hand's length, and you come after. None of you are to be seen, them by us, or you by them. Stay far enough away not to be spotted, near enough so that you can hear any disaster that might come upon us. If we can be safely rescued, do it. But if it is too late, bring the message back home, sparing neither horse nor self. Let bodies lie where they fall."

Mums nodded.

"And, m'lady," Alith finished, turning to look directly at

Snail, "if you so much as turn around to show that you are looking for someone, even by the smallest twist, I shall throttle you myself, mission be damned. These warriors are risking their lives for you. Understood?"

Snail nodded. In a way, she was glad to have something to do, even if it was a negative: no turning, no looking, no showing she was expecting to be followed. Glad and—for the first time—truly terrified.

Mums turned and left, to go back and help with the horses.

Snail waited till Mums was too far away to hear and said to Alith, "May I have a sword?"

"Can you wield it?" Alith's eyes seemed to be smiling.

"A knife, then? I killed a carnivorous mer with one but three dozen days ago. Maybe less."

"A knife it is," Alith said.

Snail suspected Alith knew that she was already carrying two knives. One in each boot. A third, though, especially one given by Alith, would make her feel part of the troop, not just a package to be delivered. She suspected Alith knew that, too.

Alith unbuckled a small sheath on a long leather thong from around her waist and handed it to Snail. "It was given to me by my father on my Gift Day."

Snail hadn't been at the Seelie Court long enough to learn about such things. She tied the knife in its sheath around her waist by the leather thong, saying, "Gift Day?"

"The day following the discovery of my gift for fighting."

Snail stared at the commander, suspecting she was being leg-pulled, but Alith was looking very serious. "And should we both get through this alive, you can return the knife— blooded or not—when we come victoriously home."

"I will," said Snail.

"And if I do not make it back, bring it to the capital and give it to my son. His Gift Day is soon. He has been studying with his father's Horse Guards and has chosen that way."

"Son?" For some reason it had never occurred to Snail that Alith might have a life outside of this small troop. That Alith was a mother astonished Snail.

Alith turned away and looked sidelong at the sun, already making its way over the firs and heading across the meadow toward Father and the White Ladies. She rubbed a hand across her head, as if her head hurt, or as if she'd a memory of longer hair. Looking again at Snail, Alith added abruptly, "His name is Alicanson, and he is thirteen years old." She turned and called to the men, "Mount up."

"I will remember," Snail said. She wasn't certain if Alith had heard her, for she made no movement to indicate she had. Just in case, Snail repeated what she'd said. "I will remember."

But Alith had already moved on.

ASPEN'S LONG FALL

*A*s he fell, Aspen screamed. He screamed first for fear that he would hit bottom. Then, that he never would. When he tired of screaming, he shouted for the Archivist. There was no answer, and though he thought they had fallen together, in the dark there was no way to know. Aspen reached for him but touched nothing. There was only darkness and the sensation of falling.

He stopped screaming and just fell.

At first he thought his eyes were playing tricks on him. A pinprick of orange below his feet, flickering enticingly in the distance. But as he fell toward it, the light grew larger, and Aspen could see that it was a fire. A big fire. In a big cavern. The light reflected off of wet, stone walls, and young stalactites drip-drip-dripped onto three figures gathered by the fire.

That was all Aspen noticed before he was consumed with watching the ground rushing toward him and wondering how badly it was going to hurt when he hit. But he looked over and in the glow from the fast-approaching firelight could finally see the Archivist, who was sitting calmly cross-legged in the air.

Whatever is happening, he does not seem too worried about it.

And, indeed, their descent slowed until they came to a stop, floating two feet above the stalagmite-littered ground. Aspen heard water and glanced behind him and could just barely see the fire reflected in the waves of an underground river. There was something familiar about the area but Aspen couldn't quite place it, and just then the figures around the fire began to chant.

"Fascinating," the Archivist breathed.

"What?" Aspen whispered. He didn't know if the figures could hear him. He suspected that he and the Archivist weren't completely there. "What is this place? Who are they?" He cocked an ear toward the chanting, but it was either guttural nonsense or in a language he didn't know. "And what are they doing?"

"I do not know," the Archivist replied, sounding as if he'd never uttered those words before. "Let us observe."

Aspen did not ask how the Archivist planned to observe without any eyes.

The chanters were old women, tall and thin, with long, stringy white hair and faces the light blue of a frozen corpse. They were dressed identically in grey-brown robes that hung past their feet and trailed on the stone behind them. Before them on the ground lay a pale figure with long straight limbs and eyes that, even closed as they were now, bulged from the head like an insect's.

"The Sticksman!" gasped Aspen, for that was the figure on the ground. He was bigger than Aspen remembered, his limbs more fleshy, his face less bony and bug-like, but it was definitely the Sticksman. Or one of the twins from the professor's troupe. They did all look the same.

He's certainly not dressed like the Sticksman, Aspen thought. The Sticksman had worn a black, hooded robe that was worn and water-stained. This creature was wearing old-style finery, good enough for the king's court.

Suddenly Aspen recognized where they were as well: the cavern below Wester Tower of King Obs's Keep. Snail and he had come through here when they had escaped the Unseelie lands. They had paid the Sticksman to ferry them down the river to the Shifting Lands, escaping both the attacking Border Lords and treacherous Old Jack Daw.

His eyes adjusting to the gloom quickly, Aspen looked back toward the Sticksman and the old women and now saw that there was a fifth figure skulking among the stalactites. The figure was squat but not short, a smallish troll perhaps or a broad-shouldered elf watching the proceedings from the shadows.

The women's chanting seemed to be reaching a crescendo. They turned their hands to face forward, and just past the prone Sticksman there was now a thin tree sprouting from the stone.

It was odd to see something green and alive in amongst all this dead, dark stone, and Aspen felt magic at work. Old earth magic: solid, stolid, everlasting.

Then the tree began to grow. It grew like any other tree, but swiftly, a season's work done in an instant. Branches shot out, budded a mere moment later. In a breath, leaves thickened, turned red and gold, fell off. New leaves appeared green and full before the old leaves hit the cavern floor. In ten breaths, the tree was as tall as a peasant's shack, a glorious young oak with thick green foliage.

The women's chanting changed tenor, suddenly lower and slower than before. Each syllable shook the tree, shaking the green leaves off.

It has stopped growing, Aspen thought.

The branches were bare of leaves now, and as Aspen watched, the branches themselves grew withered and thin. Then one by one, they snapped off with a dry crack and fell to the ground. The women's chant slowed even more and the trunk of the tree drew in on itself, becoming thin and grey. Eventually, the once-proud tree was no more than a long, thin stick stuck into the rock.

The women stopped their chant. One walked to the dead tree while the other two bent and reached out for the Sticksman. He was gaunt now, with arms and legs as thin as the just-deceased tree and still-closed eyes bulging from a bony face. He looked much like the creature Aspen had first met at the dock.

Or rather when I will first meet him, Aspen thought. *Or perhaps when I will have first met him.* Frowning, he shook the thought from his head, deciding that worrying over the correct grammar for what was happening was not at all useful. "Or had happened." Without meaning to, he spoke out loud.

The Archivist glanced at him inquisitively, and Aspen said, "Time travel is confusing." As if that explained everything.

The Archivist shrugged.

One of the women now wrenched the long stick from the ground as the other two lifted the Sticksman to his feet. His legs didn't look strong enough to support his own weight, and indeed, Aspen could see that the women were holding him up. The woman with the stick came over and placed it in the Sticksman's hand. When he grasped it, a convulsion shook him so violently, it tore him from the women's grasp.

For a moment, Aspen was afraid the Sticksman would fall, but the stick seemed to give him strength, and he stood on his own now.

Then one of the women spoke in a language Aspen finally understood.

"This is memory," she said in oddly accented Old Elven. She tapped the top of the stick.

"This is blood," said another, tapping the stick just under where her sister's hand lay.

"This is life," said the third, putting both her arms around the other two. All three turned their heads toward the Sticksman, speaking as one.

"*Never* let it go."

The Sticksman opened his pale blue eyes finally, turned toward the women, and nodded once.

"Is it done?" the skulking figure asked as he stepped into the firelight. He was grey-skinned and heavily muscled with a face that looked like it had been clumsily carved from stone. However, he wore a tunic of fine cloth, and the jeweled hilt of a huge sword poked out of a scabbard slung across his back.

"Is it done?" he asked again, louder this time, as if the women had not heard him, even though they were right in front of him. He spoke in the language of the Unseelie Court, but oddly accented, like the old women.

They nodded as one. "He has no memory of what he was," said the first.

"Nor do any of his blood," said the second.

"And he shall live forever," said the last.

"As long as he holds the staff," the skulker said. It sounded half a question.

"There must always be a Sticksman, and he always holds the staff," the first woman said. It was not exactly an answer.

The Sticksman looked up as if recognizing his new name. He focused on the skulker. Then he spoke. "You do not need passage. And shall not for some time." He turned toward the three women. "You will require it far sooner than you thought."

Then the Sticksman turned and strode purposefully

toward the river. The river was barely visible in the darkness, but Aspen swore the waters rose and began to move toward the approaching Sticksman, making a newer, closer shoreline.

One wave rose higher than the rest, cresting over the Sticksman, but without a splash. Instead, the black water draped itself around the tall creature, becoming a long, hooded robe. A simple, wooden boat followed behind the wave and settled on the shore nearby. Nobody was aboard. The Sticksman turned and faced back toward the cave, standing tall and still.

He was just as Aspen remembered seeing him the first time.

He is the Sticksman for certain.

"It is a great service you have done me," Aspen heard the skulker say, and he wrenched his eyes away from the Sticksman to see that he was addressing the crones.

"And our payment . . ." the first woman replied. The other women nodded silent assent. All three leaned in, avarice glinting in their eyes.

"About that," the skulker began, and then in one snake-swift motion whipped his huge sword out of its scabbard and lopped their heads off.

The heads clunked to the ground and the bodies crumpled moments later. The skulker gave a courtly bow to the corpses. "I am sorry, ladies, but this is business . . . and history." He swept his free arm out in a circle that encompassed the stones, the river, the Sticksman—and the fallen bodies. "And this business can have no witnesses. Nor can this history." Then he stooped to pick up the first of the bodies and carried it toward the river, whistling a pleasant hornpipe as he walked.

"Interesting," the Archivist said, and Aspen almost shushed him for fear that the murderous skulker would hear them. But the killer showed no sign of hearing anything but his own whistled tune of contentment.

Because we are not really here, are we? Aspen was now sure of it. *But if we are not here, did it* really *happen?* He was not as sure of that.

The skulker placed the women's bodies one at a time in the Sticksman's boat, then topped each corpse with a head, though whether they were the correct heads, Aspen could not tell. He doubted the skulker cared. The skulker handed the Sticksman a palmful of coins. "Give the ladies to the mer," he said, "and here are coins to smooth their crossing."

The Sticksman nodded, got into the boat, and poled it away. It disappeared into a mist.

"It appears," the Archivist continued, "that your questions have been answered."

"What do you mean, *answered?*" Shocked, Aspen shouted, "What just happened? Who is the Sticksman? And why must there always be one?"

The Archivist shook his head. "Those are not the questions you asked. I cannot answer them."

Aspen would have stamped his foot in frustration if he weren't floating in the air. "Why not? I—I am the king, and I demand you answer them!"

"I am sorry, Your Grace, but there is naught I can do." The Archivist shrugged. "I fear our observation is at an end."

"Wha—" Aspen began, but suddenly all the breath was sucked from his lungs. His ears popped and the cavern went dark. A great weight pressed on his chest and he thought his ribs would pop as well. But the weight was gone as quickly as it had come, and the lights came back on a moment after.

They were in the Catacombs of Lost Knowledge beneath the Wizard's Tower.

"I trust you can find your way out, Your Highness," the Archivist said, and pointed to the rope ladder. "Our time here is at an end." Then he put his chin to his chest and slumped his shoulders, his arms suddenly hanging limp at his sides. If he had been a torch, he would have just guttered and died.

What just happened? What is the meaning of what we saw? And why have I wasted my meager time on this when I have a war to lose? Aspen had a fistful of questions but didn't ask any of them aloud. It was clear he would get no more from the Archivist.

Shuffling to the rope ladder, Aspen climbed up listlessly. When he reached the top, the Welcomer pulled him up and asked, "Did you find what you seek?"

"I do not know."

The Welcomer nodded his cowled head. "We get that a lot."

WHEN ASPEN STEPPED through the Eldritch Door, which was blank on this side, he found himself back in bright daylight. The sun shone in the same spot as when he'd entered, as if no time at all had passed.

And perhaps none has, he thought. Shaking his head, Aspen stomped back across the invisible bridge and into his castle. He was practically trembling with anger—at the wizards with their games and their magic, at the Unseelie and their usurper king, Old Jack Daw. He was even mad at the Sticksman and the old women, though they seemed—if not entirely blameless—certainly long dead.

But mostly, he concluded, *I am furious with myself.*

8

SNAIL'S SECOND MOUNTAIN

This time when they headed out, there were only the four of them: Snap and Snaggle in the front, riding side by side whenever possible, Snaggle alone in front when the trail—which was wreathed with bittersweet—became too narrow.

Snail came next.

Alith "held the back door," as she called it.

Even if Snail had forgotten Alith's stern warning about looking backward, she wouldn't have dared. Goodspeed was strangely nervous, perhaps missing the other horses, or maybe she feared to get tangled in the encroaching berry bushes. Her leg muscles trembled, and tiny runnels of fear, like worms beneath loose soil, raced across her neck and withers.

"Shhhhhh," Snail called, even leaning over in the saddle to whisper in her ear. "Hush, Goodspeed. Be a good girl." But the horse didn't—or couldn't—listen to her rider and seemed to startle at every shadow, almost unseating Snail half a dozen times.

Yet, despite shades and shadows, despite the wind suddenly picking up, despite leaves and twigs of varying sizes scattering across the trail, they met no one and nothing appeared amiss.

At last, Snap, riding directly in front of Snail in the narrow passage, sat back in his saddle and wiggled his shoulders, almost as if to say: *Nothing to worry about now.*

Snail followed his lead, sitting more loosely, relaxing, even letting out a breath she hadn't realized she'd been holding. Goodspeed, too, took the cue. Her nervousness departed once the trail widened again and the bittersweet thinned out. Snap moved his horse up by Snaggle's side. The gap widened between Snail's roan and the other horses, and Goodspeed's gait became bouncier.

The ride continued to alternate between the two landscapes as the four horses and their riders made their way around Little Sister. The threaded forest path was littered with old leaves, reminders of past autumns, and the trees seemed to sway like ancient women at court balls whenever a breeze managed to push its way through. And then forest gave way to small meadows where the horses could lean their long necks down to grab at the tops of the grass as they waded through belly-high greenery.

But in both landscapes, Snail could not *entirely* shake off her fears. While the forest was full of shadowy places that made the back of her neck prickle, the meadows seemed somehow too open, too vulnerable for comfort, for there was nowhere to hide.

Hour followed hour, the sun moved overhead, and at last the day began to cool down.

Alith—who'd been having an intense talk with Snaggle in the last meadow, caught up with Snail and said, "Almost in sight of Big Sister. We will make our way across one final meadow, and then I'll send the scouts ahead."

Snail nodded. She didn't turn her head. She didn't have to, for she was already facing where they'd come from in order to talk with Alith. She thought she saw something at the shadowy edge of the forest they'd just left. Not a deer. They'd seen less than a handful and mostly near water, drinking or wading. The herds, she assumed, had already been well thinned by changeling poachers.

"Alith . . ." she began, "I think the Greens may be crowding us."

Turning, Alith replied, "They wouldn't dare . . ." as an arrow, red-shafted, flew between them, and another hit Alith's horse high on its rump.

The horse bolted, racing forward past Snap and Snaggle, who were both already alerted by Alith's cry and the sound of more arrows whizzing from the meadow's edge. And another sound now, a long skirling yell like the screeching of a hunting hawk.

By then, Alith had been unhorsed and was crouching in

the grass to make a smaller target of herself, shouting to the others, "Get down, get down!"

Snap threw himself to the left side and Snaggle to the right, but Snail could get neither of her boots out of the stirrups without help, and besides, she'd lost the roan's reins, so the little horse was racing away from the hurly of arrows and the cries of the invaders and into the next patch of forest ahead.

Snail had known at once they were being attacked by Border Lords. She recognized them from their battle cry, the loud ululation that mimicked the pipes they loved to play. But she didn't know how many there had been. *At least three*, she thought, *maybe a lot more.*

At the same time, she realized that since she couldn't seem to get down as instructed, her chances of escape were better in the forest than in the open meadow. The little mare had saved her with that impassioned burst of speed.

Snail knew there was a fierce enemy behind, and what was before her was still unknown. *This is a hideous game of chance*, she thought, knowing that in this instance, the unknown was a marginally better wager.

Goodspeed seemed to know that, too, and they barreled along the trail, not caring that they were leaving a huge trail of hoofprints and broken twigs that even an incompetent tracker could follow.

Branches reached out to slap at them, one leaving a welt on Snail's forehead and another opening a gash on the horse's hindquarters. Twice Goodspeed leapt over logs, both times almost unseating Snail, who managed to stay on only because she'd wound her hands in the little mare's mane.

They kept running until Goodspeed ran out of speed, out of legs, out of breath itself.

Snail could see a lighter space in the forest ahead. She leaned forward, gathered up the fallen reins, drew in a deep breath, and whispered to the horse, "Even a bit of speed is better than no speed at all." And making a clucking sound with her tongue against the top of her palate, she encouraged the roan into a fast walk.

The horse did her bidding but was houghing badly as they moved forward, and suddenly Snail remembered Alith saying, "*They will keep going if you ask them to. They will burst their hearts for you. But then they will be dead, and you will have no way to move quickly.*"

She realized this was the moment Alith had warned her of, but she'd no other options. She had to move forward or be captured.

Or die.

Or—she thought—*maybe both.*

She let Goodspeed slow down but didn't dare let her stop.

I'd weep, she thought, *if I thought it would help*, then drew in a deep breath so she could make a good next choice.

However, the little horse seemed to have caught a second wind and picked up speed on her own.

"You *are* your name, little one," Snail said, giving Goodspeed a pat on the shoulder, and began to cry in relief.

When they got to the place where the forest trail ended, Snail could see the sparkling of hundreds of early campfires, like fireflies, on the plain below. She could just about make out the form of Odds's big linked wagons in the very center of the fires. And above them all loomed the mountain, casting a huge shadow as the sun began to disappear behind it.

She wondered if she was bringing the changelings a message of hope or a thunder of Border Lords in her wake. She strained to see behind, but the dark was fast closing in.

It was then she heard a heavy thudding behind her. Glancing back quickly, she could see the black forms of two horses running flat out toward her.

Snail knew Goodspeed had nothing left to give and flung herself off the horse. This time luckily both feet came out of the stirrups, though her left boot stayed behind.

Reaching down into the right boot, she drew out her old knife. Then she stood and, at the same time, unsheathed Alith's knife that she'd tied around her waist. They would have to do.

"Come on, you blasted Border Lords," Snail cried. "I've already killed an assassin, an ogre, and a carnivorous mer. You won't find me wanting." It was an exaggeration of course. But they weren't to know that. And besides, all she really wanted to do was to survive.

But the riders couldn't have heard her anyway, over the

pounding of their own horses' hooves. They kept riding, as if to run her down. She wondered what good the knives would be against horse hooves, against the bows in the riders' hands, against the arrows.

She thought of the unmourned Groan hung on the tree by his hair, arrows sprouting out of him like spring roots, and started to tremble.

It was too late to run.

9

ASPEN GETS GOOD COUNSEL

*A*spen entered the throne room to find his mother standing alone and looking up at the throne as if wondering why her husband wasn't sitting there.

I must seem a pale replacement to her.

She had lost weight in the weeks since she'd helped Aspen and Snail escape the castle, grown weaker and perhaps even a tad frail. Probably because she'd spent most of that time in the dungeon. Balnar had carried down her special loom to keep her hands and mind occupied during the long, lonely days. It had been Balnar who brought her food and water to keep her alive when everyone else had fled, taking the dungeon key with them. It had been Balnar who told him of the queen's whereabouts.

And when Aspen had returned from the battlefield with news of the king's death—and possibly his brothers' deaths as well, for he was shining in the gold of kingship—she'd wept even as she stumbled, cramped and sore, over the ruins of the prison door he'd just blasted to pieces.

"How can you weep for the man who locked you away like a criminal?" Aspen had snarled.

"I did criminal things," she told him. "And I did them willingly. Your father only did his duty. He *always* did his duty." Then she'd laid her hand on his shoulder, which immediately began to thrum with the royal golden glow. "As you must now do."

Aspen watched her silently and wondered at a woman who could deny a monarch in order to be a good mother, yet still loved the man who denied his own fatherhood to act as the king.

Now, somehow sensing Aspen in the throne room—a mother's awareness, Aspen suspected, nothing magical—she turned and smiled.

"Ailenbran," she said in her soft voice, holding out her heart hand to him.

He stepped forward and gave her his left hand as well. Up close, he could see lots of grey strands in her ash blonde hair. *She ages not a whit for centuries, and as soon as I return, she goes grey as a harvest goose.*

"Where is that girl of yours?" she asked, as if it were a grand ball and he was short a partner.

He knew she meant Snail. "She is no one's girl, Mother. Least of all mine." He could scarcely imagine how furious Snail would be to hear herself referred to as someone's *girl*. "And I have sent her away."

His mother looked stricken. "Why would you do that? She was—"

"The only creature with half a brain in this castle?"

"I would never say that to anyone!" she exclaimed, turning away. She spoke her next words to the throne so none could say she lied. She was famous for her truth-telling. At one time, it was something the king had valued in her. "Though it may be true."

"She had to go speak to someone whom no one else could." *And who might be very angry with her.*

Aspen suddenly thought of the assassin who had come for him while he was with the professor. And how the professor had fed the assassin to Huldra the troll without a second thought. *If Odds is angry enough, he might kill Snail.*

And then a worse thought hit him. *She might already be dead!*

"Oh, Mother! What have I done?" he cried. It was as if a floodgate opened and his words were water. "I need to stop her! Go get her. I will send soldiers. I will go after her myself. I will—"

It was not kingly. But when his mother opened her arms to him, he was relieved that the throne room was empty, for he folded himself into her embrace as if he were seven again, about to leave for the Unseelie Court.

"If Snail had to go, then you have done your duty," she whispered into his hair. Then she stepped back and pushed him away, adding, "Your Majesty." It was a hint not to be ignored, and he took it.

Straightening, he wiped his eyes. Adjusted his tunic. Finally nodded to his mother.

She stared at him for a few moments before curtseying. "Come," she said, "let us eat. No one has ever saved a kingdom on an empty stomach."

His mother's logic was unassailable: he could not think of a single person who had saved anything of note while starving. Except, perhaps, his mother, who had saved the honor of the Seelie Court while in the dungeon with little food.

        ▨   ▨   ▨

IN THE GRAND Dining Room, they sat alone at a ridiculously long table, Aspen in the King's Seat. His mother, as the second most noble in the room, should have been seated in the Second Seat at the far end. Instead, she sat right next to him, in a cushioned chair reserved for "guests of the king," who on occasion had been known to be no more noble than a duke or an earl. If history was to be believed, a commoner's backside might even have dusted the pillows once or twice. His mother's, for example, before she had been made queen, though no one ever remembered that. Or at least no one ever spoke about it out loud.

"Close your mouth, Ailenbran," she snapped. "It is unseemly."

Spoken, he thought, happy for the moment, *like a mother of a seven-year-old and not the dowager queen.*

Balnar chose that moment to enter and take their orders, stopping briefly when he saw where the Queen Mother sat. She raised an eyebrow at him as if daring the old steward to say something. For a moment, Aspen thought he might. But instead, he just grabbed the setting from the Second Seat mutely and moved it to its new home.

"A full luncheon, Majesty?" he asked, addressing them both. "Or just a brief repast?"

Aspen was suddenly ravenously hungry. "A full luncheon, I think, Balnar."

His mother nodded her agreement, then touched the side of her chair. "It is tradition and formality that got us into this mess, Ailenbran," she said. "Imagine wanting to hang a child because he broke some imagined pact he had no say in."

"I do not need to imagine it, Mother. I was that child."

His mother looked at him sharply. "But you are not that child anymore."

Aspen realized that he had been wrong to think his mother's stay in the dungeons had weakened her. She'd been hardened by it, any softness in her turned to sharp bone; and the new grey hair was the grey of cold iron that would burn any who dared try to harm her or hers again.

"No, Mother," he said, drawing strength from her fierceness. "I am not that child anymore."

THE LUNCH WITH his mother was cut short by a breathless messenger charging into the dining room. Balnar followed behind, thin hands reaching for the messenger's cloak.

"I am sorry, Your Majesty," he said. "I tried to stop him!"

Aspen waved him off. "Leave him, Balnar. It looks important." *Everything at this juncture is important*, he thought miserably.

"It is, Your Majesty," the messenger said, bowing low and confirming Aspen's worst suspicions. He wore the uniform of a scout, though he was far too young to hold such a post. There was a red poppy in his cap, announcing his clan. Aspen knew he was one of the Poppy Clan boys who had refused to flee the castle when news of the great defeat had come. Instead, the entire House of the Poppy had become soldiers overnight, and a few of the other clans—some more reluctantly—followed.

Brave, Aspen thought. *Brave, but so, so young*. Even younger then I am. "Speak, then, scout. Kings have long ears and short patience."

"Outriders, sire. Our scouts have made contact with the enemy's outriders."

"How far from the castle?"

"Three days' march, sire." The scout gulped. "Perhaps a bit more."

Aspen knew the scout was trying to soften the blow with

that last bit. *Scouts three days out and the army perhaps a half day behind them.* Aspen stood, the last bites of his lunch forgotten. "That is not enough time."

"Enough time for what, Ailenbran?" his mother asked. She began to pick choice pieces from their lunches and pile them on top of a napkin.

"For Snail to return with reinforcements." *If she can convince Odds to help.* Aspen shook his head. *She has to convince him. There is no other way.* "We need to delay the Unseelie."

"Understood, sire." The young scout tucked his tunic down. Checked his sword in its sheath. "I will return to the scouts and order them to attack. We will hold them as long as we can."

"That is a brave offer, scout," Aspen said, "but we are going to need more than bravery to slow the Unseelie forces."

"Yes, sire." The boy's face shone with eagerness as he waited to be told what to do next.

"We need a plan."

The scout was sensible enough to look relieved.

"And do you have a plan, dear?" his mother asked quietly. She was folding in the corners of the napkin now, forming a roof over the small pile of food.

The scout leaned in to hear his answer, as did Balnar.

"Yes," Aspen lied.

And knew he lied.

I have no plan and even less hope. But I am sick of sitting and waiting. Every day more folk flee the castle, and those are the smart ones. If I do not give the rest of them hope and reason to stay, when the Unseelie reach us in three days, it shall just be my mother and me holding the walls. And Balnar. Always Balnar.

He looked at the old retainer, who probably should have been retired long since. Loyal to a fault.

"Balnar, ready every horse we have left and find soldiers to ride them. If there are not enough soldiers, put anyone or anything who can ride on their backs."

"Stop, Balnar!" his mother said, her voice almost rising to a shout, which startled both Aspen and Balnar. Turning to Aspen she said, "*That* is your plan?" For the first time her voice was sharp. "Ride to your death and take the last of your kingdom with you?"

"If I thought that would buy Snail the time she needs, then I would do it in an instant." Aspen shook his head. "But it will not. No, Mother, give me some credit. I have a different idea."

And suddenly he did.

"Balnar, also rig a carriage for Mishrath. Our wizard will be coming with us."

"Of course, sire," Balnar said. "But I fear he may not survive the journey."

I fear none of us may survive the journey, Aspen thought. But he didn't say it aloud. *My people need a brave and confident leader if we are going to live through the next few days.*

He almost chuckled. *Unfortunately, all they have is me.*

Drawing a deep breath, he thought: *I am going to have to fake it.*

For some reason, he thought of the skulker in the cave. The man had seemed confident. Aspen remembered the single sword stroke that had taken the heads off of all three crones. *Evil, but confident. I wonder if he was a leader? And if he was, whom did he lead?*

10

SNAIL AND THE GIANT SPIDER

The two dark riders came closer and closer, then suddenly split apart, one on either side of Snail. Before she could react, she'd been scooped up like a package wrapped for delivery.

"Let me go, you boggarts!" she cried in her fiercest voice. She tried to kick but was securely held. Her arms were bound to her side by the rider's strong arms, so her knives were useless.

"Shut up, m'lady," said the one who'd grabbed her. "And stop struggling. It scares the horse, and he needs to concentrate on speed."

"Snaggle?" She was astonished.

"Who else was you expecting? More of them Badder Lords?"

Snail was so relieved, she didn't bother correcting him and didn't mind his hand on her waist. Instead, she leaned forward over his horse's neck for balance, trying hard not to lose either of the knives.

They galloped on till they reached the path that went down into the valley, both the horses laboring mightily.

By this time Snail had managed to sit up a bit, and she saw something large, black, and long-legged straddling the way about a quarter mile down.

"Them demned spiders," Snaggle said, and spit off to one side as if to curse them.

"I don't like the looks of it, this close up," Snap called over. "Iron you said they was. Cold iron."

They pulled their horses to a stop.

"Don't worry," Snail told them, checking behind to see if anyone was following them, but there was no one in sight. "The spiders know me. Or at least their smaller mommies and daddies did."

"Not much of a coddler, are you?" said Snaggle. "Don't want to give us false hope."

"Even *false* hope would help," added Snap.

Snaggle kicked the horse forward. Not being long-sighted, the horse had only now spotted the spider and needed a second kick as inspiration.

All Snail could think as they rode ahead was the old kitchen saying: *Jump out the skillet, you fall in the flame*, which Nettle—her only friend back at the Unseelie Court—used to say whenever something was about to get worse.

Instead of telling them that, she said, "Trust me."

But she really *didn't* know how the spider would greet

them. If they were extremely lucky, perhaps the spider would run away.

But the spider didn't move.

Maybe it's died, she thought. Even luckier. But it was a made thing, and their life spans were incalculable.

The horses began to speed up as the downhill steepened.

Suddenly Snail realized that there was going to be a disastrous crash with horses and fey coming out the worst, unless she did something. And quickly.

Turning, she shouted into Snaggle's face, which was set prune-like into dark wrinkles, "Halt! Hold it. Let me go first. They know me."

At least she hoped they did.

He sawed at the reins, and his horse struggled to slow. But Snap and his horse swept by them. They could feel a wind off Snap's steed as it passed, a damp wind smelling of sweat and fear, a powerful combination.

Snaggle cried out, "Stop, you fool!" and his voice was a thunder that broke through the cloud of Snap's fierce concentration.

Snap's horse skittered, stumbled as the reins sawed at its mouth. Then it slid to a stop, its rider all but tossed over its head.

Snap looked over his shoulder. "Are ye mad?"

"M'lady's orders," Snaggle said.

Snail thought, *I hadn't meant it as an order. More like a prayer.*

Quickly they caught up to Snap and his mount, and the three confabbed for a moment.

"I'm a changeling, and the spider will sniff it on me. Then I'll tell it who I am," Snail said, hoping it was enough to hold Snap and Snaggle at this distance.

"And just who is *that*?" Snap asked before Snaggle could.

This close to the iron spider, the horses were beginning to tremble, their skins looking like earthworks in a quake.

"I'm a friend of Professor Odds, my birth is of human-kind, and I was the doctor who patched up all of the downed changelings at Bogborough."

"That should do it!" Snap said sarcastically.

Snaggle clearly didn't believe her. Worry was written plain on his face. "If that thing gives ye time to say it. And if it understands changeling speech."

His concerns were hers, but she refused to share her fears. "Stay here, and if everything is all right, go back and report to Alith, who knows what we're to say to the professor, in case I forget some of it."

"Alith . . ." Snaggle began, then his voice broke.

". . . will not be coming with us," Snap finished for him.

Snail felt her unshod foot start to wobble as if it hadn't enough support to stand up on its own. What Snap said wasn't a complete surprise. Otherwise, why hadn't Alith ridden with them? Still, Snail's body treated the news like a shock. It took all her concentration to straighten up.

"Alith . . ." she whispered, then made herself breathe more

slowly. "I'm a doctor, take me back to her."

"There's nothing for you to do," Snaggle said, and Snap nodded in agreement.

"We can't just leave her. . . ." Snail knew that in fact they could, and *had* to leave her. It was just what Alith herself had ordered.

But as to what had happened to Alith, she didn't want to know. If she knew it all, she feared she wouldn't be able to go forward.

"And the Border Lords?" she asked. That much she had to have recounted.

"All dead," said Snap.

"All that we *know* of," amended Snaggle. "Two to our arrows. And three to the captain's sword."

With Alith gone, Snail felt no need to keep the secret longer. "The Greens were following us, and Mums after them. But staying out of sight. As a precaution."

"Of course," said Snaggle.

"We spotted them early," Snap added.

"That's why *we're* the best," Snaggle said. "They're doing the cleanup."

"And *I'm* the best at this," Snail told them. "Leave me to it. But stay ready." She spoke as Alith might have. The word *cleanup* had undone her. She turned and began to walk down the hill.

Clutching the boot knife in her left hand, Alith's knife in her right, she stumbled toward the waiting spider. She knew

Snap and Snaggle wouldn't follow. They might be warriors, but they were soldiers first. And she'd barked out orders to them that—missing Alith—they had to obey.

THE SPIDER WAS as large as one of Professor Odds's wagons. It hadn't moved in all the time they'd been heading toward it, though it looked—Snail thought—preternaturally alert. If made spiders could be alert. Its jointed iron legs seemed locked, but ready.

She ignored the legs, staring instead at the carapace, or whatever that rounded thing on top was called. It seemed to sparkle, as if lit from within. She'd seen a large iron spider before—during the awful battle with the Unseelie folk—but that spider had only an iron top. *This* top appeared to be made of glass. Not the stained picture windows of a chapel, but a rounded half globe of glass big as a troll's wine cup.

If trolls ever had wine cups!

Snail wondered briefly if this spider was a second generation. Or a cousin.

As she neared the bottom of the hill, the unbooted foot was still giving her problems. She stopped to pull a thorn from between her toes. Then she started walking again, this time at half the speed. She didn't want to appear threatening, though she doubted that, limping and small, she looked like a threat to such a large creature.

When she was almost within reach of one of its legs, she

stopped and held both hands up, the knives glinting in the now fully risen sun. Bending over, she placed both knives on the ground, then stood fully erect, hands raised to show that she was now unarmed.

She heard a strange sound from the spider, not exactly a voice, more like a rasp of metal on metal. She tried to see if anything was moving, but the spider seemed as still as before.

Turning her head, she checked behind her. Snap and Snaggle had their bows up, arrows notched, waiting. As ordered, they hadn't followed, but they *were* ready.

Suddenly a silver door in the spider's belly flopped open with a loud creak.

Is it going to give birth? Pee? Do something unspeakable? She reminded herself it was a *made* thing. It shouldn't have bodily functions.

A rope ladder dropped down from the belly door, long enough to pool on the ground. She saw a face peering down but couldn't make out the features, as it was shadowed by the door.

"Are you crazed, skarm drema? Never give up yer weapons without a fight, or ye'll be fighting without yer weapons."

"Annar!" Snail finally recognized him, one of the dwarf brothers in the professor's very odd troupe. Relieved to see him, she ran over thinking to give him a hug.

"Yer weapons, girl!" he cried. "There are madmen behind you with arrows."

"No, no," she said, going back to pick up the knives, "those are my guards and guides. Sent to protect me by the Seelie king. You know—Prince Aspen."

"Prince Aspen?"

She laughed, remembering they knew him by another name. "Karl the minstrel."

"Ah, the bad singer we took into our *hule*. A prince? I always thought he was a toff. Spoke like one, smelled like one, looked down his nose like one."

"Toff indeed," she replied, "but he's not like that now."

"Not dead, then?"

"No, he's king."

"Same difference," Annar said.

She gave him the quick version of how Aspen's father and brothers had been killed, and how the gold aura of kingship had descended upon Aspen—Karl the minstrel—changing him completely.

"For the good, I hope," Annar said. "Could not be for the worse."

"For the good," Snail said, hoping she was telling the truth.

By then, of course, Snap and Snaggle had gotten to them, and there were difficult introductions, and the scouts refused to ride in the spider.

"Not natural," said Snap.

"Nor comfortable," added Snaggle. "Not like a horse."

There was no arguing with them. And because Snail had

only one boot and no pony, they accepted the fact that she would ride with the dwarf, and Snap and Snaggle would follow.

As she and Annar were climbing up the ladder, Snail heard Snaggle say, "I'll do the talking from now on, and no arguing. I'm senior now."

"Yes, sir," Snap had replied, but there was an air of unripened rebellion in his voice.

Annar heard it, too. "Trouble ahead," he told Snail as he locked the spider's belly door.

"And behind, too." She filled him in on what had just happened in the meadow, though not what she was going to say to Professor Odds. *That*, she reasoned to herself, *is between the two of us. Annar's not to be trusted with such a secret.*

"At least . . ." she added under her breath, "not yet."

ASPEN LEAVES HOME

They gathered at the great gates to the castle. It was a pitifully small contingent compared to the grandeur of the castle gates: three dozen horses, no more than twenty-five of them mounted with real soldiers and scouts, which included boys and girls from the Toad Clan who had been training for combat. The rest of the horses held old men and several youths from the palace. Aspen recognized the dog boy, a young footman, the chef's second apprentice. A single house brownie had volunteered.

There were also two kitchen maids gamely holding on to the manes of their ponies, and a queen's lady dressed in boys' trews and shirt. The queen's lady had a lance, the bottom of which she kept jammed down in her stirrup, though as it was only a jouster and not a war lance, Aspen knew it would break on contact. He hoped the enemy would not know that.

The moat troll, who had grown fat and slow under the

bridge, was there as well, looking eager and wet. He was the only one who did not ride a horse.

Hopefully he will not eat one! Aspen thought. *And it would be nice if he could keep up. He's the only creature of any size we have.* Suddenly he longed for Hulda, the troll who'd died in his last battle, defending the humans and dwarfs.

Aspen nodded at them, all fools willing to follow their young king on his mad advance, all believing that he had a plan good enough to save most of them, if not the kingdom itself. A small contingent of soldiers, six in all, were left to guard the gates and keep watch in case the castle itself was attacked by outliers, three of them riders who on swift horses could be ready at a moment's notice to race after Aspen to bring him news.

There was no provision wagon. They dared not cook hot food. Cook-fires would give away their position and their numbers. Besides, there was plenty to live on in the forest. Mushrooms, bushes groaning with berries, wild garlic and onion. Each fighter had been issued a leather pocket full of oats that were drowned in goats' milk and smothered in blueberries. There were some skins of wine as well, but only for the dying.

That should do for the troops, Aspen thought, then reminded himself to send someone for the goats. *The troll is on his own. Though if I see Jack Daw, I will offer him up to the troll as fresh meat.*

Balnar and the dowager queen were there to see them off, along with the castle cook, two cook boys, the gimp-legged hostler (both his helpers were riding with Aspen and in charge of the horses), and the elderly nanny who hadn't had anyone to care for since Aspen had been sent away as Hostage Prince.

Balnar had pleaded to go along, but Aspen needed him to keep the castle running.

"And to keep the queen alive," Aspen said, which immediately changed Balnar's demeanor. "Plus, I plan on returning," he added, "and will want a hot meal when I do."

Balnar looked ready to weep, but, of course, that would have been improper, so he did not.

On the other hand, the queen wept freely. "You had best return, my dearest son. I have already lost you twice. I cannot lose you a third time." She took something from her cloak and pressed it into his hands. It was the napkin from lunch, stuffed with leftovers. "And do not forget to eat."

Aspen just nodded and tucked the food away in his pouch. He didn't trust himself to speak lest he, too, burst into tears. *A king must not cry* twice *in one day!*

Then two oxen were led to the gates, pulling behind them a cart piled with straw. Mishrath perched atop the straw like the wizened cap of a toadstool. He was smiling, though. Three goats were already tethered behind.

Balnar, Aspen thought. *He is a gift.*

"Good evening, sire," Mishrath croaked. Still in his same

grey robe and crumpled grey hat, he smiled at Aspen, though the smile was merely a broad wrinkle amongst wrinkles. He waved a three-fingered hand. "I hope your trip to the tower was informational?"

Aspen thought about it and returned the same answer he had given the Welcomer. "I am not sure."

Mishrath chuckled. "We get that a lot."

Aspen determined that if he had time, he would tell Mishrath what he had seen with the Archivist. Maybe the old wizard could make sense of it. But for now, he had to get their small party moving.

"We ride till dark," he said in a loud voice. "We should be safe enough till then, though we shall still set a strong watch." He spun his horse around and motioned to the few soldiers to form up. "We ride hard the next day to get into position."

Swiftly the soldiers cajoled the civilians into a semblance of a martial column and spread themselves along the line. Aspen nodded his approval. Then he walked his horse to the front of the column. Where a king must ride. "And that night we stop their advance."

The soldiers and old men looked at him doubtfully. The young men and the two kitchen maids stared as if he were a hero from legend. The queen's lady seemed ready to change her mind, except it would show her a coward.

They all think me either heroic or mad. Or possibly both.

Looking down from his cart of straw, Mishrath cackled

as if mad kings leading minuscule armies to certain doom were things he had seen a thousand times in his long life. And perhaps he had—there or in the backward history of the tower.

"Companions!" Aspen called out, touching heels lightly to his mount and starting it forward. "We ride!"

They rode out the great gates, all silent except for the *clip-clop* of the horses' hooves and the racking sobs of the dowager queen, his mother, standing at the gate.

12

SNAIL IN THE ENCAMPMENT

The iron creature lurched from side to side as if drunk on the Border Lords' *Whisk of Life*.

Annar showed Snail the leather handholds hanging from the carapace ceiling and sides. "Grab on," he said. "Else you'll get flung about. Unless it's a fling you're wanting."

"No fling," she said, and grabbed on.

He pushed a button, and the lurch turned into a trot. Snail suddenly remembered Goodspeed with great fondness.

However, with those long iron spider legs, they made good time, leaving Snap and Snaggle on their winded horses far behind.

At the edge of the encampment, Annar wrenched a lever Snail hadn't even noticed, and the spider stopped mid-step.

"You'll be put down here," he told her. "I have to return to guard the path."

"Where do I go?" she asked, straining to see out the windows of the carapace. The place was aboil with people.

Annar pointed toward the north, and Snail saw the main body of the encampment lying in the shadow of the big mountain. Odds's wagons huddled together there, slightly off center.

"Himself will be in his room, plotting," Annar said, then grinned. "And spotting. Plotting and spotting. He'll know something's up, 'cause I'm here. He's got magic eyes."

"Magic eyes?" She'd never noticed *that*.

"Magic eyes that spies," Annar said. He put a finger to the side of his bulgy nose. "He holds them up in his hands and looks through and can see more than you and I can."

Now she was thoroughly confused.

He laughed. "So out you go!" He unlatched the door in the spider's belly and threw down the rope ladder. The top was tightly wound on two hooks.

For a moment, Snail thought about staying safe in the big spider, then she thought better of it and sat down beside the open belly door. Then she swung her legs through and turned over before descending one shaky rung at a time.

"Watch out for Border Lords," she said to Annar. "They were following us. We're not sure we got them all."

"Oh, we've been battling them for days," he said. "They're like stinging insects. But we swat them where they stand."

He seems so certain, Snail thought. *Surely the Border Lords aren't that easily swatted.*

Except . . . as she stepped off the rungs, she realized the

spider was the perfect swatting machine. Nothing could stand against its might.

She looked up and saluted Annar as he reeled in the ladder.

He grinned and saluted back.

How can he laugh at a time like this? she thought, remembering Snaggle's voice when he said of Alith, "There's nothing for you to do." Remembering the death of Huldra the brave troll. And the deaths and maimings of hundreds of others in those first battles of this Seelie War.

And then she thought: *Maybe* Annar's *right. Maybe we have to laugh in the face of such brutality. Isn't that really what being brave is all about?*

She shook her head. Scolded herself: *Concentrate on what you have to do.* "Which," she said aloud, "might be another way of explaining bravery—going ahead and doing what one has to do despite the odds." She giggled. "And possibly despite Professor Odds as well!"

She spotted Snaggle and Snap on the side of the ridge, a small horse between them.

"Goodspeed!" she cried joyfully.

The roan shook her mane as if in response.

Snap and Snaggle rode down to Snail, though they stayed close to the edge of the trees so that the spider could pass them by as far away as possible on its way up back up to its station.

When they got close, Snail went up to Goodspeed and

patted her on the nose, and the mare made a small chuffing sound, almost as if she was purring like one of the castle cats.

"Where did you find her?"

"She found us," said Snap. "Trotted out from the trees as if she'd never been lost."

Snaggle laughed. "And a big mound of grass between her teeth like she'd just scarfed down a huge part of the forest."

"And my boot?"

"Afraid that's lost, m'lady," Snap said. "But as you'll be aboard herself . . ."

"I'm thinking of . . . after," Snail said, adding, "though I'm sure there will be boots aplenty down in the valley." She didn't have to remind them why. Instead she said, "Turn around, give the lady some clothes-changing room. And if I see either of you peek . . ."

They turned. She took one of the two carefully packed bundles out of the saddlebags, then quickly stripped off her riding clothes, the ones she'd now been in for far too many days. What she put on were the old but laundered doctoring clothes, the skirt and shirt that she'd been wearing when the other changelings had seen her last. And the headscarf that barely covered her orange-red hair.

She stashed the dirty riding clothes against the other bundle, turned, and said, "You can look now."

They made a fuss of turning toward her, and Snaggle got down off his horse to give her a boost up.

Snap said, "Ladies and their clothing . . ."

Snaggle snarled, "Shut the bolt hole, brother."

But Snail laughed out loud. "If we want a welcome without a pike at the other end of it, we can't come to them as warriors or as toffs. They need to recognize me as one of their own, someone they remember as having saved many of their brothers and sisters, mothers and fathers, which I did in these very clothes."

Snaggle nodded, and Snap looked down at his hands. Then they rode the rest of the way down the mountainside in silence.

Snail was eager to talk to Professor Odds, rehearsing what she had to say to him in her mind. But Snaggle and Snap and their mounts were even more eager to be away from the iron spider that was once more athwart the upper path.

Guarding our backs, Snail thought, though she was certain she was the only one of them who felt that way. Ahead she could hear a bubble of noise, as a thousand or more campsites flamed into the morning; the cries of children, scolding parents, the whinny of horses and unicorns. For a few moments more she'd be above all that hubbub, but soon enough they would be in the very center of it.

Better this than the screams of the wounded, the sighs of the dying, and the awful weeping after, she thought. Though if she was unsuccessful here with Professor Odds, that, too, would come soon enough.

They were quickly on the flat and moving forward at a slower pace right to the edge of the encampment.

"They don't look much prepared for fighting," said Snaggle. "Not for a skirmish, and certainly not for a war, m'lady. There's no rhyme nor reason for how they're set up here."

Snap added, "Just higgledy-piggledy, with toddles and younglings underfoot."

Snaggle nodded. "No good lines nor the makings for a shield wall. No arms and armament. No command stations. No—"

"And yet they *have* fought," Snail said, gesturing with her head to the left where a tall iron gibbet had been set up. A body, or rather the remnants of one, the bits that crows and ravens had left, hung from the crossbar. It looked to have been a large fighting man, a Border Lord by the tangles of beard left on the ragged strips of face. Tatters of a blue-and-green kilt hung precariously from the waist bones.

How could they have left the hanged man where children could gaze at it all day? Snail was appalled. *We should be above such things,* she thought, meaning changelings, meaning humans.

She looked away.

A small buzz had begun around them. People with weapons—knives and spears, a quarterstaff or two recently cut from the forest from their fresh, fleshy look. One man carried a two-handed sword. Snail guessed the sword belonged to the hanged man, because it was much too large for the man who carried it, even though he stood head and shoulders above the rest of the mob. She wondered how many changelings the Border Lord had slaughtered before being brought down.

Standing in the stirrups as best she could, Snail waved her hands and shouted, "Remember me? I'm the doctor, friend of the professor and the dwarfs and Maggie Light. I've ridden in an iron spider to get here, and my companions have killed three Border Lords." She took a deep breath, adding, "We have news for Odds. He'll want to see me immediately."

She had no idea how many of the changelings could hear her, or even remember her. Yes, she'd nursed scores of them back to health, and saved the limbs of quite a few more. But whether any of those coming toward her had been in that old battle, or even remembered anything past this morning's meal, she couldn't say.

Just as the crowd of angry-looking changelings swirled around them and Snail began to fear more for her life than her mission, she saw Maggie Light in the crowd, behind the big man.

Maggie had opened her mouth wide. That meant she was about to sing.

Snail turned to Snap and Snaggle. "Ask no questions," she told them sharply. "There's magic coming. Deep magic. Put your fingers in your ears. *Now!*"

She was counting on them to act as soldiers. And though they looked surprised, they did as she directed. After all, she was the leader.

Snail was so busy making sure that they obeyed, she barely got her own fingers in her ears in time.

ASPEN GOES TO WAR

*A*spen led his tiny army through the ripe countryside outside Astaeri Palace. Trees dripped apples, grain grew unasked for in fields. The magic of growing things seemed bursting at its seams.

And at its seems, he thought. The six seasons from Springtide to Berrybreak ran long in Seelie lands, and one never really knew whether what was seen was real, imagined, wished for, or needed. As they passed through a small steading, he again thought about the devastation the Unseelie horde was going to bring. *Where we have seeded the ground, they will bring death's cold plow.* He had been the Hostage Prince at the Unseelie Court for half his life. Now for the first time he thought about what he had learned there— anger, heartache, trickery, fear—and wondered if any of those would serve him now.

Even if his plan worked, the Unseelie army would still trample these fields, burn those outbuildings, rip out the fence posts that lined the road.

At the end of the fence, a small, brown face poked out of a cottage door, watching the strange procession pass by.

Aspen reined in his horse and called down to the brownie. "You must leave here," he said. "Go to the palace." *As if it is any safer there*, warned his own traitor heart.

The brownie scrunched her nose up and spit in the dirt. "I'll stay in my own hame, thank ye verra much, Yer Majesty," she said, and slammed the door shut.

Aspen heard locks click and bolts being shot into place.

It will not save her, he thought. *But then—neither can the castle. Maybe it is better to die amidst your own stuff than on a battlefield.* He shook his head. *Better not to die at all.*

"There's nothing you can do, sire."

Aspen looked up to see Mishrath's wagon passing slowly by him. "I know that, wizard. But I must still try."

Mishrath stared at him then, as if seeing him for the first time. "You're not much like your father, either as boy or man."

"It would be a surprise if I were." Aspen reined his horse into a slow walk to keep pace with the wagon. "I was away from the palace for nearly as long as I was there."

"Your blood and bearing are his, but you are definitely . . . different."

Aspen wondered how old Mishrath actually was, if he'd known his father as a child a thousand years ago. "Different how?"

Mishrath seemed to consider that question carefully.

Finally he said, "Your sense of duty is not the same."

"But my mother said he always did his duty."

"That he did, sire." Mishrath curled his lips into a very small smile. "But he never did more." The wizard coughed weakly, gathering his cloak a little closer around him as if feeling a chill, though it was not cold out.

"Some would say I have done less." Aspen began ticking points off on his fingers. "It was my duty to stay at Obs's Keep. My duty to stay in Father's dungeon and be hanged. My duty to die in battle with my father. Instead, I watched him die from a hilltop nearby."

"See?" Mishrath shrugged. "Different."

Aspen snorted, unsure whether to be irate or amused.

"Tell me, sire," Mishrath went on, "do you feel you did wrong to escape the Unseelie? Or escape your Father's gibbet?"

Aspen had to shake his head. He had been tricked into leaving the Unseelie Court. *And letting my own father hang me?* It had seemed like his duty at the time. He had even felt a bit disappointed in his mother for helping him escape. But now, the more he thought about that misbegotten sense of duty, the more insane it seemed.

Mishrath nodded at him. "And if you had ridden down into that valley to be slaughtered with the rest of your father's troops, what good could you do the kingdom now?" Mishrath fixed him with eyes that suddenly didn't seem so nearsighted as before. "The land has chosen you.

Do not doubt that you are the right one for the job."

Aspen stared at the wizard for so long, it was lucky the horse knew to stay on the road without direction from its rider.

"I am certain," he finally said, sighing, "that the land could have found a more suitable choice."

Mishrath gave a barking laugh—which quickly turned into a coughing fit. When he could speak again, he said, "Perhaps doubting your own abilities is exactly what this kingdom needs. A cocksure monarch might not have come up with whatever mad plan you have to slow down Old Jack Daw's approach." He leaned toward Aspen conspiratorially. "A plan I'm hoping you will share sometime soon. Sooner the better."

Aspen nodded. "Tell me, wizard, how much magic do you have left?"

"Not enough to keep me alive much longer." Mishrath raised an eyebrow. "But perhaps enough to go out in a glorious conflagration. One that will be remembered as long as tales are told."

"I hope that will not be necessary." Aspen looked away, suddenly unable to look at Mishrath. "But would you be willing?"

There was a long pause. Aspen thought Mishrath was holding back another coughing fit, but when he spoke, his voice was clear. "Sire, I am going to give you a piece of advice, though you did not ask for it, and most likely do not want to hear it." He waited until Aspen turned back before continuing. "When you ask someone to die for you," he said slowly, "look them in the eye."

Aspen gulped. The rest of the world faded and blurred until all he could see were Mishrath's eyes, still white but clear now, staring at him unblinkingly.

To his credit, Aspen did not look away.

"Mishrath," he said, trying to match the wizard's tone. "I *do* have a plan. It might not work. And even if it does, it will only buy us a day or two. That might not be enough for Snail to bring us an army. And even if she does, *that* might not be enough. And . . ." He realized he was rambling to avoid the true question. Taking a deep breath, he looked right in Mishrath's eyes and said, "If it comes to it, will you sacrifice yourself to *possibly* save us all?"

Mishrath's face cracked open into a wide grin, and he once again looked like an old, kindly, and exceptionally wrinkled tortoise-creature. "Of course!" he shouted, startling Aspen's horse.

A couple of strong pulls on the reins got the beast back under control, and after a throat-clearing hough, Mishrath went on. "I've lived so long I don't even remember when I was born. And for the last few hundred years, I've felt positively useless. It would be a pleasure to finally do something worth putting into the histories."

Histories! Aspen thought. "Speaking of history," he said, "I need to ask you about what happened in the tower."

They rode on for some time, Aspen relating his trip to the tower and meeting the Welcomer and the Archivist, and his long fall back in time.

Mishrath didn't interrupt until Aspen described the watcher behind the rocks. "This one you call the skulker," he said, "tell me again what he looked like?"

Aspen did and then told the rest of it: the spell, the staff, the murder of the three old women, the river coming to bear the boatman away.

After the whole story was told, Mishrath grinned and said, "It seems your three questions have been answered."

"What?" Aspen exploded. "I have no idea who the Sticksman is or how he came to be other than that he was ensorcelled somehow. And I have no idea how . . ." He stopped. "The staff."

"Indeed," Mishrath said.

"The old women said there must always be a Sticksman and he always holds the staff. So if he releases the staff, he will no longer be the Sticksman." It was half a statement and half a question.

"There is your third question answered."

"But you said all three questions are answered." Aspen tried not to sound petulant.

"And indeed they are." Then Mishrath added, almost apologetically, "In a way."

Wizards! Aspen thought. *They never say anything straight.*

"First question," Mishrath said. "What is the Sticksman? Well, he is something eternal—'There must always be a Sticksman.' And unless I miss my guess, he has something to do with death."

Aspen chuckled. "I would not wager on you missing your guesses most times, Mishrath."

"Indeed." Mishrath's brow had furrowed, giving his face even more wrinkles. "The skulker said the women would need passage soon, and they were dead moments later. Therefore, the passage they needed must be after death."

"I am not following . . ."

"No matter, sire." Mishrath waved his hand dismissively. "Second question: 'How does one become the Sticksman?'"

"Through fell magic?"

"Obviously." Mishrath coughed hard after that word, and it took a while for him to catch his breath.

"Mishrath," Aspen said, holding up a hand. "Let us talk later at camp. Rest now."

Mishrath coughed twice more and snorted. "More importantly," he said as if Aspen had not spoken, "one becomes the Sticksman by being in the skulker's way." Then he finally waved Aspen off and lay back down.

"But that tells me nothing!" Aspen said, exasperated. "I still do not know who the skulker is or how the Sticksman was in his way. I do not . . ." And then it hit him. "But I do not need to know that. If I get the Sticksman to let go of the staff, he will return to his old self and can answer all those questions himself!"

Mishrath smiled and waved Aspen in close. "Now you're thinking like a wizard." He closed his eyes.

Aspen didn't know whether to feel insulted or not. But—he realized quickly—such feelings counted little on the road they were on.

Only the road counted.

And what lay at its end.

SNAIL LOOKS FOR ODDS

*W*ith the sound of the magical song keeping the mob mazed, Snail, Snap, and Snaggle and their horses followed Maggie Light. Since her fingers were firmly in her ears, Snail only managed to stay on Goodspeed by squeezing her thighs so tight against the roan's sides, she could no longer feel her feet.

The horses alone seemed unfazed by the magic. And they kept moving along, while wave after wave of the mob simply stopped in their tracks to let horses and riders through.

In a matter of mere minutes, they'd pulled up next to the professor's wagons, the unnatural green of them so familiar to Snail, and yet so foreign, too. The wagon sides were still plastered with garish posters proclaiming that Professor Odds and His Magnificent Players had performed before kings and commoners alike.

Well, Snail thought, remembering Prince Aspen's performance, *there was nothing magnificent about some of those players!* And the one performance she'd been involved with had ended in the first real skirmish of the Seelie Wars, with deaths and maimings on both sides.

She knew that on the wagon's other side, the script wrapped around a painting of one of the made spiders and read: "Professor Odds's Traveling Circus of Works & Wonders, Performance & Prestidigitation, with Occasional Flights of Fancy & Fantasy, Not to Mention a Marvel of Mimicry and Action." She hoped that Odds and his people really were up to *action* now. Though from the looks of that crowd . . . She turned and saw that the mazement had begun to wear off. Many in the mob looked stunned, wary, confused. She had to agree with Snaggle and Snap. This was no army, and there was no time to make them one.

What had the king been thinking? The only thing this mob was good for was soon-to-be-dead bodies lying between the two armies. Buying time with somebody else's blood. And that, she knew, was the sort of thing that Aspen could never countenance. But could King Ailenbran?

Snail shook off the thought and took a deep breath. If King Ailenbran could inspire the loyalty of someone like Alith—she refused to think about Alith back in the forest. She, the envoy, had one job to do. And only she could do it. *And against all odds, I'll get it done!* She giggled wildly to herself, at the repetition of that stupid wordplay in the middle of this awful situation. Clearly she was becoming part of the dwarf's *hule*, their clan. Or an apprentice to the professor's own strange wordplaying games.

Over to the left of the wagons, the unicorns were comfortably munching a mixture of hay and grass that someone had gathered into barrels for them.

Snail could feel rather than hear Goodspeed whinny, for the little horse's body positively throbbed as she tried to pull off course to get a share of the unicorns' food.

"Hush!" Snail said. "Not yet."

Something touched her right leg, and she looked down fearfully. But it was only Thridi, Annar's brother, his head barely reaching to her knee. He motioned to her to pull her fingers out of her ears.

Quickly Snail glanced over at Maggie Light.

Maggie had indeed stopped singing.

Of course, she still could be humming, Snail thought. But she knew Thridi would have been mazed if such was the case. So she took her fingers from her ears, and it was like pulling corks out of unwilling bottles. Her ears popped simultaneously. But the moment she did, the noise of the encampment rolled over her like an unwelcome wave. It took all her willpower not to jam her fingers right back in her ears.

Climbing off her horse, once more aware of how badly she did it, she signaled for Snaggle and Snap to dismount as well.

Snap immediately took his fingers out of his ears and leapt from his steed, grinning.

More careful, perhaps because caution was an old soldier's

habit, Snaggle kept his fingers in his ears and asked aloud, "Safe, m'lady?"

Snail nodded, mouthing, "Quite safe now."

Only then did he pull his fingers from his ears and dismount, though she didn't doubt that if there'd been any sort of trouble, he'd have thrown himself in harm's way to keep her safe first. She wasn't sure Snap would have done the same.

Making swift introductions, she said: "Thridi, these are Snap and Snaggle. They're the fey warriors who brought me safely through the woods. And, yes, your brother sends greetings from the top of the spider. He seems quite comfortable up there. I found it . . . wobbly and disconcerting."

"Likes being big, does Annar," grumbled Thridi. "Big without breadth. He'd best be certain he's not without breath soon." He said that last bit while looking critically up at the two elves.

"Twins, then?" said Snaggle. "Where's the third?"

Snap looked confused. "Third?"

"A dwarf *hule* is always three to start. Usually sibs. They take in others who earn it. Did ye nay pay attention in school?" Snaggle groused.

The argument made Thridi grin.

Snap saluted sharply, taking in both Snaggle and Thridi at the same time.

"Snapped to," mused Thridi, frowning now. "Snap judgment. Bound to be trouble. Snapped in two." He turned to Snaggle. "My sister is the third."

"The *true* warrior of the *hule*, then," Snaggle said.

"I've been blooded," Thridi snarled.

"Two of ye, then," Snaggle said. It was not a peace offering, more a true acknowledgment.

Thridi's quick anger was as quickly forgotten. He grinned and shook Snaggle's hand. "No one's as tough as she is."

"Families." Snaggle grinned back and gestured toward Snap with a flick of his head. "I keep him on a short rein. Sister's only boy."

Snail's head went up at their exchange. Snap and Snaggle were related? Uncle and nephew? How had she not known? Why had she not even guessed? Saying little, Thridi had found out more about Snap and Snaggle in the first moment of meeting them than she had in the entire long and grueling travel from the Seelie palace.

Was it some sort of dwarf magic? *Or*—she suddenly realized—*is it simply a matter of paying attention?* Perhaps she was believing in this *m'lady* business too much. Suddenly she remembered how it felt to be an underling in the Unseelie Court, how she hated the automatic dismissal of her wants and needs. How the toffs laughed at those they considered beneath them, used them, abused them. She decided she had to be more aware of those who served.

Like Alith, she thought. *She'd commanded but knew her*

warriors intimately and did not discount them ever. As she thought of Alith, her hand felt for the knife at her side she'd promised to deliver to Alith's son. She'd make sure he got it. *If . . .* Snail shuddered as though a spider—a real spider, not a made one—had crawled over the back of her neck. *If I live through this war.* All that stood between her and the destruction of everything she knew and had come to love was Professor Odds. She hoped he could do what Aspen thought he could.

Just then, the back door of the final wagon opened and out came another dwarf, carrying a baby so large its feet were dragging on the ground. The dwarf's eye took on an odd glow when she saw Snail.

"Skarm drema!" the dwarf cried.

"What's that supposed to mean?" Snap asked, his voice low enough to be called a growl. "Is it Dwarfish speech?"

"'Free one,'" said Snaggle. "Or 'newlywed.' 'Tis all in the tone, you know. Or you would if you listened in school." He pointed to Snail. "I think the dwarf means m'lady."

"Well, m'lady's not even promised to a husband," Snap said. "So it must mean 'free one.' Though free from what, I wonder?"

"Probably wishes she was free from you," Snaggle said with a snarl.

"Shut . . . your . . . bolt holes," said Snail, and not quietly, either. "And stand straight. This small person is worth two of you!"

Snap and Snaggle straightened and looked ahead, unblinking.

"Her name is Dagmarra, and she's to be treated with respect. She's a hero." Snail's voice was as unyielding as Alith's had been. Snail moved toward the dwarf woman, and her voice softened. "Dagmarra, that *can't* be baby Og."

"It can and is. Who else would it be?" Dagmarra said. "He'll be walking soon enough."

"Soon enough for him or soon enough for you?" Snail asked, and they both laughed.

"Not soon enough for me, obviously, my friend. But we make do." Dagmarra shifted the child in her arms. He was asleep as if the stir around him was but a lullaby.

Maybe, Snail thought, *troll babies need noise to put them to sleep.* She knew she should be getting on with her mission, but talking about the baby seemed like a safer option. Normal, even. *If a dwarf raising a troll baby can be considered normal!*

But Dagmarra wasn't fooled. Little ever got by her. "Is it Himself you're coming to see?" she asked bluntly.

Snail nodded.

"He might not want to talk to you. Raged when he found you missing. Said he'd thought better of you, thought that minstrel prince not worthy of your notice. Said you had Making Magic in your fingertips."

"I'm a midwife," Snail said. "And I dropped a baby once."

"If that's all you drop in your life," Dagmarra said, "you'll be a happy woman."

"If I live," Snail said.

"We all die," Dagmarra told her. "Dwarfs and trolls, patriots and spies, kings and kidlings, stupid fey with big mouths"— she glared at Snap and Snaggle—"and big men with swords. The problem is not how you die, but how you live."

"When did you become a wise woman?" Snail asked. "Next you'll be sealed up in a cave and making prophesies."

"Don't need a cave to see war's coming," Dagmarra said, "and that we're the least ready of the three armies to fight it. As for wisdom, it comes with watching a child grow. And this one grows fast. So I've had to be a fast learner."

"Yes, and that's why I'm here. To see Odds," Snail said. "The new Seelie king sent me as his envoy. M'lady, the warriors call me, though I don't know that I've earned the title. The king wants to join forces with the humans, to give them land for those who stay, and a high standing within the feydom. But for those who choose to leave for the human world, he promises a gift of parting."

"New king? What's wrong with the old one?"

"Dead."

The dwarf shrugged, as much as she could with an armful of sleeping troll baby. "One is like the other."

"Not this one."

"I've seen princes before. Even the good ones change

when they become king. It's that gold shine around their ears does it."

"Not this one," Snail repeated, and Dagmarra stared at her oddly.

"Hmmmmph! It's not Poppinjay the minstrel . . . ?"

Snail glared at Dagmarra, who seemed not to notice.

"I thought there were older brothers. And him a hostage from the Unseelie Court."

"The land chooses."

"As if the land is always right. Feh," said Dagmarra. "You should see some of the choices the land has made! We'd be better off doing the choosing ourselves." But she pushed baby Og into Snail's arms.

"What . . . ?" Og's weight staggered Snail, as if he was made of stone. But it was evening, and there was no sun. And it was the sun that supposedly turned all trolls into stone. Snail was careful to make no complaint.

"You hold Oggie, and I'll go and ask Himself. But you may not like the answer."

"At least he'll have to say *something* that way," Snail said, shifting the heavy baby to her shoulder. "There's hardly a Seelie army left, and so nothing stands between you and the Unseelie folk. Trust me, you don't want to be conscripted by *them*."

"Maybe not," said Dagmarra. She hopped up into the wagon and was immediately gone from sight.

"Well, that went well," Snaggle whispered in Snail's ear, the one farthest from the baby.

"Well as could be expected," Snail replied, meaning it hadn't gone well at all. "And now we wait."

Snap snorted. "Waiting is what warriors do best."

"I heard that was fighting," Snail said.

"Then you heard wrong," said Snap.

❖ ❖ ❖

BUT THEY DIDN'T have to wait long after all. Dagmarra was back quickly, and the news was neither good nor bad. "He said he'll give you his answer in the morning. Meanwhile, you bunk down in the wagon and your warriors under it. They won't be disturbed. I'll make sure of it." She took baby Og back into her arms, and he stirred comfortably but never woke.

So Snail went in, found her old room, lay down on the bed. She heard a snuffling from the floor. The bowser lay curled there, looking ragged and unwashed.

"I'll give you a scrub in the morning," she promised aloud and was immediately rewarded with a loud snore.

She fell asleep quickly herself and dreamed of the three dead Border Lords in the forest, with Alith beside them. The Border Lords began multiplying, wearing faces she knew and faces she didn't want to know. Suddenly she found herself in a green meadow where there were three stone cairns, the topmost stone on each carved with a name.

She moved closer and read them: Alith, Odds, Snail.

Shivering, she woke up, smelling like Goodspeed after a long gallop.

I don't believe in dreams as prophecy, she told herself. But afraid to fall asleep again into that same dream, she got up and opened the door, expecting deepest night.

It was morning. The encampment was a-bustle with cook-fires and a low hubbub of voices.

Snail walked around the outside of the wagons until she came to the one which she knew to be the professor's. Snap and Snaggle were there eating fresh journeycake with the dwarfs. They seemed like old companions now, part of the *hule*. Snail was surprised that she felt left out.

"Morning, m'lady," said Snaggle.

Snap nodded, his mouth too full for a greeting.

"Is he in?" Snail asked Thridi.

"Definitely in but not up," he replied.

"Up but not out," said Dagmarra.

"Out but not by," said Snap, having swallowed the jour-neycake and followed it with a swig of hot cav.

"Out, out, out!" gurgled baby Og.

"There!" said Thridi. "I told you he'd get the swing of it."

They all laughed, except for Snail.

"In, in, in!" Og said, trying for another laugh.

"You're corrupting him," Snail said.

The door of the wagon opened. "Not corrupting," said Odds. He was in a morning robe that was dotted with twinkling stars. "Teaching him grammar instead of grammary."

Snail glared at him.

"A fine choice if he is to become one of us," Odds continued.

"He's a troll," Snail said. "Remember—huge and hungry, eats people, turns to stone in the sun."

The professor pointed to the sky where a sullen sun sat on the shoulder of Big Sister. "Sun." He pointed to the baby. "Troll." Then he smiled. "Not stone."

Snail felt her jaw beginning to drop, closed it. *How had she not noticed?* But she didn't stop glaring.

"People can change," Odds said. "Trolls can change. Countries can change, too."

And suddenly Snail knew what to say. "That's what I've come to tell you." She forced herself to smile.

Odds opened the door more widely and ushered her into his room.

15

ASPEN ON THE ROAD

$\mathcal{W}$ith the road clear and no enemies expected until late the next day, Aspen didn't call the halt until well after the sun went down. They had reached a sparsely treed hilltop with a clear view in all directions, and a lucky full moon that lit the countryside for miles around.

We are not likely to find a more suitable spot, he thought. Even if he hadn't noticed how perfect the place was, his soldiers were casting meaningful glances at the ground and occasionally giving exaggerated yawns. *They do not dare give advice to their king. No matter how much I may need it.*

"We will make camp here," he called, watching the soldiers breathe a sigh of relief. "If my soldiers agree." He picked one at random, an older elf in the muted colors of the Toad Clan. "Does this spot suit you?"

The old soldier balked for only a moment at being addressed directly by the king, but recovered quickly. Glancing around, he said, "Good sight lines," then nodded at the few trees and occasional scrubby bushes. "Bit of cover." He nodded again, even shallower than before. "Suits well, sire."

"Then we make camp here," Aspen said, loud enough for all to hear. He started to dismount, then paused. The Toad Clan soldier was still looking at him. *Or rather he is looking at my horse's left ear and occasionally flicking his eyes in my direction.* "Is there more, soldier?"

The soldier nodded again, so shallow that it was as if he hoped Aspen wouldn't notice.

"Well, please speak freely," Aspen said. "And quickly. We are all tired."

Despite that instruction, the soldier paused, possibly collecting his thoughts. He pursed his lips as if to spit, then remembered he was in the presence of royalty and swallowed awkwardly.

"Um," he finally said. Another pause, though no pursed lips this time. "Your Majesty said a strong watch earlier?"

Aspen had the feeling this was rather a large amount of words for the soldier to string together all at once. The Toad Clan was not an overly talkative group. "Yes?"

"Might I suggest five and five for three apiece? We'll ring the hill and still be good as gold on the morrow." He got it all out in a rush, sitting his horse stiffly, his cheeks noticeably red even in the moonlight.

Aspen had very little idea what any of that meant. "An excellent idea," he said anyway. "Set the watch!" he called. "Five and five for three apiece!" He thought he sounded properly military with that last bit.

The soldiers conferred quickly, a knot of twenty. They must have agreed easily, for almost immediately, they saluted Aspen smartly and dismounted in unison. Their horses were hobbled in an instant, and then five of them were off, spreading themselves out along the hillside's perimeter at equal distances apart, three of them easy to spot and the other two well hidden. Another five plopped onto the ground, wrapped their cloaks around themselves, and were asleep at once. The remaining ten fanned out to set up their meager camp.

Five and five for three apiece? Aspen thought. *Must be five to watch and five to sleep. I bet they go three hours each watch, and we will travel again after six hours.* He looked at the sleeping soldiers. *I suppose when you only get three hours to sleep in, you learn to make the most of them.*

Aspen thought he should follow their example, but first he helped the civilians hobble their horses and bed down for the night. They took longer, most being unaccustomed to caring for horses on the road or sleeping rough. Except for the moat troll. He had no horse and bedded down on the most uncomfortable-looking boulder on the hilltop. He was soon asleep and snoring loudly, almost as quickly as the soldiers. Being a day troll, he would sleep through the night and be ready to travel again in the morning.

Aspen had slept rough often since escaping the Unseelie Court—and most times without the luxury of being guarded by soldiers. He was also exhausted from travel and worry. But even after he lay down in the softest grass on the hilltop, where the queen's lady had made him a bed with straw from the wagon and her own embroidered cloak, sleep still eluded him. He tossed about, feeling every pebble beneath him as if there were no straw or cloak between him and the ground.

In fact he felt like a princess from a story his nanny had told him in the long ago. Escaping from an enemy, the princess had slept in a dragon's cave atop a treasure. After a sleepless night, she had said a miser could figure out the creature's fortune by counting her bruises. "Counting her bruises!" The nanny always said it twice. He remembered how they had both howled with laughter, but he was not howling now.

After a long hour listening to the troll snore and watching the stars dance around in the sky, Aspen arose and went to check in with the sentries.

He exchanged soldier's talk with them.

"Any sign of the enemy?"

"No, sire."

"Have any family at home?"

"My mother."

"My sister."

"My wife and a newborn babe."

"You will return to them soon," Aspen assured them, hoping it was not a lie.

He learned their names and their clans: Fortuna, her hair

dyed the green of House Clover; Snarl and Bite, brothers of Clan Wolf; young Alicanson of the House of the Poppy, who had brought the news of the Unseelie approach that afternoon; and Fading Crocus of the Toad Clan who had been the one who suggested a five and five watch for three apiece.

"You gave me good advice, Fading Crocus," he said to the fey warrior. "I will not forget it. Kings always need good advisors not afraid to speak their minds."

"Croak, sire."

"Pardon?"

"They call me Croak," Fading Crocus said. Then quickly added, "Your Majesty!"

"I will not forget, Croak," Aspen said.

Finally he looked each of the soldiers in the eye and thanked them for watching over him and his company throughout the night.

Only then did he feel ready for sleep.

I will learn the rest of my companions' names in the morning, he thought, nestled in his makeshift bed. It was his last conscious thought of the evening, and a fine notion to fall asleep on.

Much better than pebbles.

SUNRISE CAME TOO early, as it always does for those who march to war. They were up and away with the light still slanting hard across the land. One of the girls had milked the goats so their complaints wouldn't give away the small army, and the milk was shared amongst the whole company. Eating oats from their leather pockets and berries gathered from the high hilltop bushes by the moat troll satisfied all their bellies.

In fact, the troll had not just gathered the berries, but ripped the bushes from the ground, shaking them roughly until all the fruit fell off for the others to pick up. Then he stuffed the bush whole into his wide, wide mouth.

So moat trolls are vegetarians, Aspen thought, happy to know that neither the horses nor the small company would become troll dinner.

Mishrath looked a little better after sleeping so long.

Well, not exactly better, Aspen concluded, *but when he closes his eyes, I actually expect he will manage to open them again.* Aspen hoped the wizard would have the strength they needed come the morrow.

True to his promise to himself, Aspen passed the morning riding up and down the line, first learning the names and clans of the other soldiers, and then interviewing the civilians. Most were a bit awed to speak with a king but warmed up quickly to his honest interest and earnest smile.

Molintien, the queen's lady, was surprisingly tongue-tied in his presence, and Aspen realized that she was much younger than he had thought at first. Her hair had fallen down in the night and she had not pinned it up again, and her face was now clear of the kinds of paints a woman at court usually applied.

Why, she is no more than a child herself! Then he smiled ruefully, for Molintien was probably just his age—and Snail's.

The moat troll grunted unintelligibly and pulled a sapling up by its roots, offering it to Aspen like a bouquet of flowers. Through one-syllable words and simple hand gestures, Aspen managed to convey that he was indeed honored by the gift but had nowhere to keep it at the moment, thank you very much.

The troll nodded, and made the sound of wind whistling through his unevenly spaced teeth, which Aspen took as a troll thank-you. They bobbed heads at one another for a moment more, and then Aspen trotted back to the head of the column, riding on in silence for a while as the troll ate the tree just like the berry bushes, in one big gulp.

⬛ ⬛ ⬛

By midmorning, Aspen realized they were going to have to move faster. *It will do us no good to hold up Jack Daw while still so close to the palace.*

"Croak!" he shouted, and the old soldier spurred his horse forward.

"Yes, sire?"

"Pick the two ablest civilians to take turns driving and guarding Mishrath's wagon. The rest of us must ride hard till nightfall, and the oxen cannot keep up."

Croak gave what for him was a positively enthusiastic nod—his chin moved nearly a full inch! Then he rode back to pull Molintien and one of the old men out of the line.

Fal is his name. Retired woodsman. Aspen was glad to have learned it. Fal was very old, but his chest was still broad and powerful and looked plenty capable of pulling the well-worn bow he carried. There was a newly sharpened ax at his waist.

"Press on in darkness till you reach us," Aspen told them. "The trail we leave will be easy to follow. If it gets too hard, I will send back soldiers to guide you."

Then turning to Mishrath, he said, "Rest up, wizard. I shall need your strength in the morning."

Standing high in the stirrups, he addressed the others. "Come, my good warriors! It is speed we need now!" Heels to horse, and he was off at a gallop, his companions kicking their own steeds to follow.

For the first time, Aspen felt like a soldier. And a king.

THEY COULDN'T GALLOP all day, of course. Even Aspen knew that. But he pushed both warriors and horses as hard as he could.

With the sun setting, he finally let the tired horses stop.

"Croak," he said, no longer needing to shout for him. Croak now rode next to him at all times. "What do you think of this spot?"

Ahead of them was a wide plain, sloping gently down to a swiftly running stream. There was thick forest off to their right, and rockier, broken ground to their left. Hills in the distance concealed any sign of the Unseelie host that must lie just beyond them.

"No good," Croak muttered. He offered no further explanation.

Aspen explained it for him. "Because if we are going to stop Jack Daw and his army, we would need someplace confined, a ravine, perhaps, or a mountain pass. Something to funnel them into a small space so their numbers will not count against us so badly."

Croak nodded.

"Even then, Croak, could we possibly stand against them for more than a few moments?"

Croak looked sour. Then shook his head.

"I agree," Aspen said. Then he looked out over the plain. "But what if we had an army? An army big enough to give the Unseelie a fight."

He looked over at Croak and could see him eyeing the field anew, this time placing soldiers in strategic spots, calling up imaginary units to defend this location or attack that one.

"What then, Croak?"

Croak paused, then spoke quietly. "'Tis good." He nodded toward the stream. "Skirmishers attack their crossing." His gaze traveled back up the slope. "Make 'em attack uphill." He glanced left, then right. "Flanks protected." Then back at Aspen. "'Tis a good spot, sire."

"Yes, it is." Aspen dismounted and called for the rest of the party to do the same. He waited, but Croak said nothing more. "Go ahead and say it, Croak."

"We've got no army, Your Majesty."

Aspen laughed. "Do we not?"

Then he sent everyone back into the woods to gather firewood.

"We're to have fire tonight, sire?" Croak asked, sounding completely confused.

"Oh, yes," Aspen replied, enjoying the bit of mystery. "We're to have fire tonight. Lots of fire. I *want* them to know we are here." He chuckled, then jogged off into the woods to gather wood with the rest.

I hope Mishrath is resting well in the wagon, for he will get none tomorrow. And the rest of us will get none tonight.

16

SNAIL LAYS OUT THE PLAN

Odds's room hadn't changed as much as he had. He seemed to have aged badly since she last saw him, his hair like cloth left out too long in the sun, his face more weathered than it had been only days before.

But the room was still recognizably his. The desk piled with oddments and ends of things, half-made manikins, glass balls that swirled in the light, two puzzles like the one she'd taken apart that had so engaged her attention. The bell pull hanging motionless by the desk's side, waiting for his hand.

Odds sat down heavily in his big chair and motioned for her to take a seat as well, but as there was only the bed to sit on, she continued standing.

"I have a plan," she said, quickly amending it. "*We* have a plan. The Seelie king and I . . ."

He interrupted, "That venal fool? What do you have to do with him? I thought you were too bright for that one. The only good thing he ever did was marry the commoner."

"He married a commoner?" When had Aspen had time? She'd just been gone a few days. And he'd never said . . . She realized with a start that she was about to cry. Turning her back to Odds for a moment to get control of herself, she bit her lip. Hard. So hard she almost drew blood. Pain would help her keep her feelings under control.

When she turned toward him again, she concentrated on her lip and the thought that at least Aspen had married someone interesting and thwarted convention. *Even if he hadn't said a thing to me. Even if he'd kept a secret, and why did he marry so young anyway? And moments away from a war? There had to be something to be gained by it. Maybe his mother had wanted it, or the wizards or* . . . And then she thought—and it made her miserable all over again—*No wonder he wanted to send me off on a mission.*

She glared at Odds. *You never thought much of Aspen!* And of course she herself had always believed that the royal bloodlines had to be pure. Certainly in the Unseelie Court the toffs always made a huge fuss about that.

"So the king married a commoner, had sons with her, and then he never listened to her again," Odds added.

Had sons? Never listened to her again?

Finally Snail realized what Odds was saying. He was talking about the *old* king, Aspen's father. And then she thought of the queen, that strong, elegant woman who had braved her husband's wrath and the laws of the land to save Aspen, her son—and Snail as well. *The queen a commoner?*

Hardly. If people like her were common, there'd be a lot less trouble in the world.

"No, no," she said, raising her hands for emphasis, "that king is dead. A new king is on the throne."

"One fey king is much like another." He looked at his fingers, and she saw that he was somehow making a coin move under and over each finger as if the coin were dancing. For a moment she was mesmerized by it. Then she shook her head to wake herself up.

"People change, you just now said." Her voice sounded tight to her, even overeager. She carefully lowered it again. "And no one has changed more than *this* king."

He looked up at her with renewed interest, simultaneously palming the coin. Then, folding his hands, he sat like a statue, giving nothing away. "The old king had two sons," he said carefully, "grown tall and handsome as all full fey do. Sons of the first wife. But you say that the one now king—has changed? I find that unlikely."

And then the coin was back dancing along Odds's fingers.

Snail became mesmerized again, had to push herself to look away in case it was some kind of magic that would force from her more than she meant to say.

"No," she replied. "Not them. The older brothers may be dead as well. Or not. We don't know. But the land has chosen a different king."

Odds closed his eyes, stuck the coin in a pocket, folded his hands over his belly, leaned back in his chair. He ignored her, pretending sleep, but she knew he was thinking. She could see the shadow of movement beneath his eyelids.

She decided to outwait him.

It didn't take long. His eyes flicked open, and they were not sleepy eyes at all, boring into her as if he could read her entire life with that one glance. He no longer looked old, bleached out. He looked . . . ready . . . the way a wolf or fox would look when ready to pounce.

"*Not* the minstrel prince?" he said. Less a question than a statement.

This time, despite the pain in her lip, Snail smiled broadly. "The very one."

"People change," he said, "but not always for the better. He's glowing gold, I suppose."

"He sees that as a burden."

"Hmmmm. I suppose he would. He got that from his mother. And the years in the Unseelie Court. A rough wooing that, with no wedding promised at the end but to death." Odds brought the coin out of his pocket again, this time flicking it into the air, where it spun over and over. When it hit his open palm, he slapped it onto the back of his other hand. "I'll listen if you can guess the coin's face. Odds or evens."

"A game, Professor? You'd chance the fate of your people on the flip of a coin?"

"Not a game. A puzzle!" Odds grinned at her and raised his hands closer to her face.

She didn't hesitate then. "With you it's always odds. But you may have charmed it to evens as a trick, But no, you are too full of yourself, of the professor, of Odds. And that's what we want."

"We?"

"The new king, the new kingdom." She drew in a deep breath. "And me." She said the final bit with ease because the speaking of it sat easily on her bruised lip.

He showed her the coin. It was, indeed, odds.

"Tell me the plan. But don't think you guessed right by chance." He turned the coin over, and she saw it had odds on the other side as well.

"A trick . . ."

"It's the only way you are going to win this war," he said. "With a trick. You have too few soldiers, and my people are not an army."

Her voice rose again, and this time she let it. Best he hear excitement, not caution, from her. "And that's what I came to tell you. The king has a plan." At any rate, she hoped he had. "But he needs *you* and your people to make the plan work. He will give much in return if you help him accomplish it."

He leaned forward in the chair. "How much of a much?"

She told him about the rise in status, the payment of land, of gold.

He laughed. "We need no status if we are the only ones alive at battle's end. And faerie gold is nothing but dried leaves in the wind."

"He will help those who wish to leave as well."

"And how could he stop us?"

Snail had only one last card in her small deck, and she played it now. "Only Aspen and his small band of fey stand between you and the Unseelie horde. He is willing to die with his people. Are you willing to die with yours?"

His first hesitation was a rapid blinking of his eyes. "We have our own magic. The iron spiders . . ."

"Ropes can trip them," she said. "I realized that possibility when I climbed up in one."

"We have our Singer of Spells." His voice had an edge to it, but it trembled.

"Bog cotton in the ears. How quickly will they figure that one out? Or if she's silenced by an arrow or a sword, what have you then? Small trickeries, cold iron, and mirrors? The horde will overrun you in a moment, and those not killed will be taken off to the Unseelie Court as slaves."

He was silent. And then blurted out, "The Unseelie have trickery as well."

"But the king knows all their tricks. He lived amongst them from the time he was small, and they think him weak."

"He *is* weak!" Odds squeaked.

"You're wrong," said Snail. "He's young. But youth is not a disease, nor is it a weakness. It's a promise. And Aspen keeps his."

Odds nodded. "But the women and children . . ."

"Stay behind," she said.

"Not Dagmarra and her kind."

"Someone will have to take care of Og," she said.

"Someone will," Odds said.

That was when she knew that she had won the battle with Odds.

But there was still the war.

ASPEN MAKES SOME MAGIC

By dark, Aspen figured they had collected over half the wood they would need. He gave new orders, putting most of his crew to work setting up pyramids of firewood stuffed with kindling all across the field in preparation for lighting. The remaining few kept gathering wood. Work slowed a bit as darkness fell, but the bright moon kept at least the pyramid builders working at a pace that Aspen thought might serve.

The moon was well up in the sky when Mishrath's wagon finally rolled into camp. Molintien galloped ahead and when she spotted the king, leapt off her horse to greet him like a farm girl and not a well-bred queen's lady-in-waiting.

"Sire," she said, bowing, "he is not well."

Aspen stopped stuffing twigs and leaves under a pile of wood and rushed to the wagon. Fal was trying to grab Mishrath and lift him out. The wizard, pale and shaky, waved off any assistance.

"I need no help from youngsters like you!" But even that

sentence seemed to exhaust him, and he fell back into the straw.

"Fal, a moment," Aspen said quietly, and the old forester bowed and stepped away from the wagon. "Molintien, start a fire. And when you see Croak, send him to me."

They hurried away, and Aspen turned back to the wagon.

"Mishrath," he said, and waited for the wizard to open his eyes. Then he waited a few more moments for them to focus. It took longer than he had hoped. "I understand pride. And I understand not wanting help." He thought about Snail and how not so long ago he would have thought accepting help from her unacceptable. *But now*, he admitted to himself, *I feel quite lost without her here.* "However, we have no time for that. I need you to let Fal lift you from the wagon. You are going to rest by the fire. To warm your blood. For we must have all of your strength tomorrow."

Mishrath peered up at him with his cloudy eyes. "There may not be much left, sire."

"Then we are probably all doomed anyway." But Aspen smiled when he said it and waved Fal back over.

This time, Mishrath nodded to the forester and stayed quiet as he was lifted from the wagon. He looked tiny against Fal's broad chest, and Aspen thought, *I hope I am not wrong to put all of my hopes in the care of this one old wizard.* But then he remembered the stone in Mishrath's voice just yesterday and he believed that with rest now, he could do what was needed.

I have to believe.

He followed Fal and Mishrath to where Molintien had started the small fire. Fal set the wizard down next to it, spreading his own cloak on the ground close by, before moving the old wizard onto it. Not to be outdone, Aspen took off his royal cloak, which had fur at the neck and the wrists, and covered Mishrath.

"Bring my saddle," he said to Fal, "so that he has something to sit up against until he is completely warm and ready to sleep."

"At once, sire," Fal said as Aspen sat down by the fire next to the old wizard.

"So you have a plan then, young king?" Mishrath said, his voice rough and weary.

"Yes, I believe I do."

"And you think Old Jack Daw won't see it coming?" He frowned into the fire as if something he saw there displeased him. "He has counseled three kings, and survived centuries in a court that—I am sure you know—is particularly unforgiving."

"I do not think he will guess it." Aspen pulled the royal cloak down a little so it covered the wizard's feet. He collected his thoughts, trying to think of the proper way to explain them. "Jack Daw," he finally said, "has been playing a game where only he is allowed to move the players."

Mishrath peered up at Aspen, his eyebrows lowered, his mouth quivering like a petulant child's. "I don't follow."

Aspen spoke carefully. "He has known exactly how all the players in this war would react to his moves. So, in a sense, through his actions, he controls them and has moved their pieces into the positions he wants."

"Ah," Mishrath breathed. A smile began to gather on his lips. "And he thinks he knows what the Seelie king will do."

Aspen nodded. "Of course he does. The Seelie king will ride into glorious battle with whatever forces he has left." He thought of the one battle he had actually been in. *Blood, death, chaos. And guilt.* There had been nothing glorious about it. "Because that is what Seelie kings do. Honor before all else." He took a deep breath. "But I am not just the Seelie king. I am the Hostage Prince. I was raised in the Unseelie Court. And I am going to use a few things that I learned in my years there, things I learned from Jack Daw himself, though he never knew he had taught me so well."

"And those are?" Though Mishrath had been lying in a partial faint on the ground, he sat up now, atremble. Though with excitement or fear or just with the coldness of his own approaching death, Aspen did not know.

But one thing Aspen did understand—Mishrath had already made the mental leap to where he was, though it was good of the old wizard to let him say it out loud.

"Trickery," Aspen said. "Trickery, lies, and deceit."

Mishrath made a strange sound then, something between a wheeze and a throat clear. It took a moment, but Aspen finally recognized it. The old wizard was chuckling. It seemed to make him younger, stronger. "And illusion, do not forget illusion, the greatest deceit of all. It is why I am here."

Aspen nodded. "Yes, my fine wizard. That is why you are here."

Mishrath closed his eyes. Pulled the cloak a little closer around him. "Do not put me back in the wagon like an old man. I will stay here and doze by the fire, remembering days when I did this kind of thing for glory and adventure. I will gain strength through memory. Wake me when I am needed. "

Getting to his feet, Aspen whispered, "I will."

At that very moment, Fal returned with the saddle. Aspen nodded again, this time in thanks, and at the same time saw that Croak was just coming from the forest with a load of wood.

"Stay a while with the old wizard," Aspen said to Fal. "Help him sit up if that would be more comfortable." Then he walked away to have a talk with Croak.

Croak was placing his wood on the ground, his back to the wizard's wagon. But he was totally aware of the king's presence at all times. When he turned, he bowed his head, all in a single movement.

"Croak," Aspen began, thinking hard how to cushion what had to be said, then realizing Croak needed no cozening. "I have an impossible task for you and the other warriors."

Croak smiled slowly.

Aspen could not tell if the smile was because he had used the word *warriors*, or because *impossible* was not in a warrior's vocabulary. Aspen pointed downhill. "We know that out there in the dark, enemy scouts approach. They cannot be allowed to cross the stream. No matter how they outnumber us, no matter if they outflank us, they cannot cross the stream." He peered intensely at the old Toad Clan soldier. "Do you understand? They *cannot* be allowed to cross over. If they do, and find out how few we are and what we plan, then all is lost."

Croak nodded. "I understand, sire."

"Good. You will scout in two-man groups. When you spot their scouts, one from the group comes back for me." Aspen gritted his teeth in what he hoped Croak would see as a carefree smile. "I am your reinforcements. I will repel the attackers whilst you make sure none slip past me. Do you understand?"

"Two-man groups. Retreat and reinforce. Repeat." Croak spit on the ground. "I understand, sire."

"And no one gets past the stream."

Croak nodded. "None will pass the stream."

"Now," Aspen said, adopting a light tone that he did not feel, "I believe I promised you an army." He called out, "Fal! Take Fayeth and Fennel with you and light the fires." Fayeth and Fennel were the two maids. *They will have some kitchen magic to help with the burning.* "Light them all!

Quickly, now!" Then he turned to Croak. "Do you see?"

Three at a time at first, and then more scattershot and separate, fires sprang to life on the sloping plain, like will o' wisps in the season of Trout Rise. Not one or two or ten or twenty but . . .

"What do you see, Croak?"

Croak's teeth glowed orange in the firelight as he smiled. "An army, sire."

Aspen nodded. "Now the hard work begins. Gather your men. No one crosses the stream."

Bowing without speaking, Croak turned and hurried away.

But Aspen was already gone, jogging to an unlit fire on the opposite side of the field from where Fal, Fayeth, and Fennel worked. He breathed sparks into the kindling and waved the fire to life. Then he ran to the next. And the next. Before long the entire field was alive with campfires. Not just will o' wisps now, but the cook-fires of a thousand hungry warriors.

A great host camps here, Aspen told himself, saying a small spell that the words should make it so. But of course, he had not that sort of magic. It was only a wish.

Still, the trickery might suffice. It must *suffice! For a while. At least for the time it takes for Snail to bring the real army.* He thought about Snail. He could always count on her. It was Odds, that crafty old human, he worried about.

He thought about the trickery the skulker must have used to get the crones to do all his work for him. *And why did he need the Sticksman so much that he had gone through all that?* He had a sudden thought. *What if the skulker hadn't needed the Sticksman? What if he had needed to get the Sticksman out of the way? Or rather get the creature who became the Sticksman out of the way?*

He had no idea who the Sticksman had been or why the skulker needed him gone, but the idea intrigued him. However, there was no time to think about that now. There was too much work to do. So he went back to the central fire where Mishrath slept on.

The civilians had gathered around that fire as well, most sprawled exhausted on the ground. Only Fal and Molintien were standing.

Even the moat troll was lying down, though he kept himself a safe distance from the fire. Aspen thought briefly of sending him to the stream, but feared it might complicate or compromise the trickery.

"Do not get too comfortable, my brave companions," Aspen said to them in as kingly a fashion as possible, "for we still have a long night ahead." There were some groans, quickly stifled. "I need you to keep the fires burning all the way till dawn."

No one asked why, but Aspen knew they were curious. "If we can keep the scouts from getting too close, we should be able to convince the Unseelie army that we, too, have an army."

"But in the morning—" one of the civilians began. Aspen didn't see who it was before he interrupted.

"In the morning," he said, "we will see how much magic Mishrath has left in him. Up now. Up and to the fires. Keep them lit; keep our hopes alive."

They grumbled and stumbled as they all got back up to their feet, but they did their duty, spreading out into the darkness. All except the moat troll, who stayed put and stared sheepishly at his gigantic, mossy feet.

Oh, Aspen suddenly realized, *he will be no help with the fires.* Trolls hated fire.

"Troll," Aspen said, "you are with me. There is a stream to visit."

The troll's aspect was suddenly almost jolly. It did not improve his looks at all.

And truth be told, Aspen thought, *I may have need of him before this night is over.* He sighed heavily, once again picturing the Battle of Bogborough, when last he had borne sword and flame into battle. *I do not relish what I will need to do tonight. A very large and very quiet companion may be just what is needed. For the chaos. And for the guilt.*

Aspen heard muffled footsteps approaching swiftly behind him. Turning, he saw Snarl, one of the Clan Wolf brothers, appear out of the darkness.

"Sire," he said, his voice a guttural rattle. "We have con-tact. Mixed squad of bogles and Borderers belly-crawling toward the stream on our left flank."

Aspen nodded to Snarl. Beckoned to the troll.

"Take me to them," he said.

It was time to go to war.

SNAIL READIES FOR WAR

*B*efore cleaning up the bowser, Snail went outside to speak with Snaggle and Snap. She found them by the front of the lead wagon. Snap was sitting on the wagon, along with Thridi and baby Og. Og was on Snap's lap, wearing a rather large helmet that probably came from Snap's saddlebag.

Og was grinning toothlessly and banging his fist on the helmet over and over again. It made the helmet ring, and probably his ears, too, but he sang out gleefully, "Ding! Ding! Ding!"

"Who knew troll babies were so cute," Snap said.

Snaggle grunted in disgust. He and Dagmarra were on the ground beside the wagon, where Snaggle had been ignoring the baby while showing Dagmarra a few fancy cuts with his sword. When Dagmarra punched his arm with her fist, he laughed but rubbed at it with his other hand, so Snail knew the punch had left a mark.

Small but deadly, that's Dagmarra, Snail thought.

"You two!" she called out, and it was clear that Snap and

Snaggle knew who she was speaking to, for Snaggle immediately sheathed his sword, turned, and saluted her.

"M'lady." His voice was firm and his eyes were firm, too. She gathered he'd slept well.

More slowly, Snap gave baby Og back into Thridi's hands. "I think he's made a deposit. . . ."

Indeed, Snail could smell it from there.

Dagmarra shook her head at Og. "You know you're supposed to say when . . ." she began.

"Ding! Ding!" Og said. It was clearly the only thing on his mind at the moment.

Snap jumped down and gave Snail a quick salute as well. Even though he was younger than his uncle, he was not as sprightly. Nor as quick.

"Time to earn your keep," Snail told them. "You two are the only true warriors here besides Dagmarra, who is . . . um . . . otherwise engaged. I need you to go with Thridi through the camp and choose all the strongest-looking men and boys . . ."

"And girls," Dagmarra called over her shoulder as she lugged Og into the wagon to change his clouts. "Don't you dare forget the girls. I know them. They are strong and smart and . . ."

Snail nodded and said, "And girls," remembering Alith and what a warrior she'd been. "Begin teaching them the rudiments of war."

"They already know the rudiments for ordinary folk: run,

scream, fall, die," Snaggle said, his voice without malice but with a kind of grave politeness. "I believe you mean, m'lady, we should teach them some sort of defense."

"Defense or offense, they need to know how best to handle weapons, how to bind themselves together to make the most of what they have, how to—"

"And how many years do we have to do this in, m'lady?" asked Snap. *His* tone wasn't polite.

Snaggle cuffed him on the ear.

"You already know that," she said wearily. "We only have today and the few days after, as we march to the aid of the king." Her mouth was now thinned down in a line. Snap was tiresome and, she thought, deserved every cuff he got. "So best to start at once. I assume you've eaten already?"

They nodded. It could have meant either that they knew she assumed it or that they had actually eaten. Or any number of other things as well. She was learning it was hard to tell what warriors meant—or thought. For all they were experts with weapons, they weren't practiced talkers. And they knew how to keep secrets.

"Then go. Have them make weapons out of whatever is handy, and you two take orders only from Odds or Dagmarra or the made woman who sings, Maggie Light. No one else. And—"

"And you, m'lady," asked Snaggle, "where will you be?"

"Cleaning a filthy, unhealthy, and altogether disgustingly nasty rug," she said. "Dagmarra will know where."

"A rug, m'lady?" Her title in Snap's mouth had turned into a whine.

Snaggle gave him another cuff on the ear. "We've got our orders. Are you a mouse or a warrior to squeak so?"

As she went into the wagon, she heard Snap's retort. "No need to keep swatting the same ear, uncle, or I'll soon be unable to hear any orders at all." Presumably, Snaggle cuffed him again, because Snap added, "OW!"

⬚ ⬚ ⬚

THE BOWSER WAS drowsing uneasily on the floor of the twins' room in the last wagon, the one in which Aspen had slept. Little runnels ran along his coarse hair, and every now and then he made a growling sound, as if dreaming of prey, though she doubted he ate anything.

The twins also drowsed, standing up in the semi-dark, looking just like two long capes hanging on separate pegs. Snail knew little would wake the two of them until nightfall, when they would rouse, eat, walk about by the backside of the wagons. She'd never understood why they were part of Odds's troupe. They neither performed nor helped set up for a performance. They didn't make the kind of magic that quieted mobs or turned away snoopers. They just . . . were.

She wondered if they would fight. Indeed, she wondered if they *could*.

Sitting down next to the bowser, which was much more than a simple animate rug, she thought about how he'd greeted her originally—with a snarl and the baring of almost a hundred teeth.

The bowser, so Odds had warned her that first time, didn't ordinarily like females, though she and the rug had become friends of a sort soon after. Right now it was hard to believe he had any teeth—or any mouth—so hidden were they in the greasy grey folds of his body.

She put her hand on his matted fur. "Who left you in this awful condition?" she said softly. "Has no one bathed you since the king and I went with you through those first skirmishes?" When there was no response, she added, "Want a bath now?"

The bowser shifted, or rather he scrabbled on the floor and pushed a section of his dirty, grey, limpish body onto her lap.

"I'll take that as a yes," she said, trying to push the filthy creature down. "But first I've got to get some water and some soap, and then you and I will have a wash."

The bowser still didn't move, so she stood up quickly, and he tumbled back onto the floor of the wagon. "Back soon."

She got her riding clothes out of her saddlebag. She had to save the m'lady clothes for addressing audiences and speaking to toffs. And that meant the first thing she had to do was brush off some of the filth the bowser had left on the skirt.

Then she changed back into her smelly, unwashed clothes and went outside. There she found a big wooden bucket and filled it to the brim with tepid water from a barrel. She uncovered a stiff brush—probably used for the unicorns' manes—and some yellow soap.

When she returned to the bowser's room, the twins were hanging from hooks closer to the door, possibly to avoid the inevitable splashing water.

The bowser had spread himself out flat so that she could reach every bit of his body.

"Good," she said, dumping some of the water in the very center of his back—or front. Without the teeth showing it was impossible to tell. Then she got onto her knees, scraped some of the rose-scented soap onto the brush, and got to work.

The work wasn't hard but it was repetitive, very like scrubbing a birthing room in preparation for the blessing event, which was what midwives often called the bloody mess of newborn babies.

As she continued scrubbing, adding water and soap when needed, the bowser turned light grey, and then a kind of warm tan. On the third full wash she began to see gold shining through. She knew that once he was thoroughly gold on both sides, he'd be ready for his role in the days to come.

Now it was just soap, water, push, pull, and a lot of bowser purr.

WHEN THE BATH was finally done, the bowser—miraculously dry from some inner heat—draped himself over her shoulders. His rough tongue, rather like a cat's, licked her cheek. She hadn't known he had a tongue, only teeth.

If he has a tongue, she wondered, *can he taste things?* Then a more important idea passed through her mind. *If he has a tongue, can he talk?* Other made things in Odds's troupe talked—like Maggie Light. The iron spiders mostly grunted. *But*—she wondered—*if the bowser can't talk, why give him a tongue?*

Just because he'd never talked to her didn't mean he was mute. *Perhaps,* she thought, *he's spoken to Aspen.* Of course, Aspen had never mentioned it, and she believed that he told her everything. *But then*—she remembered with some shame—*I thought he'd gotten married without saying a word. So what do I really know about him?*

She might have stayed there, wrapped in the warm comfort of the bowser's gold body, but she heard a vaguely familiar sound: a kind of thump. And then a grinding noise followed closely, after which the entire wagon shook.

At once she understood—Odds had pulled the rope that set the stage in motion.

He was going to give the performance of his life.

And possibly all of theirs.

SNAIL KEPT THE bowser over her shoulders and walked out of the door onto the grass. Snap and Snaggle were gone, as were Dagmarra and baby Og. She assumed they were together, working to form the ragtag army. At least she hoped that was what they were doing.

Shifting the bowser even higher on her shoulders and telling him how beautifully he shone in the sunlight—for he was ever susceptible to flattery—she made her way to the front of the big stage.

The one big iron spider not on guard in the forest was surrounded by a dozen smaller ones, each the size of a war horse. They were pulling the panels and the parts of the stage out to its broadest.

Maggie Light came over with her strange gliding walk, stopping not a handsbreadth away. "Shall I carry the bowser for you?"

It made sense. Maggie was taller and had shoulders made out of some unimaginably strong material, but for some reason Snail resisted the offer. The bowser had chosen her, and she needed that connection to strengthen.

"Thanks," she said to Maggie Light, "but we have business later, the bowser and I, and should not be separated, not even for comfort's sake."

Maggie bowed her head. "The professor chose rightly. Even before he knew you, he knew what you could do."

"And what is that?"

"You will find it for yourself," Maggie said. "To tell you sets you on a path not of your choosing."

She walked off, leaving Snail to puzzle that out. *If I am already chosen by the professor*, she wondered, *does this mean my path is of my own choosing, or his? Am I free to not do what Odds wishes? Is my asking for his help part of Odds's plan or the king's?* Thinking about all of this made her head swim, so she stopped.

Just then she felt the movement of a thousand or more people around her pushing toward the stage.

If I'm not ahead of them, she thought, *I'll be left behind.*

She moved to the left, climbing back into the wagon, and then went through the linked rooms till she came to Odds's own bedroom. She entered without knocking and found the professor himself standing at the far end, holding open the door that was the entrance to the stage.

"I thought you'd never get here," he said. "I was about to send Maggie Light out to—"

"To sing your people into submission?"

"*Compliance* is a better word."

"Not," she said sharply, "if you're the one complying."

He laughed. "You didn't complain before, not when it helped you plow through the crowd."

She knew he was right, but didn't thank him. Being beholden to him gave Odds power over her she didn't like. "Are we ready to begin?" she asked brightly.

"Oddly ready and ready against all odds," he said, then preceded her through the door, saying, "Stand to my right, neither ahead of me nor behind."

She thought that a good idea. That way they would be seen as being of the same status. Even amongst the humans, for whom status seemed to be more changeable than in the two kingdoms, that was probably the best way to present themselves.

Once out on the stage with the sea of people in front of her, Snail's knees suddenly went weak. But the bowser growled in her ear, which made her giggle. *At least I have him right-side up.*

Against the stage was a knot of handpicked strong men and a handful of gawky boys standing beside Snap and Snaggle. They were all attentive but not at attention, obviously placed there by Dagmarra, who was even now conferring with Maggie Light. She gestured with her left arm to the small force. Her right arm was full of baby Og, who was napping in the midst of all the commotion.

Snail pretended she saw none of them, nor did she try to pick out faces in the crowd she'd known before. If she fogged her eyes, they all seemed to disappear into a kind of mist. But even that wasn't enough to distract her from the mass of them following her every movement. So, to distance herself even further from the vast audience, she shifted the bowser from her shoulders and took a long while spreading him out on the stage floor.

"Soon," she crooned. "Soon, golden one."

The bowser gave a little shiver and a shimmer, then lay quiet.

One of the iron spiders, a small one only the size of a wildcat, hauled out a box twice its size to the center front of the stage, grumbling in its clanky voice. Then it clumsily unfolded three short steps from one side of the box. Once the box was ready, and steady, Odds walked over and climbed up carefully.

The crowd cheered him as he rose to the top, planted his feet widely, then raised his hands.

Almost directly in front of him, but standing sideways against the stage, so she could watch Odds's movements and catch Snail's eye as well, stood Maggie Light. As soon as the professor's hands were in the air, she put two fingers in her mouth and gave a shrill whistle that cut through the cheers.

The crowd went suddenly and totally silent.

"My friends, my people," Odds thundered.

Snail was surprised at how strong his voice was, stronger than any man's had a right to be, till she noticed Maggie's mouth was wide open. The sound of Odds's voice was issuing out through her, amplified in some magical way Snail didn't understand.

"All of you are my partners in this *human* experiment," Odds said, hands now before him, palms up. His gesture encouraged them to roar their approval back at him.

The roar was so loud, it shook the stage, and the bowser scrunched up a bit closer to her feet.

Odds raised his hands again, Maggie Light whistled once more, and the crowd grew silent for a second time.

Professor Odds got right to the meat of what he meant to say.

"You all know we are in a war not of our choosing. That it's a war of faerie factions is not lost on any of us. And maybe you're thinking: What do I care if an ogre kills a brownie, or a Border Lord maims a troll?"

At the mention of a troll, Dagmarra looked up and bared her teeth at Odds but was otherwise silent.

Odds never noticed her protest and kept on speaking. "But we're caught in the middle of this muddle. We don't have wizardry and dark magicks on our side. And so we are more vulnerable than they. We have already seen this, having so recently buried loved ones."

"But we got some of them buggers ourselves!" someone called out, and the sea of people started to call out examples of the same.

"Me and my brother snagged a Borderer!" Two large men, gap-toothed and looking far too jolly to have beaten a Border Lord, held up their arms as if in victory.

"And then we hanged him," shouted an equally large woman.

The midwife in Snail made her wonder if the large men and woman were halflings: part human, part giant or troll.

"I cut off a drow's head," shouted a young lad in Snap and Snaggle's group. "Well, after my da beat him to his knees with a shovel."

"And we brought down an ogre with ropes around his ankles, and when he fell, he went face-first into the fire," cried out a group of men, each of whom was not much larger than the dwarfs.

Odds let the crowd exhaust itself with its bloodthirstiness before putting his hands up again, which got most of the crowd's attention. Maggie whistled the rest back to silence.

Snail was still not sure if there was magic in Maggie's whistle or just a shrill call to attention. Either way, it worked.

Odds went on. "Yes—one or two of the fey company we can manage. But we aren't an army, not one that's organized. Not soldiers. Not *warriors*, as the Seelie troops call themselves. Not the *monster hordes*, as the Unseelie are known."

There was a mumble and groan around the stage as the listeners took this in. Not anything they hadn't known before, but being spoken by Odds made it more real somehow.

The professor raised his hands again, and this time he needed no whistle from Maggie. The crowd hushed at once. "We can be at the mercy of the winner of this war or we can be merciless and dictate our own terms."

"Dictate!" cried the big woman. Suddenly she lifted a large shovel over her head. It had, Snail noticed, an iron blade. Snail was used to wooden-bladed shovels, of course. No fey would have been able to use iron, so the Unseelie had none.

Maggie's whistle forestalled any reaction, and Odds said quickly, "As I have already done. Our doctor here . . ." And he pointed to Snail, who rashly raised her hand, and then regretted doing so when the entire audience swiveled toward her. "Our doctor," Odds reiterated, "has come back to me with many concessions from the Seelie king, who promises us much if we will support and hold the backs of his army. The *backs*, my friends, not the fronts."

A huge roar went up, and even Maggie's whistle had trouble controlling it. But at last the roars and shouts died down.

"Not only freedom and complete equality with the Seelie folk, but gifts of estates and fortunes for all to work side by side with the fey. As equals. Plus anyone who desires to leave Faerie and go into the human world, will be given a pocket of gold for the journey, plus a fine steed to ride."

Snail was astonished at the professor's amazing soup of half-truths and part-lies made from the thin broth she'd brought him. And then she was amazed that she was astonished, given what she knew of him.

But then he added, "Though I warn you that you'll live a much shorter life out there, and a softer one here if you stay."

"Shorter than dying in their bloody war?" shouted a green-jacketed woman on the edge of the crowd.

"Some of us will die anyway," Odds told her. "Whether we support this king or not. Worse even than dying would be living under the barbarous Unseelie folk, should they win. You have seen them and know what they can do."

The green-jacketed woman was having none of this and shouted again, and now there were several yelling along with her, "Why not just head for the Door?"

Snail assumed they meant the Door out of Faerie and into the human world.

"The Door! The Door!" her followers chorused.

But just as the crowd was about to cross the border into mob, Maggie whistled so loudly they were stopped in an instant. And then she began to sing.

"Right!" Dagmarra handed baby Og off to a startled Snaggle, who immediately passed the little troll to Snap. She jumped onto the stage and ran to Snail. "Fingers in ears."

Snail had already done so, though the first few words of Maggie's song-spell still drifted through her mind.

> The gate between the trees is open.
> The way will be quite steep.
> Stones as hard as hearts the markers . . .

She remembered as if in a dream the familiar next line, *Do not weep, child, do not weep.* But with her fingers in her ears, there was no longer power in the words to enchant.

Dagmarra looked at her and smiled, turned, and went back down off the stage. As she turned, Snail noticed the bog cotton in her ears. Dagmarra had been ready for such an eventuality.

As Snail watched, the dwarf strode through the crowd, found the green-jacketed woman, who was as entranced as the rest, and hauled her off. To where, Snail had no idea. Nor did she want to ask. Not then, at any rate.

When she was positive the danger was past, Maggie stopped singing. And when Snail realized people were coming around again, she took her fingers from her ears, though she still heard the line *Do not weep, child, do not weep*, over and over again in her head.

Odds was haranguing the newly awakened crowd about the Door. Snail turned toward him just as he said, "But since we have yet to find the Door, better to work with the king who knows where it is and how to go through it. He has given his promise, written on this paper . . ." At that, he raised a scroll in his hand that Snail had never seen before, and certainly doubted the king could have sent. "This scroll in which he promises to put together a troop of fey explorers and an equal number of our people to find the Door. But all these concessions are for naught if the Seelie can't beat back the Unseelie tide. And without our help . . ."

From somewhere off to the side—the side where Dagmarra had gone to deal with the green jacket and her followers,

Snail realized—a single voice rang out. "See-lie! See-lie!"
She knew that voice.

That single voice was quickly joined by two and then
three voices, some from the back and some—she noted—
from the front. The front voices had been started by Snap
and then Snaggle, and their handpicked crew. And finally,
the cry was taken up by an avalanche of fervid tongues.

Odds let the sound rise and rise and then tumble down
the mountainside of his people's desire for peace. When it
was all but finished, he pointed dramatically at Snail. "Go,
our doctor, our sister, our comforter, our skarm drema,
and tell the Seelie king we will hold his back." He smiled.
"We will hold to our purpose. *And* we will hold him to his
promises!"

She knew the time had come. Nodding, she sat down on
the bowser, put her hands in his gleaming fur, formed a
picture in her head of Aspen's palace, and said, "Take me to
Astaeri, golden one. As fast as you can manage."

Just as the bowser began to tremble beneath her, Snaggle
leapt onto the stage.

"M'lady," he called as he ran toward her, "how shall we
get you in safety to . . ."

The bowser had already lifted a hairbreadth off the stage
floor, and then two. Before Snaggle could reach Snail, the
bowser suddenly lurched upward at a high rate of speed and
began to circle toward the south.

It was all Snail could do to hold on. Waving at the people below was impossible. She inched closer to the edge of the rug and cried out to Snaggle, "Do what Alith would have done. . . ." But the rest of what she tried to say was taken by the wind.

Edging back to the center of the bowser, she knew she had to trust Snaggle, Snap, Dagmarra, Thridi, and Maggie Light to do as Odds had promised.

She wasn't sure she trusted the professor at all.

ASPEN MAKES A NAME FOR HIMSELF

*A*spen crawled through the rocks behind Snarl, silently cursing every sharp pebble that scraped his palms or bruised his knees or found its way down his breeches.

The indignity alone would have killed me not too long ago.

The Wolf Clan warrior was wearing a cloak with reeds and grasses woven right into it so that he'd look a part of the ground. He stopped suddenly and motioned Aspen to him with the smallest of waves.

"There, sire," Snarl breathed, barely audible, even with his mouth nearly touching Aspen's ear. He pointed toward a group of rocks on the far side of the stream.

"Where?" Aspen said.

"The rocks, sire. Watch them."

It took a few moments, and he certainly wouldn't have noticed if Snarl hadn't pointed it out, but the rocks were moving. And they weren't rocks.

"A dozen of them, sire."

Now that he knew what they were, the rocks resolved into

a dozen figures making their own way through the *actual* rocks on their bellies much like he and Snarl had just done. The moat troll waited at the top of the broken ground, ordered to stay still. He certainly couldn't sneak, but if he kept still, he looked much like one of the boulders strewn about.

"There is none else, yet," Bite said into Aspen's other ear, startling him.

Aspen kept his teeth gritted. *A jump by me would spoil the ambush . . . just a bit.*

"A long-run scouting party," Bite continued, "well in advance of the others."

"They'll be fast, sire," Snarl said. "And we weren't in position quickly enough to see their approach."

"What does that mean?" Aspen said.

"They may have already seen an empty fire."

"Why would they come on, then?" For they were definitely still coming forward. Slowly, oh so slowly. But coming nonetheless. "Why not report back immediately?"

"One empty fire is a curiosity. They'll want to know more before they report."

"If any escape . . ." Aspen said.

"Bite and I will work our way round behind them to keep that from happening," Snarl said. "If it pleases you, sire," he added after a moment.

Probably hard to remember I am the king when we are all facedown in the mud.

Aspen nodded. "Go."

Bite pulled the hood of his cloak up and disappeared as if he'd never been there. Snarl, only slightly more visible in grey-and-black-spattered leathers, crawled off after him. Neither made any sound.

Aspen realized belatedly that they had chosen no signal for when the Wolf brothers were in position and he should attack. He looked at the advance scouts crawling toward the stream. They were close enough that he could now see the broad shoulders and kilts of the Borderers, the ragged fur on the backs of the much smaller bogles.

I need to attack before they see another empty fire. Like Snarl said, one is a curiosity. He shook his head. *Even one is too many. I cannot have any doubt enter Jack Daw's mind.*

They were almost to the stream, and signal or no, he had to attack now.

And I am done with crawling.

He stood and gathered the flame to him, trying to think only of what was at stake. Why he needed to do what he was about to do.

Think of Snail. Think of your mother. Think of all the Seelie peoples who are counting on you to save them from the horrors of an Unseelie invasion.

Instead, all he could think about was the Battle of Bogborough and all the foes—and some friends—who had died horribly by his hand.

"I am sorry," he said quietly to the scouts, who were just now looking up at him, eyes reflecting the red glow of the regal flame.

Then the fire rained down on them and their eyes shut forever.

"OH, THAT WAS well done, sire!"

"Not a one escaped, Your Majesty!"

"I've never seen the like. Sire?"

"Your Majesty?"

"Is he . . . weeping?"

Aspen's eyes cleared, and he saw that Snarl and Bite were there again, upright this time. The moat troll was there as well, looking at Aspen with concern in his giant yellow eyes. He had no memory of any of them arriving.

I only remember fire.

Shaking the tears from his eyes, he somehow found his voice. "Find me sooner next time." He wanted to say more, thank them for their dangerous work, tell them he never meant to be short with them but that he was having a bit of a hard day. He was afraid, though, that if he spoke, he would start crying again and never stop.

He turned and walked back up the hill, the moat troll lumbering behind.

ASPEN WAS CALLED on six more times that night. Snarl and Bite had obviously spread the word to the other scouts, and each time he was able to make contact with the enemy well beyond the stream. They had no chance to see any empty fires, and since they were scouts, more interested in acquiring information than doing battle with the king of the fey, Aspen was able to drive most of them off instead of slaughtering them. Still, he killed five more Unseelie before they stopped coming.

He wept for each one.

As he lay by the fire, wishing now he hadn't given his cloak to Mishrath, he heard one of the soldiers—he was too tired to identify which one—whisper to another, "The Crying King."

It did not sound like an insult. The whispers were passed from soldier to soldier in awed tones, until Aspen heard Croak's voice.

"No," Croak said. "He is the Weeping Warrior."

The soldiers muttered their consent, and that was that. The reign of King Ailenbran, the Weeping Warrior, had begun.

I hope it is not too short a reign, Aspen thought as he closed his eyes. Moments later, or so it seemed, Molintien was shaking him awake.

"It is almost sunrise, sire," she said. "And Mishrath says he is ready."

"You told him what we need?"

She shook her head. "He knew already."

Aspen was unsurprised that Mishrath had figured out his plan. *It only matters that Old Jack Daw does not*, he thought to himself.

Aloud he only thanked Molintien and looked across the fire at Mishrath, who was sitting up with a cup of something steaming in his hands.

"Are you truly ready, wizard?"

Mishrath adjusted his grey hat, nodded, then held his drink up to Aspen in salute. "By sunrise," he said, "this hill will seem to hold the greatest host the Seelie have ever assembled. And at my death, the illusion will take hold until you need it no more." He took a sip from the cup. "Or at least it should. And that *needing it no more* . . . may mean when you are dead or when the battle is won or lost or . . ." The old wizard took a deep breath. But before he could add what else might threaten the illusion, Alicanson, the young House of the Poppy soldier, ran into the firelight.

"They come," the boy said breathlessly.

Aspen hoisted himself to his feet, feeling pain in nearly every part of his body. "How many this time?" he asked, hoping for a small group. They were easier to drive off. The bigger groups tended to have at least one overly brave warrior who would charge and end up dead.

"Thousands!"

"Oh," Aspen said. He turned to Mishrath. "I will have that army now, if it please you."

Old Jack Daw had finally arrived.

SNAIL RIDES THE WIND

Once again Snail settled herself on the bowser's back. She could tell they were heading south and west, which made sense. But did the bowser really know where they were going? Even if she asked, she knew she'd get no answer. She simply had to trust him as she had to trust Snaggle and Snap and the rest.

At least, she told herself, *I can relax a bit and enjoy the ride*. There was nothing else she could do till they got to Astaeri Palace.

Peering carefully over the edge of the bowser into the fading light, she saw they were passing over a river that coiled like a serpent, then a series of three meadows, and at last they sailed over the top of Little Sister, which looked rather fiercer this close, its rock face jagged with intricately balanced stones.

There was an eagle banking to one side of them, which then circled back around to check them out. Snail could see its yellow eyes assessing both rug and rider, as if measuring them for food, before it turned sharply and dove down. Next time she spotted it, the eagle was coursing along a narrow meadow that was shaped like a hammer. Suddenly the bird swooped down, landing on its prey.

The bowser, too, was now banking, and Snail had to grab on more tightly.

Even in the coming darkness, she could see in the distance the outline of the palace alight with hundreds of candles. So the bowser *did* know where they were heading.

She grinned. "Good boy," she whispered.

Suddenly a different fire caught her eye. A blaze of light was shining far to the west. She squinted hard, leaning dangerously over the bowser's left side.

No—not a *single* light but *many* blazes.

She knew what that had to mean. The Unseelie horde was camping not more than a day's march, two at best, from the palace.

For a moment she considered going closer, scouting the size and weight of the army for Aspen. Then she realized what danger that might put her in. An arrow or a catapult could easily bring her down, and then how would she tell him what she knew? Dead scouts can't report.

The bowser, not part of her inner conversation, simply headed now for the palace. Snail knew they wouldn't get there until well after dark, but at least the candlelight would show them the way.

"Faster!" she hissed into the bowser's fur. "*Faster!* We have to warn Aspen. He needs to know it will be several days before the human reinforcements can make it to Astaeri. Somehow, we have to find something to hold off that horde.

"But the changelings," she shouted into the thin air, "the humans and their iron monsters are on their way! They *are* on their way!"

The bowser must have understood what she was saying, for it put on an extra burst of speed.

That speed called up a fiercer wind, which hit Snail with such cold power, she was afraid she would faint. Trying to snuggle deeper into the bowser's fur, she glared down at his back as if that alone would let him know that *nothing*—not even being turned into a snow fiend, one of those creatures of northern legends—would stop her from telling the king that she'd successfully carried out her mission.

She could feel droplets of ice forming at the corners of her eyes, told herself she was being fanciful, worried she was not. Then, just as she just closed her eyes, the bowser dropped so precipitously, her legs flailed behind her in the air, and she was frightened she might pull out hanks of his hair and be set whirling into the wind on her own.

But his hair—like her hands—was well anchored. They sped along the lower lanes of sky, sometimes barely over the treetops. She warmed up enough to open her eyes just in time to see the palace lights rushing toward them at such a fast pace, her newest worry was whether the bowser would stop in time.

SNAIL HAD NO idea how long the whole ride had taken them, but the moon stood above Astaeri like a round lantern. From gripping so hard in the cold wind, she could barely feel her fingers. But when the bowser settled into a long, slow glide, she lay more fully against him, and they rode down as one being until he landed on the Queen's Walk, which ran around the top allure of the castle.

The actual landing happened so quickly, she had the breath knocked out of her and had to lie on the bowser for a moment simply to catch it again. But now that they were out of the wind, she was measurably warmer.

After a bit, she could even feel her fingers.

Pushing herself up to a sitting position, she patted the bowser. "Well done, golden one. Wait here till I tell the king. Then I will come for you, and you will lie in state, be bathed in warm water and admired by all."

That should hold him for a while, she thought.

Then she found the door to the stairs and hurried down.

She was surprised at how quiet the palace was, and even more surprised that she passed no one along the way. Normally a palace is a noisy place, even in the fullness of night:

servants, guards, footmen, ladies in all sorts of waiting, cleaners, pot boys, servers, cooks would be awake and busy. It was said in the Unseelie Court that "the king's castle never sleeps." And even in the smaller Astaeri Palace, with few enough people left, she could always hear movement outside her bedroom as she tried to fall asleep.

In fact, going down the three flights of stairs, she met not a single soul, which was odd and a bit frightening. She wondered if everyone had fled.

But if they have, she told herself, *who was it lit all the candles? And where is Aspen?*

When she turned into the throne room, only Balnar and the queen were there, conferring at a long table. As Snail came closer, she realized they were looking at a series of maps.

As always, Balnar was in an impeccable black tunic with silver buttons, and black hose. His storm-cloud-colored hair was carefully brushed back and tied with a dark bow, and on his shoulder was a golden bar pin from which hung medals.

Well, Snail thought, *the bar and medals are new.*

The buckles on Balnar's shoes were silver and so well shined, a courtier could see his face in them.

If—Snail thought—*anyone wanted to bend over that far.*

The queen, too, was impeccable in a dress so full of mourning black lace and flounces, it was hard to realize how thin she was beneath all the puffery.

"Here!" the queen was saying, stabbing her finger at a place on the largest map.

Balnar's nose was almost right at the spot she was pointing to, and for the first time Snail realized that he was probably half-blind with age.

"Where is Aspen?" Snail said.

The two jumped and spun around. Obviously, they hadn't heard her come in, so engrossed with the maps. "I have news for him."

"Gone," the queen said solemnly.

"Gone?" Snail felt the shock of it in her chest. "How can he be gone? How did he die? How could I not have known it here?" She touched a hand to her chest, feeling as if once again she'd had the wind knocked out of her. Wind she'd never be able to get back.

She glared at the queen.

"Oh, my dear," the queen said, coming quickly to her side. "Not dead. But gone with a small . . . um . . . force to try and give you time to . . . um . . ." She put her hands on Snail's shoulders.

The queen had never seemed flustered before, and Snail wondered what it meant.

"Then who is guarding Astaeri?"

The queen turned to Balnar, who had the grace to look at his feet. "Why, *we* are," she said. "Along with a loyal force of six soldiers, seven underage pot boys, three ladies-in-waiting, several counselors, a cook, and the royal smith.

The smith has a bad leg and can't walk far. He has made us weapons, and we have practiced barring the gates at a moment's notice."

"And the rest . . . ?" Snail asked.

"Ah, well, the rest have fled, to the north, and the mountains. I fear they will find no comfort there."

"My queen, perhaps you have forgotten the three house brownies, the hedge witch, the farmwives, and their young children from the outlying towns getting in what harvest they can. Oh, and the woman in white, ma'am," said Balnar, adding as an aside to Snail, "the upstairs ghost. Though I suppose she will do nothing but weep. That is what she does, you know."

Snail had once caught a glimpse of the woman in white, and indeed that *was* all she did, that and wring her transparent hands.

"Madam," Snail said, using her best court language, which felt like pebbles in her mouth, "the regiment of humans will be a few days yet getting here. They are walking and riding. Mostly walking." She took a deep breath and added in a rush, sounding more like the old Snail, "I flew. There's a huge camp of Unseelie troops a day's pace, possibly two, from here."

"You *fly?*" The queen looked puzzled. "I was not informed you had wings. Nor have I ever seen any." She gave Balnar a quick look.

He shrugged back. "The *bowser*, ma'am, the animate rug.

Your son and the . . . m'lady . . . made their escape from the Great Battle on its back, arriving here when you were . . . discommoded."

Discommoded. Snail almost snorted. Balnar meant the time that the queen had been in the dungeon, sent there by her own husband for letting their son escape. *She is,* Snail knew, *a tough woman, for all the lace, ruffles, and trimmings.*

Snail explained further. "The bowser had fled back to the human encampment, madam, where I found him again and persuaded him to bring me here with the news for the king that the humans had agreed wholeheartedly to fight for the Seelie cause." It was a long sentence, with a bit of a lie embedded in it, and she felt every word of it like the knell of a death bell, when all she really wanted to do was speak to Aspen and tell him everything that had happened straight out. So they could laugh at it, make fun of it, make *sense* of it.

Then she added, "Where is he? I can fly to him and . . ."

"We will fly together," the queen said.

"Madam . . ."

"Ma'am!"

"The queen needs to stay in the palace," Snail said, glaring at Balnar.

In response, Balnar said, agreeing, "The queen is still too frail to go gallivanting about on a flying carpet."

The queen drew herself to her full height, which in fey terms was not high at all.

"As you know, Balnar, I am *no longer* queen, but the dowager. When Ailenbran marries, there will be a queen again on the throne. So—not a queen, but still a mother. And it is the mother who is going, not the queen."

She turned to Snail and added, "If you are right about how close the horde is, then my late husband's one remaining son—*my* son—and his small troop are in terrible danger. I could not help my husband or his other sons when they left this realm. But I will be there for Ailenbran."

Balnar recovered quickly. "Who will hold the palace, ma'am?" he asked.

"Why, you, dear old friend," she said. "You always have. You always will. We just lived here at your leave, you know. It was you who have kept its ticks and tocks moving all these years, and shall do so till the end of its time and yours."

Then she turned to Snail. "Now, have you eaten today?"

When Snail began to protest, the queen said, "I take that as a no. You cannot go off to war without something warm in your stomach. Balnar will get you some of today's soup. It was new mushrooms and old venison, stirred with wine and garlic and herbs. Not cook's best, but perhaps better than we had any right to expect."

Balnar bowed, and within moments returned with the soup, not quite as warm as the queen intended, but Snail gulped it down and felt positively refreshed.

The queen waited until Snail had wiped her mouth on the

cloth that Balnar proffered, then said, "Now, where is this flying rug of yours? Do I need a cloak for the ride?"

"It's quite cold up there, madam," Snail replied. She didn't add that what the queen was wearing was not at all what she needed when flying on the bowser's back. Or going into a war zone. Just as she was about to mention this, the queen spoke.

"Then a cloak *and* gloves, please, Balnar," the queen said. "The green, I think." She looked at Snail and shook her head. "The same for m'lady. And be quick about it, for we have no time to waste."

"And boots," Snail said, pointing at the queen's silken shoes.

"Of course," the queen said, nodding at Balnar. "And for m'lady as well, who seems to have but one shoe."

"At once, madam," he said. "I will wake the ladies who should have been in waiting."

"They need their sleep."

"As do you, my queen."

"The old need little sleep. Mourners need less," she said.

It sounded to Snail like an ancient argument between them.

"We will be up on the Queen's Walk," Snail told Balnar, pointing a finger into the air. "I will be introducing Her Majesty to the rug. He's not fond of girls. But I'm *certain* he will make an exception for the *queen*."

Once on the allure, the moon already beginning its downward descent, Snail and the queen sat close together on the bowser. Despite her worst fears, the rug had taken to the queen at once. *And she to him*, Snail thought, feeling a small pang of jealousy.

"And now what?" the queen whispered.

"Now we ask him to find Aspen," Snail said.

The queen bent over and whispered into the rug's fur. "Find me King Ailenbran Astaeri, Bright Celestial, Ruire of the Tir na nOg, and Lord of the Seelie kingdom. Find me my son."

"That's not . . ." Snail began, meaning to say the bowser knew him as Aspen and as Karl the minstrel, before remembering that Aspen had also flown once as the king.

Seeming to flex himself, the bowser rose the merest fraction.

"We have warm clothes coming!" Snail said quickly. "Don't fly just yet."

The bowser gave a tiny shudder and settled back down on the stones.

Just then Balnar arrived with two cloaks, two pairs of gloves, the queen's walking boots, and a pair for Snail as well. She was glad to see the boots were sturdy ones, not just for show. Gathering the cloak around her shoulders, she pulled on the gloves. She thought, *This time the cold air shouldn't be much of a problem.*

"Twist your hands in his fur," Snail said to the queen, showing how it was done. Then she bent over and whispered to the bowser, "Let's fly,"

The bowser shuddered.

"And quickly," Snail added.

The queen was a fast learner, and just as well, for the bowser had already begun to lift up, but slowly, as if the double burden he was carrying was an especially heavy one.

"You carried the king and me before," Snail whispered to him, the words a bit venomous, "and now you grunt over this slighter burden?"

The queen put one gloved hand on Snail's shoulder, as if to hush her, but then set the other hand onto the bowser's back, fingers deeply entwined in the mass of the fur.

Snail realized the queen had not heard her and only touched Snail's shoulder to keep herself steady.

"Don't be afraid, madam," Snail said.

"A queen is never afraid," came the answer. "Only occasionally out of sorts."

It made Snail laugh, and the queen joined her until both women, mouths wide in merriment, faced the wind, the cold, and soon the slow rising of the sun.

21

ASPEN FINDS AN ARMY

The fires were burning down, soon to be replaced by the sun's light. All but the four soldiers who continued to patrol were gathered around the central fire, where Mishrath sat with a collection of herbs and wildflowers in front of him. Everyone looked exhausted, though the soldiers hid it well.

"Are you sure that is all you need, Mishrath?"

Aspen looked at the small pile of dried leaves and uprooted plants sitting in front of the wizard. The dried leaves Mishrath had pulled from a pouch hidden in his robes; the rest he had Fayeth and Fennel gather for him from the field and the forest's edge. It looked pitifully inadequate to the job of creating an illusion big enough to fool an army.

"Who is the wizard here?" Mishrath said snarkily, "and who is the insolent boy king?"

Molintien gasped, surely having never heard a king spoken to in such a way. The soldiers' hands went automatically to the hilts of their weapons, ready to punish such rudeness.

Fal's eyes widened in surprise, but Aspen thought he saw a slight twinkle in them and the hint of a smile in the corners of his mouth.

And why should a blatant insult to your king be amusing, forester? he thought angrily. But then he remembered the wizard's tower, and how they seemed to send messages beyond the obvious in everything they did. Suddenly he understood, and snorted out a laugh. He mused for a moment for the perfect reply. And then . . .

"The first is yet to be determined," he said, "and as to the second . . ." He raised his nose archly. "I have no idea of whom you speak."

Mishrath howled with laughter. Molintien looked horrified. The soldiers looked confused. Fal looked to burst something in his forehead as he kept trying not to laugh.

"Do you not see?" Aspen asked the onlookers. He explained. "You know the saying 'On the day you die, you may speak to the king any way you please'?" They nodded. It was an old saw, the joke being that if you spoke too impolitely to royalty, then that day was almost certainly the day you would die. "Well, guess what . . ."

Mishrath bared his few teeth at them in a grim smile. "This is my day."

No one is smiling now.

"And it will begin soon," Aspen said. "Let us begin before it does."

Mishrath nodded. "This," he said, pointing to his plant pile, "is just to help me concentrate. For the spell . . . how much do you know about major illusion, sire?"

"Not a great deal."

"Not many do." The wizard sighed. "After all, we fey all have a touch of glamour at our disposal. And once we make ourselves look good, what else do we need?"

Aspen might once have agreed wholeheartedly with that last bit, but now he realized how vain and vapid his former self had been. Even as a hostage, he had been a prince, acting—and dressing—accordingly. Or as much as was possible for a hostage prince in the Unseelie Court.

And how vain and vapid most of the court was, he thought. *Both courts, really.*

Though Unseelie courtiers had a very different idea of what physical beauty was from their counterparts in the Seelie Court, they still spent more time before a mirror than before the king and council advising them how to govern.

And advising is supposed to be their duty!

"The illusion?" Aspen prompted.

The old wizard gave his shoulders a shake and continued. "I will use the fires as a base for the illusion. Thanks to all of you, there are plenty of fires about, and they will provide both loci and fuel for the spell. Keep them burning and the spell will go on as long as it is needed." He nodded to

Aspen. "As the king will attest, fire is the most powerful of the five energies, though it can be burned through quickly. The dying fires are actually better for this type of spell, for I need the duration of coals rather than the explosive spark of true flame. But *afterward*, you must stoke them all, through both day and night." He did not have to explain *afterward*. It was written on all their faces.

His professorial tone reminded Aspen of Jaunty, his old tutor in the Unseelie Court, whom he had last seen in the Unseelie camp before the battle that killed his father.

I hope Jaunty is still alive. Aspen shuddered. *Unless Old Jack Daw discovered that he spoke to me in his tent early that morn. If so, then I hope he managed a quick and painless death.*

"The trees that fuel the fire," Mishrath continued, "were once alive." He motioned Fennel forward and pointed at his pile of plants. She spoke the tiniest word of power and set them alight. Strangely, the flowers were burning strongly before the dried leaves even caught. "In a sense, this spell brings them back to life. But in a different form." He frowned in concentration for a moment, staring into the small fire before him. "And not truly alive, either, I suppose." He cocked his head to one side, and the burning flowers now shadowed his deeply lined face into crags and canyons that mapped the millennia he had practiced his craft. He chuckled. "But you'll see something today, children. You will certainly see something today. And any of you who are left alive after . . . tell what we do here today. That will be my glory—and yours."

Then he stood, creakily at first. But when Aspen stepped forward to assist him, Mishrath waved him away angrily. Throwing off his cloak, he puffed his chest out and began to speak. His voice was bold and clear, with none of the sputtering and coughing of the last few days.

"I am Mishrath of the Five Mountains," he said, giving name to a region far to the south where neither the Seelie nor the Unseelie had ever reigned.

I wonder what brought him here, Aspen thought, *and why he stayed*. And he suddenly realized that he would never know. Would never have a chance to ask. He was deeply saddened by this new knowledge, and it surprised him.

"Slayer of the Kolkorath, the Wyrm of the Wastes, and the Guardian of Dreadstane."

More names Aspen did not know.

"I turned the One Who Awoke into the One Who Will Never Wake Again and stole the treasure of the Fire Crèche from under their soot-blackened noses." The words seemed to make the old wizard grow taller before them, though whether this was an illusion or not, Aspen could not say.

And yet he will die for me. Aspen looked around at the small company he led. *For all of us*.

"Bear witness to my last spell," Mishrath intoned, "and

tell your children's children that you were there at my passing."

He looked at Aspen, eyes white and unreadable. Aspen
nodded solemnly. There were tears in his own eyes, and he
could tell he was not alone in this.

But not Mishrath. His eyes were dry and his voice strong
as he began a deep humming way back in his throat. It
rumbled and tumbled through the deep octaves, lower than
any voice had a right to go. At times, it sounded like more
than one voice, as if he had summoned dozens of dead wizards to join him in the making of the spell. The humming
kept going, creating low harmonies that bypassed the ear
to shake the very bones of the listeners. Smoke from the
dried leaves roiled up before him, and Aspen thought he
saw small images in it: swords and spears, silver armor and
polished shields, tiny elven warriors to wear and wield them.

He is putting the pieces together.

There was a mist on the ground now, and Aspen saw that
it was spreading out across the field.

No, he thought, *it is pouring out from the dying fires.*

The mist quickly covered the whole field, and figures were
rising out of it: the warriors from the smoke now life-sized
and armored, bristling with weaponry. There were also
creatures of war: horses and unicorns and hippogriffs, their
bardings covered with clan badges surrounding the Seelie
sigil.

It is incredibly detailed, Aspen thought, for now came camp followers and supply wagons as well as specialized troops: dwarven sappers, gnomish engineers, skirmishers, scouts. A hardened old trooper in the blacks and tans of the Basilisk Clan, the so-called turncoat clan that had left the Unseelie side and joined their old enemy eons ago, stepped up to Aspen. He saluted, and Aspen could hear the snap of the trooper's boots slapping together, the creak of old leather shifting. He could even smell the soldier stink of him: sweat and dust and musty horse, with just a hint of olive from the whetstone oil of freshly sharpened weapons.

"It is done," the trooper said in Mishrath's voice.

Aspen looked over at Mishrath. He bowed to the old wizard, something a king rarely does. "And *it* is amazing."

"Yes," the wizard said, "it is." Then he paled and toppled, collapsing from the ground up, legs buckling, back arching, head wobbling loose on his neck. Fal caught him before he hit the ground, lowering him gently the rest of the way. Rushing forward, Aspen knelt by the wizard's side and put a hand on his forehead. His skin was already cooling.

Apparently, having waited so long to take the old wizard, death was not going to be slow about it.

Aspen knelt with his hand on Mishrath's forehead for a few more moments, then got to his feet. He was suddenly very tired. Looking over his small group of companions, he saw that they were all crying openly, whether in great wracking sobs like Fayth and Fennel or in the silent tears that trickled down Fal's stoic face. Even Snarl's and Bite's eyes shone with something other than martial fervor. Yet there were no longer any tears in his own eyes.

You cry for your enemies, but not for your friends? It was a good question, but he had no answer for it. *I have no answer to* any *questions.* He thought about burying the old wizard, but they had so little time.

"Put him in the cart and wrap him in my cloak," Aspen said. "If we all survive till this evening, we will bury him then."

"Perhaps," Molientien said carefully, "we should leave him unburied and within view of his army in case we break that connection."

"Surely," Fal said just as carefully, though there was an edge in his voice, "death has already broken that connection."

"I take both your meanings," Aspen said quickly. "But the truth of it is that we really do not know if he needs to be nearby. So to err on the side of caution, we will keep his body unburied and safe as long as the army exists. Quickly, you, Master Moat"—he pointed to the troll—"take him to the wagon."

The troll moved forward, nodded at Aspen, then picked up Mishrath's body as if it weighed no more than a sack of grain, though he carried it with great care to the wagon. Then he wrapped the old wizard in the king's cloak, his broad hands the size of shovel heads surprisingly gentle as he did so. Afterward, he stood up, squared his boulder-sized shoulders, and returned to the others, seeming—Aspen thought—more animated than he had been since leaving the moat.

Aspen looked again at the army Mishrath had died to create. He tried desperately to find something more inspiring to say to his companions than *This had better work.*

Nothing sprang to mind. Before he could think more about it, the sun finally peeked over the hilltops and revealed another great host just coming over the hills across the stream.

And that army is real. He did not mean to shiver, but a shudder escaped him. If anything, Jack Daw's army looked bigger than when it had defeated Aspen's father.

Perhaps because I am closer to it. He had watched his father die from atop a mountain.

Much closer.

"Molintien," Aspen said, hoping his voice didn't quaver, "prepare a flag of parley. It is time to talk to Old Jack Daw."

Molintien nodded quickly, but then asked, "Will he, sire?"

"Will he what?"

"Talk."

"Almost certainly." Aspen took a last glance at Mishrath in the wagon. He looked withered and even smaller wrapped in the cloak, with no hint of the power he had so recently wielded.

That is not Mishrath any longer, he thought. *Just the vessel that once held him.*

Aspen worked hard not to let the weariness take hold of his voice. "We have given the virtual Unseelie king something unexpected. A major army at my back. He will want to know all that he can before he makes his next move."

At least I hope that is true, Aspen thought. *I cannot say Jack Daw is cautious, having taken over one kingdom and now moving on another. But he does like to plan things out far in advance.* Suddenly remembering how Snail and he had escaped Jack Daw's clutches, he added to himself, *And he hates surprises!*

"My friends, Mishrath has bought us time. Good time. Let us not waste it." Turning, Aspen strode to his horse, hoping he looked kingly. "Molintien, Croak, Snarl, and Bite: you are with me." The gentlewoman for courtly reassurance, three real soldiers to add power and authority. At least he hoped so.

He mounted his horse, and the four he had called mounted as well, Molintien with a white cloth tied to her lance. *We look martial enough, I suppose.*

The illusory soldiers looked even more so, but he didn't want Jack Daw to get too close a look at them. He had no idea what the old drow knew of major illusion. The moment Jack caught a sniff of it, they were all dead.

But before Aspen could lead his contingent toward the enemy's lines, there was a commotion back by the fire. He spun his horse around to see what was happening, afraid the Unseelie troops might have sneaked around behind them.

The young Poppy Clan soldier—*what is his name, again? Oh yes, Alicanson*—was muscling his way through Mishrath's soldiers.

They do not disappear when touched. Aspen allowed himself a small smile. *Mishrath, you have outdone yourself!*

"Sire, wait!" Alicanson shouted. "You'll want to see this."

"Is it important?" Aspen said, letting impatience turn into anger. *I sound like my father*, he thought. *That is not good.*

"They seem to think so, sire," Alicanson said.

Then Snail and his mother burst through the crowd, and Aspen felt like the sun was rising for a second time that day.

22

SNAIL ADDS TO ASPEN'S PLAN

*T*he queen, who'd been by Snail's side, wrapped in her cloak and her royal presence, suddenly took three quick steps forward and then ran toward Aspen, arms out.

She gathered him in, almost drowning him in the folds of her heavy cloak, and saying quite audibly, "Oh my son, my dearest son."

He squirmed out of her reach and whispered something to her.

Snail was sure it had to do with decorum or danger. Or both. Either way, they pulled themselves apart, and the queen handed him a shiny object, which he put on his head.

A crown? For a battle? So everyone will know where to aim? Snail could hardly credit it. With an army on their doorstep, the queen had taken time to bring his crown, as if Aspen was a small boy who'd forgotten his warm coat or gloves.

Suddenly Snail wondered whether she'd ever noticed the queen carrying the crown. Only then did she realize that the queen had a crown perched atop her head as well.

It must have been Balnar's doing, she thought. *He must have hidden the crowns in secret pockets in the queen's cloak. He might not be a wizard, but clearly he does know sleight of hand tricks.* She smiled, thinking, *He and Odds will like one another.*

Snail caught up with Aspen and the queen but didn't force her way into their intimate circle, until Aspen, seeing her waiting, signaled her to him.

This king stuff, Snail thought, *is incredibly annoying. It was so much easier when Aspen was the prickly Hostage Prince. Or even the needy minstrel, Karl.*

Nonetheless, she went over to them.

"Why did you bring the queen here?" Aspen said, his face fighting between joy and anger. "She should not be set in the teeth of an ogre, though we may all be there soon enough."

"Because *she* insisted," Snail hissed. "Have you ever tried arguing with a queen? Or the *mother* of a king?"

"Do not talk about me as if I cannot hear," the queen said. "I may be getting old and worn down by my stay in your father's dungeon, Ailenbran, but I still have all my faculties. Besides, I have some magic I can add to this army's meager supply."

"I did not know you had magic, Mother," Aspen said, turning slowly to look straight at her.

"All the Astaeri royal family has magic." The queen allowed a small smile to play across her lips, but Snail could see that she controlled it. "Minor nobility has some as well. Have you not retained any of those history lessons your first tutors drummed into you?"

"The only tutors I remember, Mother, are facing us across that stream. I hope it is river magic you have. Raise the river and drown them all."

She shook her head. "Alas, no. I have . . ." She hesitated as if telling him might spoil her surprise. "I have woman's magic. Never to be scorned, of course. But not highly cultivated. Your father did not approve of me using magic at court. I am not sure if it will work in battle, but I am certainly willing to try."

Snail found she was liking Aspen's father less and less. *Just as well he's dead*, she though savagely.

"I practiced it a bit in my . . . um . . . discommode."

The dungeon, Snail reminded herself. And then she grinned. The queen had practiced magic in the dungeon. She vividly recalled her own stay in the Unseelie king's dungeon. *I could have used magic—even woman's magic—there*, she thought.

"Woman's magic, Mother?" Aspen asked, almost through gritted teeth. "Curdling milk? Pulling herbs? Hedge witch tricks? And why did I not know this?"

"Well," Snail said sensibly, "how *could* you have known? Stuck away in the Unseelie Court and kept under Obs's lock and key." She was beginning to lose her temper with all of them. "Maybe you should just ask her to show it to you, not dismiss it unseen. Oh, and ask me what news I bring of the professor and his army of changelings."

The queen's hand went up to her mouth. If Snail didn't know better, she would have said the queen was smothering a smile.

Like a weathercock, Aspen turned back to Snail. "Yes, yes, I meant to ask—what news?"

He was flustered now, and Snail pitied him. Pitied them all. They were outmanned and outmastered. *Though . . .* she thought, sounding—even in her own head—a bit too much like Odds, *though not without mastery of manners!* But at least she could give Aspen some good news, even though it might—like the human army—be coming too late.

"Odds and his people are perhaps two days behind." She looked around at the army spread out across the field. "With them and this army you should be able to drive Old Jack Daw all the way back to King Obs's Keep. Though," she snapped, "he's probably renamed it Jack Daw's Keep by now."

Aspen looked momentarily confused, then followed her gaze to the army Mishrath had made, who were still as firm as an actual army. "Oh. Them. They are not real."

"What?"

"It is a wizard's trick, an illusion cast by a dying wizard and made the stronger thereby. Or so both he and I hope.

It's a long story. I will tell it to you at battle's end."

"You didn't . . ." She trembled even thinking about it, but asked anyway. "You didn't kill him?"

"*Me?*" Aspen's voice broke on the single word. Then he added, "How could you think . . ."

"I never . . ."

"He was already dying and he said his death in the making of the illusion might give it added strength and he was willing to try."

She let out a breath she hadn't realized she was holding.

"He said he would be remembered for it."

"*If* it works."

"So far . . . pretty good." He suddenly scrunched his eyebrows. "Two days away, you said?"

Snail nodded. "Yes. And they are pledged to you as long as you fulfill your promises to them." She'd never doubted his promises, just doubted whether he would have the luck and time to make them come true.

"Freedom, land, equality?" Aspen said. "Yes, of course. As long as I and mine live, that promise stands. I shall put it in writing and send it through the Seelie lands. As soon as . . . as soon as . . ."

"I promise as well," said the queen. "For what that is worth."

"Madam," Snail said, before Aspen could answer, "it means everything."

The queen looked at Snail in a manner that seemed to

suggest she was measuring her. Snail could only wonder what her final reckoning would be.

Smiling, the queen inclined her head gracefully. "You do not credit yourself enough, Snail. You are smart, courageous, sometimes willful, and always speak your mind. You will do, girl. You will most certainly *do*."

Do what? Snail wondered. She knew she had no magic to offer the army and no knowledge but that which was in her hands. She'd already done what she could, convincing Odds to bring his people here. But she'd no guarantee they'd arrive in time. She didn't know if Odds would actually keep his pledge any more than she could be sure Aspen would be *able* to keep his. All she could do now was sew up what wounds could be sewn, give comfort and herbal sleep to those who would die, and . . . She bit her lip. *And hope to live.* That was all.

But before she could think further about this, there was the loud clarion of a war horn.

"Jack Daw!" Aspen said, and turned to face forward, with the rest of his army of make-believe warriors at his back.

He looks, Snail thought, *young and vulnerable. He looks frightened. He looks . . . ready.*

She hoped that the wizard hadn't died in vain.

And that Odds would get there in time.

ASPEN FACES AN OLD ENEMY

cAspen rode toward the enemy lines, Snail on his left side. Behind him rode Molientien, still bearing the flag of parley, as well as Croak, Snarl, and Bite, who bristled like hedgehogs with the innumerable amount of weapons they had managed to clip to their belts or sling over their shoulders or stuff into their boots, gloves, helmets, and sundry other hiding places.

The moat troll kept pace with the horses, though he did not look as if he was enjoying himself.

And my mother is coming with us as well, Aspen thought, glancing quickly to his right. He was slightly ashamed that she had insisted on riding to the parley, but a bit comforted, too, though he would never admit it aloud.

"I will keep silent, dearest," she had said, "I promise."

He did not believe her.

Though in truth, he thought, *she is probably the most sensible of us all. And if she were given control of both the* kingdoms, then both kingdoms would be well fed, watched over, and wearing something sensible for the weather.

"Would that Seelie mothers were in charge of the world," he muttered.

As they rode, Aspen told Snail a bit more about Mishrath's sacrifice and the spell he cast.

"So really all we have is these four soldiers and your mother?" Snail said, keeping her voice low.

"Oh, no," Aspen said. "There are almost forty more back at camp." He knew he was exaggerating but not by much. "Though only twenty are real soldiers." He bit his lip, look slightly discomforted, and added, "And about half of those are boys, probationers. From the Poppy Clan."

"The Poppy Clan!" Snail said. "Then we are in good hands." She didn't elaborate, but she turned and glared at Aspen as if he was at fault.

For some reason the look on Snail's face cheered him immeasurably. *Snail is furious*, he thought. *All is right with the world*.

"You mean," she hissed, "that there are just three dozen Seelie folk facing that?" She pointed across the stream where Old Jack Daw's army was arrayed.

"Well, you and my mother are here now, so that's two more," he said, looking where she was pointing.

The Border Lords were in the vanguard, colorful in bright tams and battle kilts and armed with a frightening array of overly large weapons. Bogle skirmishers ranged in front of them, testing the ground before the stream for traps both magical and mundane so that nothing would impede their fearsome charge when it came. For the life of him, Aspen could not tell if he wanted that charge to come early or late.

For the life of me! He sighed, wondering idly if his last words were going to be a joke.

On the left flank of the Unseelie army, heavily armored ogres stood with blank looks on their faces. Though he had to admit it was better than their usual expression—a horrible sneer.

On the right, a troop of kelpie cavalry snorted mist from their nostrils, impatient for their own charge.

Jack Daw will hold them till the end. Use them either to break us or to ride down those already broken.

The rest of the ranks were filled out with a motley array of fell creatures, some bearing weapons, others armed only with claws and teeth. But as different as they looked, he knew what they shared was a lust for blood and slaughter.

And there will be more hidden in the woods, strategic reserves of creatures unable or unwilling to come out in the daylight. Jaunty had taught him that. He called it the Ranks of War. Aspen had had to memorize them, make lists, create small wooden sculptures to set out on a battle map. He grimaced. *Who knows what foul beasts lurk there?*

But he knew. He'd grown up with them, after all. Dark elves, goblins, boggarts, cannibal ogres, vampyrs, banshees,

Red Caps, duergar and drow, nickneven and neugle . . . The list went on and on, each creature of the night more horrible than the last.

"But yes," he said to Snail, "those numbers sound about right."

She sighed. It was not a comforting sound.

They called a halt fifty yards short of the stream and waited, white flag waving lazily in a weak breeze. They didn't have to wait long. There was a commotion in the army across the waters, and then the Border Lords' ranks began to split down the middle to make room—reluctantly, Aspen thought—for a small troop of riders. They were all drow, regally appointed in gleaming armor and blood-red cloaks, hard to tell apart. *Probably nest brothers.*

At their head rode an ancient one of their race, thinner and greyer than all the rest, wearing not armor but the black robes of a senior councilor. He did not wear a crown. He had no need for it. But even without it, he moved like a king.

Old Jack Daw had come to talk.

"You and you," Snail suddenly said, pointing at Molintien and Croak. "Stay in front of the king at all times. Old Jack Daw is a traitor and a poisoner. He can't be trusted even under a parley flag."

"Snail," Aspen said as Molintien and Croak moved in front of him.

"You and you," Snail went on, ignoring him. This time

she pointed at Snarl and Bite. "If anyone makes a sudden move, kill them. Immediately."

"Snail . . ."

"Troll—if that happens, take Their Majesties back to camp." She hesitated. "No, all the way back to the palace. Carry them if need be. They will both try to talk you out of it. Don't listen."

The moat troll smiled, though whether he understood the instructions or was just happy to be addressed, Aspen wasn't certain.

"Snail!" Aspen practically shouted. "Jack Daw will not kill me."

Snail spun and faced him, her face red with anger, her eyes bright. "Why not? He killed your father! He killed your brothers!" Aspen heard his mother's breath catch as if fighting back a sob when Snail mentioned her murdered sons. "You're just an obstacle to him. And he will kill you if given half a chance."

Aspen shook his head. "He will not kill me today."

"Then you're a fool, Aspen!" This time it was the soldiers gasping to hear their king addressed this way.

"That is why he will not kill me, Snail," Aspen said calmly. "In his mind, I am a fool. A young, inexperienced, vain fool, whom he has already tricked once." Aspen glanced back at Mishrath's illusory army. "Who does he want at the head of this unexpected host? A general? A wizard? A new, adult king picked by the land?" He stared hard at

Snail. "Or a fool whose every move he knows so well?"

She said nothing for a moment, and Aspen watched the storm pass from her face. "Still," she said, quieter now, "those two stay in front of you."

Aspen smiled. "Of course. It would not do to take *foolish* chances."

They said no more as they watched Old Jack Daw and his drow brothers pick their way across the stream. Drows could cross running water, though they were not particularly fond of it. When they were within a dozen yards, Snail called out, "That's far enough, Daw."

A few of the group took a few more defiant steps forward, then Jack Daw raised his hand and they stopped.

Aspen had wondered what he would feel when he was finally this close to Jack Daw again. Anger? Fear? Sadness? He had thought the old drow his friend, and had been betrayed. But strangely he felt nothing.

Perhaps because so much has happened since the betrayal.

Leaning forward on his mount, Old Jack Daw peered at Snail. "Oh, it's the little changeling girl!" he said happily. "Slug or something, right?"

"Snail," she spat at him. "And still alive, despite your best efforts."

He sat straight again, dismissing her. "Let your betters speak, girl."

Aspen felt her stiffen beside him, but he laid his hand on her arm. His plan didn't involve her acting foolish, only him.

"Old Jack Daw? Is that you?" Suddenly his mother was beside him and then past him, drawing her horse even with Molintien and Croak. "Oh, it is *lovely* to see you!"

"Mother!" Aspen hissed, but she ignored him. *So much for staying silent.*

"Your Highness," Jack Daw said, sketching a bow from atop his horse. "You look as radiant as ever."

"Oh," the dowager queen tittered, "it is kind of you to say so. I wish I could say the same for you. You look *so* much older than last I saw you. Perhaps it is time for you to leave the keep and retire to your caves. I know the drow do not do well as they age. They get fusty, get feather fungus, the eyesight goes. And the cunning."

The drow brothers behind Jack Daw rustled their feathers as if the queen had cursed them. But Jack held up a hand, and they were silenced. Then he sighed expansively. "Would that I could retire, Your Highness. I see you have no need to do it yourself. But I must serve for a while longer. And besides," he said, looking at Aspen, "I have some business to conclude at Astaeri Palace."

Aspen barely suppressed a shudder. *Fear*, he thought. *Definitely fear.*

His mother sounded unfazed. "Oh, that *is* a shame. Perhaps I could come with you and we could discuss your business back in Unseelie lands?"

Aspen suddenly realized what his mother was doing. *She is*

offering herself up as a new hostage. He also knew it wouldn't work. Old Jack Daw was not interested in peace. Or an old dowager queen with no power. *It's time to end this,* he told himself.

"Enough!" Aspen shouted, and spurred his horse forward, pulling even with his mother. Molintien and Croak struggled to stay ahead of him as ordered, and drow hands crept toward their weapons as the Seelie folk grew nearer.

Old Jack didn't move, however, as if he knew there was no chance that a Seelie king would break the rules of parley. Especially not a weak and foolish king who had already seen the consequence of breaking the law of hostages.

"I have heard enough," Aspen said, trying to make his voice sound deep as the sea and dangerous as cold iron. "You see my host. You may leave my lands tonight, for if you do not do it peacefully, tomorrow I shall drive you from them. You have till the morning to decide."

Then he spun his horse and began trotting back toward the lines of his make-believe army. He didn't look back, for fear Jack Daw would read the lie in his face, but he was certain that his companions would turn and follow him.

And hopefully none of us will get a poisoned arrow in the back.

He suddenly had a dreadful itch between his shoulder blades where he imagined the arrow would lodge. It was with great effort he kept his hands on the reins. But he heard galloping, and moments later, Snail was by his side and his mother, too, and his soldiers were around him, with the moat troll forming the rearguard, walking backward and staring daggers at the drow.

Aspen was as certain as he could be that Jack Daw wouldn't try to kill him yet, but he certainly felt safer with his friends and family around.

"*That's* your plan?" Snail said, her voice low but angry.

"Well, it will hold them for today and tonight, at least."

"How can you be sure?" Strangely, she sounded curious, not sarcastic.

Perhaps she is starting to trust my judgment?

"Tell her, Croak."

Croak frowned, apparently unhappy at the thought of pushing words past his tight lips, but he obeyed his king. "Higher ground," he said.

"What the loquacious Fading Crocus is trying to say is that if Old Jack Daw wishes to attack us, he will have to attack uphill." Aspen smiled. "It is my understanding that most commanders try to avoid that if at all possible."

Croak nodded and spit. "Stream, too."

"Also, he would have to get across the stream," Aspen explained. "Certain members of his army have trouble crossing running water. Jack himself is not partial to it, but it will not hurt him as it would some of the others."

Snail looked back at the stream and the army behind it. "And why would he do that, since you have just promised to cross the stream and attack him tomorrow so he needn't go uphill or into water. All he has to do is wait for the foolish Seelie king."

"Exactly. And furthermore, he knows Seelie kings have magic that the land gives them, and he will want to know what my power is before he tests those waters."

Aspen barely had time to feel proud of how well his plan was working before Snail spoke again.

"Then why didn't you give him *two* days to decide?"

"I . . . um . . ."

"Or three or four?"

Because I am an idiot?

"I . . . um . . ."

As if inspired by Snail's biting words, her horse nipped at Aspen's mount. He had to rein it in to keep control, and Snail pulled a little bit ahead of him. "If you'd done that, Odds could have had his army here before we had to *talk* to Jack Daw again."

"Yes . . . er . . . those are all good points but . . ."

Snail looked back over her shoulder at him, one eyebrow raised, waiting for what came after the "but."

He had nothing to offer as an excuse. "I did not think of it."

"Hrmph," Snail said, or something like that. Then she kicked her heels lightly into her horse's flanks and spurred it faster toward their camp.

I am the Seelie king. I shoot fire out of my fingertips. And

I have just outwitted—albeit temporarily—the greatest threat the Seelie kingdom has ever faced. He watched as Snail reached the fire and dismounted. *Yet I am still unable to impress a midwife's apprentice.*

He wondered if other kings ever had similar problems.

He shrugged almost imperceptibly. *Seems unlikely.*

Heaving a great sigh, he kicked his horse ahead as well. They had a day and a night to rest up and plan. He didn't want to waste a moment of it.

24

SNAIL LEARNS A LESSON

*T*hey rode away as if they didn't mind that their backs were targets. Or at least everyone else didn't seem to mind. Snail felt even more vulnerable than she had in the Unseelie king's dungeon. But then, she wasn't a warrior. *Though*, she thought, *I've certainly been a fighter. And I don't want to die today—honorably or otherwise.*

The Seelie folk rode without haste but with a certain determination, and the moat troll kept pace with them, though he was huffing a bit by the end.

When they got back to camp, Snail saw that all the fires had been rekindled so that the high ground was alight with the flames. *Enough for about fifty fires per real Seelie warrior.* She stopped and glanced around. It was as though little flame imps were dancing on the hillside.

And then she thought: *If the flames aren't carefully tended, the entire hillside could become a pyre.*

Aspen and the queen walked away to the perimeter where

they were talking to the live guards and nodding at the illusions. Close up, the differences were clear. The illusions had better armor and armament. They didn't speak, didn't eat, managed to stay on their feet interminably. But if you didn't know they weren't real . . .

Snail hastened to catch up with them.

"Just in case"—Aspen was whispering to one real guard—"there are spies close enough to see."

The queen had actually walked over to two of the illusions and was carrying on an animated conversation with them. The illusions nodded as if they could actually hear what she said.

And perhaps, Snail thought, *they can. One never knows with magic.*

"I sure hope your fires keep your illusion warriors warm," Snail told Aspen. "There's certainly enough fire for the lot of them."

"Keeping them warm *is* important," Aspen said as his mother joined the conversation.

"Really?" Snail realized that sounded irritable. She hadn't meant to say that aloud. But knowing she might be dead in the morning seemed to have sharpened her tongue.

"The fires feed the illusion," Aspen said blandly.

The queen added, "The illusions have been made of light. In total darkness, they will simply disappear and need remaking."

"And alas, our illusionist is dead." Aspen pointed at the

cart, where Mishrath's now-shrouded body lay.

"Why can't *you* remake the illusions, Aspen? You're *the king*!"

The queen looked shocked at this outburst, but Aspen merely shook his head.

"I am a fire-mage, Snail. A gift I was evidently born with. Illusion is a different school, one which takes years to learn. No one taught me any magic when I was a Hostage Prince. Why *would* they?"

He shrugged as if it had been no true matter, but Snail knew it mattered a great deal to him. And by his mother's face, Snail knew it mattered to her, too.

"Well, then we're about to lose a lot of men," Snail said quietly. They both looked at her in alarm. "In case neither of you have noticed, it's going to rain before nightfall."

"How do you know?" the queen asked.

"I could tell you it's a changeling thing, and that it's *my* gift, but just look at that sky."

Aspen looked up hastily at the dark, gathering clouds. "Oh no," he said. "What can we . . . ?"

"Snail," the queen said, "can you go up on the bowser and see if Odds's army is anywhere close?"

"In a storm?" she and Aspen said as one.

"Is a storm any more dangerous than a war?" asked the queen.

Snail had no response for that.

"Never mind," the queen said, "I shall go."

"Absolutely not," Aspen said. And Snail added, "I just needed to know how important it was."

"We have to know," Aspen told her, "how long we have to stall. Without the illusion of a larger army . . ." He left the rest unsaid.

"I'll go and try to convince the bowser . . ." Snail tried to sound spirited, ready. But all she felt was dread.

The queen shrugged out of her heavy cape. "If the rug will go up, you will need this for the cold and the rain. It is made to repel them both."

"*You* will need it down here, madam . . ." Snail began.

"I will have little sleep tonight," the queen said. "This is where my small magicks must try their best.

"What *are* those magicks, Mother?" Aspen managed to look dubious and hopeful at the same time.

"Party magic," she said, "the sort of thing a queen needs to be able to do. And now, if you please, send your men to bring me a dozen house-tall trees from the far side where there are no watching eyes."

"Trees, Mother?"

"I can't make trees, my darling boy, but I can make everything else we need."

He sent the Poppy Clan under Fal's direction to get what his mother required.

But at Snail's insistence, she and the queen traded capes. There was no way she was going to let the queen stay out in the rain, even at some magical party, without any warm clothes.

THE BOWSER WASN'T as easy to convince. He'd been enjoying his time by one of the fires and at first had bared his teeth at her, snarling at the suggestion.

Snail had heated up some water on the flames and given the bowser a quick bath, thinking all the while that they both would be wet soon enough once the storm broke.

However, again clean—although not entirely a true gold—the bowser wrapped himself around Snail's legs like a large, shapeless dog.

A minute later, Snail was sitting on him, and then they were off.

It was a colder and rougher ride than before, even though they were only skimming the treetops. Snail could feel ice in the air. And once the storm, which was advancing from the mountains, started spitting at them, hurling raindrops as hard as pebbles, neither she nor the bowser was happy. She apologized to him over and over, in between explaining where they were heading.

Darkness and rain made it almost impossible to see how close they were to the trees, and twice she could feel the tops of firs brushing the bowser's belly, and he shivered uncontrollably for what seemed like hours. It felt as if there were a river running beneath her as they flew.

SOME TIME LATER, a chance strike of lightning showed her the huddled hordes of changelings below, and further back, the linked wagons of Odds's troupe. *Maybe,* Snail thought, *a day away from Aspen's camp. Not more. But probably not less.* The storm was slowing everything down.

"Down there," she whispered, and the bowser dropped so precipitously in his hurry to get out of the rain, Snail was almost thrown off. But she'd been ready for such a maneuver and clung to his fur, though the queen's cape was ripped from her shoulders by the wind and lost in their descent. She wondered how she'd explain it to the queen, to Aspen, then realized that in the larger view of what was about to happen, it was too small a thing to worry about.

Soaking wet and miserable, they landed not five large steps from the front of the wagons.

Snail got up off the bowser, and he humped and hunched his way to the back end of the wagons, disappearing through one of the doors. Then Snail went in the door she expected belonged to Odds.

It was not Odds's room at all, but Maggie Light's.

"I hate," Snail said, "how the rooms keep changing around."

Maggie was sitting, unmoving, in front of the table, looking into her mirror so that it seemed as if there were two Maggie Lights sitting there, both equally still.

Or perhaps I'm hallucinating from the cold, Snail thought, for even though she was now indoors, she was shivering.

"Maggie . . ." she began. Her teeth began to chatter, and she couldn't say another word.

Maggie turned quickly, stood, and came over to Snail with the coverlet from her bed in her hands. She wrapped Snail in it and said something softly.

Snail realized it was a song and knew she should put her fingers in her ears because Maggie always sang her spells, and this was not the time for her to become spellbound. But she couldn't move, swaddled as she was in the blanket, and besides, suddenly she didn't care.

Maggie sang:

> *Sun warms earth, and secrets grow,*
> *Deep beneath the winter ground.*
> *Shoots and stalks and roots reach up*
> *Until the springtide can be found.*
> *Find the sun, child, find the sun . . .*

As the song burrowed into her, Snail felt an inner spring-tide filling her with warmth. Not just the warmth of the blanket. She knew it was the spell because she was warm in places the blanket didn't touch—her feet and hair tickling with the warm. Where she had been soaking wet, now she was dry. Dry and distraught.

She had come to hurry Odds along, to get him to Aspen

before Mishrath's phony army faded. But with the storm there would be nothing she could do. The changeling army would move as fast as it could and no faster.

This time her mission was sure to be a failure. *In fact*, she told herself, *it already is.*

But then she thought, *Maybe the bowser brought me to Maggie instead of Odds for a reason.*

Snail knew what she had to do.

"Maggie," she said, "come with me. On the bowser. Help me help the Seelie king."

Maggie cocked her head to one side, looking slightly demented. "I do not do well in the wet," she said.

"If it settles before morning?"

"Then I will go."

"Should I ask Odds?" Snail said. "Will he give his permission?"

"I serve the professor's purpose," Maggie said, "but he does not own me. He only made me." She looked straight at Snail. "His purpose was for me to give you whatever you ask for, whether it is spoken or unspoken."

"Thank you," Snail said. She began to shuffle toward the door.

"Where do you go, child?"

"To keep an eye on the storm."

Maggie smiled. Snail could not tell if it was an effort. "You sleep; I will watch."

Snail opened her mouth to resist, then realized Maggie

could just sing her to sleep. "All right," she said, "if you promise to wake me once the rain lightens."

"I promise," Maggie Light said.

That was enough for Snail. She climbed onto the bed, still wrapped in the blanket, and fell immediately into an exhausted sleep.

* * *

IT WAS STILL dark when a hand shook her awake. Snail sat up, disoriented for a moment before remembering all that had happened. "Has it stopped raining?"

"It has," a voice said, but not Maggie Light's. "And I am going with you, too."

Dagmarra grinned. "I canna leave you to fight a battle without me."

"But what about baby Og?"

"My brother will take care of him," the dwarf said. "He's not much of a fighter. And Og's too young to be in the front lines of a war."

"And Maggie?"

"She's cleaned up the bowser, so stump your sticks, girl. We have a flight to make, prisoners to take."

"Done with sleep, promises to keep?" asked Snail.

"You'd make a great dwarf," said Dagmarra, "if only you were shorter."

She held out a cape that could wrap around Snail three times. "This belonged to Huldra the troll," she said, adding in case Snail had forgotten, "Og's mother."

Snail nodded. "I brought him into this world," she reminded Dagmarra.

"So you did. But wars often make us forget things. And forget our friends."

Snail ignored that, saying, "I'm not sure the bowser can carry us all."

"Maggie will take care of that."

Snail nodded. She was sure that Maggie could convince anyone of anything. So she got out of the bed, rumpled and hungry but not complaining about either. And took the huge cape.

They went outside, where Maggie was waiting for them. The bowser, now completely golden on the top, lay spread out on the still-wet grass.

Maggie sat down first, lacing her fingers in the bowser's fur. He seemed to shiver with joy. Dagmarra was next, snugging up to Maggie and putting her arms around Maggie's waist. She looked only at Maggie's back, and Snail realized the dwarf was terrified—not of the fighting but of the flight—though Snail was sure that nothing would shake that admission out of her.

Snail was the last to sit down, sandwiching Dagmarra between Maggie and herself and wrapping them both with the troll's cape. Then she grabbed two handfuls of the bowser's fur. "You know where the Seelie king is," she told the bowser. "Take us there as quickly as possible."

Dagmarra said something. At first Snail thought it might be a prayer. But then when Dagmarra repeated it, Snail understood what she was saying. "Maggie's left a note."

"A note?"

Dagmarra looked back at her long enough to say, "For Odds. So he knows she's gone and where she's going. He won't be long in coming after."

And then the bowser lifted, and Dagmarra said nothing more, just clung even tighter to Maggie.

They headed toward the west, the sun just beginning to shed its light upon their backs. Snail held on to that small light and the smaller hope that she'd taken a tiny step toward helping Aspen win his war.

ASPEN LEARNS A LESSON

*U*nder Fal's direction, the boys of the Poppy Clan found ten wind-harvested trees lying on the forest floor, so they only had to take down two. Or rather, Fal, at least four times the age of any of the lads, only had to take down two. The boys watched as he brought down each with five expertly placed swings of his ax. Then the old forester measured the trees with steady strides and trimmed off the bottoms till they were all of a size.

The boys hitched two of the oxen that had pulled the wagon to the downed trees. The great beasts hardly strained as they dragged the trees, in pairs, to the center of the encampment.

It all took more time than the queen would have liked. But since the rain had not yet begun to fall, only hovering heavily in the sluggish grey clouds streaming in from the north, she soon had the boys setting up four of the trees along the camp's perimeter, at the four corners.

Aspen realized that those trees now marked the farthest of all the fires.

"Oh, Mother . . ." he whispered. "I think I am beginning to understand."

Now the queen began to weave magic in the air with her fingers. It spun out like spider's silk, winding about each standing tree, anchoring each to its spot. Once the first trees were steady, the queen had the boys set up four more well inside the area designated by the first four.

"Sire," whispered Molintien, "she's making a . . ."

"Hush," he said, finger to his lips.

Again the queen's spider fingers spun out their silken anchors till those four trees held themselves up in sturdy splendor.

Then the final four trees were hauled by the oxen and placed by the boys under the queen's direction. The trees marked an inside space where—if Aspen had brought along his throne—a throne would have been set.

When all the trees were solidly situated, by fey and magic, that old companionship, the queen wove a silken canopy over the whole, acres and acres spun out of her fingers, though it was no soft covering to be brought down in any passing breeze.

Aspen put a hand to a piece of the tent closest to him. "Ah . . ." he said. His mother had spun a pavilion as solid as stone. *But at what cost?*

He turned and saw her collapse into Molintien's arms, looking as drained and frail and grey as the woman in white who haunted the upper halls of Astaeri Palace.

"Mother," he whispered, near to tears.

"I may have overdone," the queen said faintly.

"No, madam, it was *well* done," Molintien answered, loud enough so that Aspen could hear. "You can rest now. The fires are saved."

Aspen had the wagon brought into the pavilion, pushing aside the crowds of illusory soldiers. He ordered four of the Poppy Clan boys to move the wizard's body to beneath the wagon. One boy shuddered at touching the corpse, which, he said, was no longer stiff, but the rest of the boys seemed to have no problem handling the dead.

Then Aspen told them to stand at each corner of the wagon to keep a constant watch.

"On the dead man?" the shuddering boy asked.

"On the queen," Aspen growled.

The moat troll picked the queen up and carried her to the wagon, placing her carefully on the straw. Everyone else was surprised at how gentle he was with her, though Aspen was not.

Then Molintien climbed in with the queen to keep her warm. Aspen covered them both with Snail's cloak and his own as well.

"Does she breathe?" he whispered to Molintien.

"Shallowly, sire. But steady. All she needs is time and some hot tea."

Tea they had. Time . . . that was a different question. Aspen sent one of the brownies for a mug of tea.

"Are you certain she will recover?" he asked Molintien.

"As certain as one can be in the middle of a war, sire," she said.

Aspen worried that she was trying to make him feel better. Snail would have told him the truth.

Suddenly at his side, Croak said, "I'll take first and last perimeter watch. You, sire, should stay here and keep watch over the queen." Those were the most words in a row Aspen had ever heard from him.

Aspen shook his head. "The queen would never allow it. I will take second perimeter watch with one of the boys and the troll. Wake us."

"But, sire . . ."

"No buts. I am the king. In some lands, my word would be law." Aspen's lips thinned and set in a determined scowl.

Croak saluted and left.

Aspen made the rest of the real soldiers bed down. He stared up into the pavilion roof that his mother had spun out of magic, need, and love. The fires cast strange shadows, which a wizard might have been able to parse. He kept thinking that if he looked long enough at the shadows, something about this war might make sense.

At last, he lay down, knowing he would probably not be able to sleep. But he had underestimated how tired he was. As soon as he was horizontal, he was out.

HE DREAMED OF the Sticksman's cavern. Not as he had seen it with the Archivist, but as it had been when he had escaped the Unseelie Court with Snail. The stalagmites were gone, and there was a dock, a boathouse, and a crowd of Border Lords charging toward the shore. But instead of Old Jack Daw urging them on, this time it was the skulker. And then, as they got closer, Aspen saw that it was King Obs, not the skulker.

Wait—it is *the skulker.* He changed his mind several times more, then realized something: *They look the same.*

Aspen shot awake and sat up. "They are the same!" he said aloud, knowing that some dreams could be prophetic.

No, not the same, he corrected himself. They could not be. Obs wasn't old enough to have been alive at the time the Archivist had brought him to. *But they could be related. Was the skulker related to King Obs?* Aspen thought that was an awfully big leap to make from a physical resemblance. *But what if he were?* King Obs traced his line back to the first Unseelie king: King Arl, the Uniter of Clans. At least he said he did. *Was the skulker King Arl? Did the Archivist and I actually go back that far in time? Why did the skulker need to rid himself of the Sticksman? And how will this knowledge help me delay Jack Daw till the changeling army arrives?*

Sleep was obviously not going to return, so Aspen got wearily to his feet. He had no answer to any of that. And now it was starting to drizzle. He could hear the patter on the pavilion roof.

"Sire?" It was Molintien, sitting up in the wagon, though the queen did not move. "The men have gathered more wood and are standing by the fires in case the queen's roof doesn't hold. We'll keep them lit while you and the soldiers keep any scouts at bay."

If it started raining in earnest, he was not sure he would be able to summon his own fire, but it was nice of her to say so. And also to take initiative while he slept.

"Thank you, Molintien," he said. "The queen's roof *will* hold. It *must* hold. How does Her Majesty?"

"Breathing steady, sire. But colder than I would like."

He nodded, but once he had heard his mother still breathed, his mind began its own conversation, and whatever else Molintien said disappeared into the patter of the rain.

What I need, he thought, *is to hold Jack Daw off another day. Then hopefully Odds will be here.*

He decided to walk about the camp to see if anything came to him. *I need to make certain no scouts get too close, anyway. I do not want them loosing any arrows and seeing them go right through my soldiers.*

He wandered down the hill, already slippery underfoot

with the small rain. He sensed rather than saw some of his own scouts nearby. It was comforting to know they were close, but he wondered if any of them had slept. An exhausted soldiery was not going to help hold off the horde.

He saw at once that Jack Daw's army had pulled back to the edge of the forest, which made sense. They expected an attack in the morning and were digging into a defensive position, cutting down trees and making a perimeter around their camp with sharpened logs and trenches. Aspen looked but didn't see any magical means being used.

They must have lost all their wizards when they fought my father.

That was often the way of it with battle-mages. The energies they commanded were so powerful that mutual destruction was often assured. In a few ancient wars Jaunty had told him about, the wizards on *both* sides had refused to fight because of this. *Would that we all could just refuse to fight.* Aspen smiled despite the poor weather and his impending doom. *Sorry, Jack, my old friend, I just don't feel like fighting today. Some other time, perhaps?*

He didn't think that would delay the old drow for long. *Might confuse him for a bit, however.* Aspen stopped walking, struck by a thought. *And that might be enough.*

Jack Daw was a schemer, a planner. He didn't like to make moves until assured of victory. *Maybe if I confuse him, it could buy us enough time.* He looked at his ranks of illusory soldiers, some very convincingly shivering in the cold. *Buy us enough time to replace this fake army with a real one.*

He looked up at the sky, which showed no sign of light. Dark clouds still hovered over everything.

Unless the magical soldiers disappear before then.

With that cheerful thought, he headed back up the hill.

He was nearing the central fire, which Fal had stoked up to great height, when he heard Molintien call, "Sire, come get something hot with us!"

Us! He ran the rest of the way.

When he came back into the pavilion, pushing past real soldiers and fake ones without making a distinction, he saw his mother sitting up, a mug in her hand.

Aspen hadn't thought he was very hungry until he saw that mug. Suddenly he was ravenous. *I have not eaten since yesterday.* He rounded the flames and found that somehow, in the middle of a soldier's camp and in the middle of a war, his mother—or more probably Molintien—had managed to put out a spread worthy of a king.

Balnar, he thought. The old steward could perform magic when packing a sack for travel. *Probably real magic.*

Aspen stood next to the wagon while his mother instructed Molintien to pile a plate for him. He tore into it with no decorum and very little of the reverence a meal of that quality deserved.

"So, Aspen," his mother said, her voice no more than a whisper, "do you have a plan for the morning?"

The question stalled any questions he might have made

about her health and whether she should be sitting up.

Aspen shrugged. "The beginning of one."

"Good. I shall sleep better knowing you have a plan."

Calling it a plan may be glorifying it a bit. I have a stratagem that might buy us a couple of hours.

"Then sleep well, Mother." He grabbed a last starfruit and popped it in his mouth. It tasted of cool night and sugared dreams. "But before you are off to that land of shadows, do you know anything about King Obs's ancestry? Is he truly descended from Arl the Uniter?"

His mother took a sip of whatever was in her mug, then said in the same whispery voice, "They all say they are, do they not?" Another sip. "But Obs's claim might have more merit than most."

He thought her hand looked as if it were shaking, and indeed Molintien took the mug from her. His mother made no protest and finished her thought in her whisper voice. "The wizards in the tower thought so, at least. What of it?"

"Most likely nothing. Is it true Arl brought the lawless clans together to form the first Unseelie Court?"

She shrugged, a gesture that once might have been almost coquettish but now made her look exceedingly frail. "No one knows for certain. There are no records from that time."

"That ever strike you as odd? *We* have written histories as far back as then."

"But the Unseelie are very different from us, my son." Frowning, she held out her hand for the mug. Molintien gave it to her, and she took a long draught. "And we had not yet discovered the Unseelie folk then, for the river crossing was too desperate, filled with carnivorous and very hungry mer. Plus the Shifting Lands swallowed up our explorers, so *our* histories tell us nothing of the Unseelie then."

He feared tiring her further, but he knew this conversation was important and she would finish it even if he would not. "I am not so sure how different we are," he said. "My father tried to have me killed. That seems pretty Unseelie." He thought of Snail. "And some from that land, like Snail, are brave and trustworthy and noble."

His mother nodded solemnly, her eyes in the shadows thrown by the fires now dark and unfathomable. Like the eyes of a prophetess. "There are some who say we were all the same long ago. *'All the rivers in Faerie are one, and so are its people.'*" Tilting her head, she said, "I do not remember who said that. I am getting old and this travel does not agree with me. I believe I will turn in now." She bowed slightly to him. It had to be an unfamiliar gesture for her, who had been queen for so long, but she performed it gracefully and naturally.

"Good night, Your Majesty," she added. Then she winked and fell back into Molintien's arms, leaving him alone with his thoughts.

All the rivers in Faerie are one, and so are its people. Aspen moved off to stand by the closest fire. He frowned. *Then what* was *the skulker doing with the Sticksman in that cave so long ago?* He plucked a piece of grass and threw it into the fire, watching it curl up and burn, wishing all of his troubles would just burn up and drift away like ash.

26

SNAIL JOINS THE WAR

"*There!*" Snail shouted, pointing to the final milestone. "After Little Sister, and the next few meadows, there's a high plain where our troops—the real ones *and* the illusions—are camped. You'll know it by the cook-fires."

She managed to make out the mountain as they passed by it through the driving rain, but only just, and pointed.

Snail hoped the bowser knew where they were. They were flying rain-blind. The only thing missing was lightning. "And thank the gods for that," she said under her breath, confident neither Maggie nor Dagmarra would hear her.

"I don't see an encampment anywhere," called Maggie Light from her place at the head of the bowser. "And no fires." Her voice seemed rusty, worn.

"Oh no." Snail was devastated. "Without the fires, the illusory army will disappear."

Dagmarra spit out a short, sharp word. "*Vrest!*"

Snail assumed it was a dwarven swear.

The meadows below, or what they could see of them from this height, looked more like ponds from the amount of rain that had fallen.

The bowser headed downward, until he was skimming the treetops, possibly because of the weight of his three passengers. But also his rain-soaked fur must have added even more weight.

Snail patted him for reassurance, her hand getting even wetter than it already was. She hadn't thought that possible.

THEY DIDN'T SPEAK for the next few leagues. It was too difficult and too wearing. Besides, the closer they came to their destination, the more they feared being overheard by the wrong soldiers. If they were spotted, what fell weapons might be fired at them, what flying monsters might take to the skies to chase them down?

Now Snail tried to see more than just the grey rain and failed. Even rubbing a soggy sleeve across her face didn't help.

In fact, she thought, *it only makes things worse.* She wondered if they'd gotten lost; if they were going to suddenly find themselves in the midst of the Unseelie horde. Her mind spiraled out of control with bad thoughts.

"No camp," Maggie said suddenly, "but I see a shining pavilion ahead."

"Pavilion?" Snail couldn't imagine what she meant.

Maggie Light added, "Smoke from all sides. The whole illuminated with . . ."

Snail strained to see through the storm, but she didn't have the kind of made eyes that Maggie had. But that description was enough to frighten her.

"Turn around, turn around!" she shouted at the bowser, certain that what they were seeing was the kind of Unseelie magic that she'd been fearing. Any minute, she was sure, they would be surrounded by dragons and drows, by ogres reaching upward to pluck them from the skies.

But the bowser was already dropping well below the tree line and clearly coming in for a landing.

"You stupid excuse for a foot wipe!" Snail screamed. "You'll be our deaths."

Maggie lifted her head and took a deep breath. "I smell no Unseelie here," she said. "Though I *do* smell royal magicks."

Smell? Snail thought. *Maggie Light can* smell *magic? Why hadn't I known that? Can Aspen use it?* When she drew in a deep breath herself, all she got was a nose full of wet air.

They landed with a bump, skidded across the wet grass, till the bowser ended with his head—at least Snail assumed it was his head—resting against a tall tree that was posing as a pavilion post.

A very large set of feet and legs stood by the post.

Snail looked up and up.

"Troll," Dagmarra said, almost happily.

"Why, Master Moat," Snail said, "I think we've come home." She stood up, as did Maggie and the dwarf. "Though it doesn't quite look like the home I left."

The moat troll grinned. It almost improved his looks. Almost, but not quite.

Then he picked up the bowser as if the rug was no more than a nose wipe, and the three passengers followed behind.

Snail didn't know what to make of the pavilion, its shimmering light, the fact that it kept the bucketing rain out. The grass beneath the pavilion's roof was dry, and all the fires—magic or real—were merrily crackling away.

Even more important was the crush of soldiers in full armor, swords at their belts. Snail knew they were only an illusion, but a couple of times when she brushed by them their armor felt solid. She wondered if their swords were sharp enough to run an enemy through and had to stop herself from asking, or from testing out the swords' points.

The wizard was gone, but his magic not only lingered, it had powered an illusion that fed every sense. She could see, hear, touch them. She thought she could smell them, too. And they hadn't dimmed one bit since she'd been away. But of course, such an army didn't dare leave the tented place, not as long as it was raining.

She shared none of her fears with Dagmarra or Maggie Light. She guessed they'd already figured it out for themselves.

Ahead of them, but still beneath the pavilion's sheltering roof, was the wagon, with a buzz of real soldiers around it. The Poppy Clan, and a few of the Toad Clan as well. Sitting in the wagon and holding court was the queen, though she looked older, shrunken, and pale.

How she has faded in a single day and night, Snail thought.

The queen's voice, though, was still powerful, and when she spotted Snail, she called out, "Give way for m'lady."

Dagmarra turned and looked up at Snail.

Snail shrugged. Winked.

Maggie Light said nothing. She didn't have to. Dagmarra's face said it all.

"Snail!" From behind, the familiar voice welcomed her back.

Snail turned, resisted curtseying, stepped forward, and was enveloped in a big hug. She stood rigid, afraid to give in to his brotherly affection, when all she could see was doom ahead.

"I'm soaking wet," she warned Aspen.

"But you're here," he said. "With Maggie Light. And Dagmarra." He grinned. "Everything is going to be all right now."

Snail thought about the Unseelie army awaiting them. The Red Caps and Border Lords, the ogres and bogles, the swords and arrows, lances, talons, teeth. And all they had was a handful of real soldiers and a regiment of shadows.

"Everything . . . all . . . right," she whispered, lying to her king and knowing she lied. And when he gave her a second hug, she allowed herself to forget fear and instead to breathe hope. It was a small victory. Perhaps the only one that she'd have in this night before battle.

ASPEN CHOOSES THE WAY

"*H*ow far away is Odds's army?" Aspen said as he watched Snail tear into a hearty soup Molintien had provided. She had provided a spoon as well. He had no idea where the ingredients for the soup had come from, and decided not to ask. He assumed the spoon had been sent along by Balnar.

Dagmarra and Maggie Light sat on either side of Snail protectively, neither looking entirely comfortable being surrounded by so many fey. Dagmarra had a smaller bowl of soup that she was simply drinking from as if it were a cup.

Maggie Light did not eat at all, and no amount of argument from Molintien could convince her to. Finally Snail said, "She's a made woman, like your soldiers in the tent. She neither eats nor sleeps." Only then did Molintien stop trying.

I wonder when last Snail ate? Aspen thought.

"A day," Snail replied, after a quick swallow.

It took Aspen a moment to realize she was answering the question he had asked aloud, not the one he had thought.

"If you can call it an army." She glared up at the silken roof that still held despite the now-pounding rain. "Might be longer if this storm continues."

Aspen nodded. "I think I can give them a day. Then we can all retreat to the palace. I think we will feel better with walls around us and an *actual* army beside us."

Snail nodded in agreement and went back to shoveling soup into her mouth.

But Dagmarra looked furious. "Retreat? How can you think of retreat? We'll have the numbers to go forward. Retreat is no treat. It's just a stupid rout. The route to despair and defeat. Arms carry us forward; backward-running feet make for a defeat."

Aspen thought about what he had learned from Jaunty about an army in retreat. It was not much. But he did remember that a retreat was the most dangerous time, even if the army wasn't running from a lost battle. The mere act of moving backward made soldiers lose heart, and any attack launched at them then could have a disastrous effect. It would be even worse for Odds's men. They were more rabble than army, lacking the training necessary for an orderly retreat.

"Weapons," he told Dagmarra. "Bloodthirstiness. Battle-savvy. Brute force. It's what they have and we do not." He shook his head. "We need the palace walls around us for strength, to give us room to maneuver. This was never about fighting the Unseelie face-to-face, but about buying us time to outthink them, outrun them, and outscheme them."

I will lend Croak to the changelings, he thought. *If Odds heeds his advice, they should be able to make it to Astaeri Palace safely. And with the changelings manning the walls with us, we will at least have a* chance *of victory. Or at least a chance to outwit defeat.*

He knew it wasn't *much* of a chance, but not too long ago defeat was a near certainty. He glanced over at Snail, and the sight of her eating cheered him. She was done with the soup and was now tearing off bits of the black bread the bowl was made of to sop up the remnants. Laughing at something Dagmarra said, she pushed some flyaway orange hair back behind her ear. She noticed Aspen smiling and saluted him with the last of the bread.

I could stay by this fire forever, he thought. He was warm and happy and mostly dry. He had friends and family near.

But—he thought—*a king's duties pull me away.* Maybe it was like that with his father. The man his mother had loved had been consumed by the role he had to play. *If so, I forgive you, Father.*

Because now he understood. He knew he had to check the perimeter and make sure no enemy scouts got too close. He had to check on the fires and see that they were well fed. No, he couldn't stay by the fire forever. He couldn't stay for more than a few more moments.

Who would ever wish to be king? he mused. The answer came to him immediately. *All those who are not.*

Turning his eyes away from the fire, he looked out into the darkness toward where Jack Daw was encamped with his army. *And many of them will lie, scheme, betray, and kill to become king.* He thought of the skulker and the three crones he had killed, the Sticksman walking to the water with no memory of what he once was. *Did the skulker do all that to become king?* There was no way to answer that question. But having seen the terrible lengths Jack Daw had gone through to make himself the virtual king of the Unseelie . . .

If they only knew how little the prize is worth.

"Sire," Croak said, stepping into the firelight and interrupting his reverie. "Scouts."

Aspen nodded and stood. He thought about asking where the scouts were and how many. Keep the old Toad talking so he could stay in the warmth of the fire for just a little longer.

Instead, he said, "Show me," and followed Croak out into the dark.

THE SCOUTS WERE gone by the time Aspen arrived. All that was left were their footprints, already half filled with rainwater.

"Must've just wanted a peek at Her Majesty's weaving, sire," Alicanson said, crouched behind a rock, still gazing downhill toward the stream. The red of his Poppy Clan emblem looked black in the low light. "Went back to camp when they saw it's just to keep us dry." He smiled and brushed a few strands of soaking wet hair off his forehead. "Well, most of us, anyway."

Aspen suddenly realized that while he sat safe and dry by the fires, his scouts had been working far away from the silk cover and firelight, crawling through mud and darkness to make sure the rest of the small army stayed alive through the night.

"Pull your scouts back under the cover, Croak," he said. "Let them dry out as well."

Croak stared at him for a second, then spit on the ground but away into the dark so as not to offend. "No," he said. "Sire."

"Umm . . . what?"

Croak shrugged. "No."

"If I might explain, sire," Alicanson said, talking to Aspen but looking to Croak for permission to speak. The old Toad soldier nodded imperceptibly. "You probably think being a warrior is about killing. And, sure, that's a part of it. But nobody becomes a warrior just so's they can kill." He paused, lips pressed thin. "Well, some do, I suppose. But most don't. Not Croak, here. Not me. Not anyone in your company. We became warriors for one reason: to keep our friends and family safe. And a bit of discomfort is nothing if it lets us do that."

Aspen looked to Croak, who nodded his agreement.

"Very well," Aspen said, "but cut the watch by a third. I think Old Jack Daw will be content to rest most of his soldiers for the battle he thinks is coming tomorrow."

"Yes, sire," the two warriors said in unison.

He left them there and marched back up the hill alone.

◆ ◆ ◆

ASPEN WAS CORRECT; Jack Daw only guarded the Unseelie lines that night and left the Seelie to their own devices. So the king was not called upon again till dawn. And if he'd been able to sleep, he would have started the day well rested.

As it turned out, he was tired and cranky from a fitful night of nightmare-filled catnaps. He scowled at Molintien when she brought him hot spiced tea just before daybreak, and barked at Fortuna, the Clover Clan soldier who gave him a stuttering morning report that all was clear.

He would have snapped at Snail, too, but she looked even crabbier than he did.

"Do we have a plan to live through the day, Your Majesty?" Her voice was emotionless, as if they were talking about a walk around the castle grounds.

"Yes," he said, "though it will not sound like much of one."

At that, she smiled. "They never do."

"This one even less so." He cleared his throat. "Today, I plan for us to do nothing. But bravely."

"What?" She gawped. "Nothing?"

"Bravely," he reminded her.

She ignored him. "*Nothing?* How is that a plan?"

"That is why I added the *bravely*. I toyed with *gallantly* for a while, but I think *bravely* is better."

"Bravely? Nothing?" Snail sputtered. "You . . . I . . ."

Aspen threw back his head and laughed. It felt good.

"How," Snail said, "can you laugh at a time like this?"

"How can I not?" Aspen said. "I am trying to face down the greatest threat the realm has ever faced with a midwife, a moat troll, and an army of illusions. And my only hope is that a man who hates me arrives with reinforcements in time for all of us to run away together."

"Well, when you put it that way . . ." Snail showed the smallest of smiles. It was only a rueful, slightly cynical twist of the lips.

But nonetheless—Aspen thought—*a smile.*

"I know, it is like the beginning of a joke. A midwife walks into a tavern with a moat troll on her head . . ."

Now it was Snail's turn to laugh. She laughed and Aspen laughed with her until they were both coughing and crying and bent over from sore bellies. Several of the soldiers looked on with concern but were too polite or perhaps too disturbed to interrupt.

Dagmarra was neither. "In Odds's name, what are you two doing?" she asked, striding up boldly, Maggie Light close behind.

"Moat troll," Aspen said, then broke off in a giggling fit.

"On my head," Snail said, unable to stop laughing.

Dagmarra frowned at them for a few moments, then stomped off, muttering, "Worse than my brothers, they are."

Maggie Light peered at them curiously, then eventually followed Dagmarra.

Snail regained her composure first. "But seriously, do nothing? And don't say *bravely*!" she said, raising a finger to forestall him.

Aspen cleared his throat of humor. "Old Jack Daw will not know what to make of it. He will spend all day waiting, but nothing will happen. No attack. No talk. Nothing."

"So, that's the day. Why won't he attack that night?"

"Well, that is the weakness in my plan." He went on quickly before Snail could pounce on that statement. "But I am betting he will not. His defensive position is so advantageous, I think he will give me another day to attack. And by then, hopefully Odds will have arrived."

Snail was quiet, obviously thinking hard. "It is," she finally said, "a shockingly good plan. Especially considering it involves doing absolutely nothing."

"But bravely!"

She nodded sagely. "I can see why you added that."

"I will go tell the troops."

THE TROOPS—ALL thirty or so of them—took the news better than Snail. The storm had passed and all looked forward to spending the day drying out. And it looked like the thought of doing nothing while their enemies braced themselves for an attack that would not come appealed to them. They ate their food slowly and with great relish, guessing they were being watched.

Aspen tried to join in their nonchalance, but he found he could only nibble at his journeycake, and grew more nervous as each hour passed.

Tonight, he thought, *tonight will be the test.*

At midday he made sure his scouts were resting, not talking or drinking or playing nine-man.

"I will need you tonight," he told them. *As if I have not needed them every other night as well.*

He checked in on his mother several times, but there seemed to be no change for the good. If anything, she looked thinner, paler, less aware. As if magically holding the pavilion up in case the rain should return was draining her of everything that made her who she was. He was painfully aware, actually shivered with the memory, of how the old wizard had killed himself doing such hard magic. He would not let his mother wear herself away on his watch.

He ordered the queen's brow wiped with a cool cloth and checked in on Snail, Dagmarra, and Maggie Light. They discussed whether another flight to check on Odds's progress was wise. Aspen decided against it.

"I do not want Jack Daw to see anyone leaving this camp. If he suspects reinforcements are coming, it will force his hand."

Halfway to sundown an Unseelie herald marched to the middle of the stream. The rain had started up again, and his parley flag hung sodden and limp from his spear. Aspen sent no one to deal with him.

"Let him soak his boots. And his head, too," he said to the great delight of his soldiers, especially Snarl and Bite. Eventually, the herald returned to the Unseelie camp. No other heralds came. And Jack Daw's army stayed encamped on their hill.

When darkness fell, Aspen sent out his scouts. All of them.

No one sleeps tonight, he thought. He had special orders for them.

"As usual, no one crosses the stream," he said. "Except for us. Tonight I need eyes on the enemy camp. I need to know if they move."

The soldiers all nodded, and young Alicanson said, "Yes, sire."

"But there is more." He swallowed. His next words might

send his soldiers to their death tonight. But it had to be said. "If they move, I will need you to attack." He watched the words hit them, but none flinched. "Just a feint! But I need you to do enough damage to sit them back down behind their lines to wait for morning."

Croak spoke for all of them. "It is done, sire."

There was nothing more to be said. Everyone there knew that an attack—even a feint—by so small a force against an army as big as the one the Unseelie had fielded was suicidal.

So this is what it is really *like to be king*, Aspen thought. *I get to make new friends, then send them to their deaths.*

Remembering what the wizard had told him, he looked each soldier in the eye, letting them know he knew what he was asking. Letting each one of them understand that he did not do so lightly. Then he bowed to them as if they were all kings themselves. They bowed back, then disappeared into the dark.

ASPEN RETURNED TO the central fire, where Snail looked a question at him. He shook his head, not trusting himself to speak. Crossing his legs beneath him, he stared at the fire and waited for the distant sound of clashing arms to tell him that his friends were dying.

The hours could not have passed more slowly if they had been dipped in treacle. *Or, more likely, blood*, he thought.

His flippancy from earlier in the day was long gone, and now he worried constantly. He worried that Odds would not come at all, or would come too late to do anything but bury the bodies. He worried that his soldiers would be killed, had already been killed, would die uselessly, and the Unseelie would attack at night anyway. He worried that Old Jack Daw had seen through his plan and outflanked him in the night, slipping past them to put Astaeri Palace to the torch. He worried that the old drow had *not* slipped past and was still there in the dark, and knew that most of the Seelie army was illusion. He worried his mother would never recover, that Snail would die horribly, that all his friends' trust in him was misplaced, and that he was a fool who would forever be known as the king who lost the Seelie kingdom.

Like his scouts out in the rain and darkness, he got no sleep that night.

※　※　※

BUT THOUGH TIME was slow, it still moved, and eventually the sun returned and with it his soldiers. They limped into camp scratched and bruised, most wounded in some small way, some in bigger ways. Snarl was missing half an ear, and Fortuna of the Clover Clan had an arrow in her calf that Snail would have to remove, but they were all alive.

"They did not move," Croak said, standing plank-straight in front of his king, even though he was obviously exhausted and his ankle looked black and swollen enough to be broken. "They. Did. Not. Move."

"Thank you, Croak," Aspen said. And if tears filled his eyes, he figured they were used to it by now. "I—" He was interrupted by Snail.

"Aspen!" she shouted, forgetting decorum in her excitement. "Look!"

He followed her pointing finger and saw cold iron spiders cresting the hill, and behind them changelings, hundreds of them, thousands even. They were a rabble, armed haphazardly and lightly armored if at all, but there were a lot of them.

We can go home, he thought. *I can take Snail and my mother and my brave, brave warriors home. If we die, we die where we lived.* He ignored—and knew he ignored—the fact that he had lived most of his life as a hostage in the Unseelie palace. For him, Astaeri *was* home.

Everyone cheered to see them, even the illusory soldiers.

"Snail!" he shouted over the noise. "Find Odds. Tell him to form up to our rear. It's time to go home. I would like some walls between us and Old Jack Daw sooner rather than later."

Snail nodded, looking around for the bowser. But he was dirty and hiding under the cart. She turned back to say something, and Aspen saw her expression change from joy to horror as she pointed behind him, at the changelings. He turned around and saw what she saw. Instead of marching sensibly toward the Seelie encampment, the changelings seemed to have stirred themselves up into a killing frenzy. Not realizing that their allies were mostly illusion, they were charging right toward the Unseelie lines.

Toward certain death.

"You did not tell him how few we were," he said, not accusing, just stating a fact.

"Would he have come if I had?"

They both knew the answer to that. Odds was no fool. He looked to play the greater game. The better Odds, he would have said, if asked. If he had thought for a moment that Aspen's army was only thirty or so strong, he would have left the Seelie to the teeth and claws of their enemies.

A bigger spider than the rest appeared on the hill now, and Aspen—guessing Odds was at the helm—waved his arms frantically. He had no idea if he could be seen from such a distance. He did not know how to signal the professor to call his men back. Did not even know if Odds could do any such thing. Battle rage was upon the changelings, and Aspen knew how powerful such a thing was.

"I won't be able to get the bowser into the air," Snail said. "He's too filthy and cold from the rain. I'd no time to wash him."

Aspen didn't hesitate. "Take one of the horses." They were all kept saddled and bridled, just in case.

Snail nodded and chose the smallest of the horses, a black

with a white blaze on its nose. As Aspen watched, Snail put her hands on either side of the horse's head and whispered something in each ear. Then she blew softly in the horse's nostrils.

He did not ask. He had seen some of the soldiers do the very same thing and assumed she had been taught by one of them.

Leading the little mare over to the cart, Snail climbed up—careful not to disturb the dozing queen. Using the cart as a mounting platform, she vaulted onto the horse, the motion hardly graceful as she landed on the mare's back with a huge outtake of breath.

"*Ouffff!*" she said, and the queen stirred at the noise.

Using the reins to turn the horse so that they faced the far-off charging changelings, Snail kicked her into a gallop.

Aspen was surprised. Though he knew her courage, he had not known the extent of her riding ability. But surely she knew the danger. Though this time she had not glared at him, which was her usual way of signaling that she was furious or that he had done something absolutely stupid. She had to know—that she would never make it in time.

He hoped he was wrong. However, after a night of doubts and worry, he finally understood exactly what he needed to do. It was most likely futile and almost certainly fatal, but all his other options had fled down the hill with the charging changelings.

"Croak!" he shouted, though the soldier was right next to him. "Gather your warriors. No one sleeps today but the dead."

"What are your orders, sire?"

Aspen drew his blade and felt the fire building inside of him. His allies sped toward slaughter, but he would not abandon them to it. *I will shed no tears today.*

"We attack."

Croak grinned. As if excited. As if delighted. As if relieved. "Yes, Majesty," he said. "We attack!

28

SNAIL FALLS

The little mare ran the long distance between the encampment and the hill and meadow where the changelings were charging. She never made a misstep. She never faltered, not even when the iron spiders came close enough to be identified, their strange metal filling her nostrils with their alien smell. However, her gait was not as smooth and gentle as Goodspeed's had been, and Snail found herself wishing she had that old pony back.

Still, she had to pay attention to this nameless mare, so she gathered the reins and gave her an extra kick, hoping it would smooth the ride out.

All that did was encourage the mare to stretch further and run faster. There was no smoothness in either gait.

Suddenly Snail remembered what Alith had warned. *The horses will keep going if you ask them to. They will burst their hearts for you. But then they will be dead, and you will have no way to move quickly.* She thought perhaps she should rein the black in, but they were closing the gap quite swiftly, and so she hesitated. After all, Alith had been talking about all-day runs. Not a sprint across a long meadow. The horse didn't seem at all winded, even seemed to be enjoying herself. Probably annoyed with having had such a long rest between outings.

Besides, what good would one live horse be, Snail asked herself, *if everyone else died because we didn't get there in time?*

Then she scolded herself roundly, first for the hesitation, next for the sentimentality and how little she understood about horses, then because she'd dismissed the horse's probable death with such offhandedness, and finally because she really *didn't* know what she should do.

How can I hope to advise the king when I have such small knowledge? she thought, without once ever letting herself think that if everyone died, there'd be no one left to rule and no one around to advise anyway.

All the while she argued with herself, the little mare blazed across the landscape, the wind of their passage flinging her black mane in all directions. The horse alone seemed to be without fear of consequence.

Blaze, Snail thought. *Whatever her soldier name is, she will always be Blaze to me.* She bent over Blaze's shoulder and told the horse her new name.

Pricking her ears back and forth as if she understood,

Blaze ran faster still, the sound of her hooves on the wet meadow grass a soft drumming.

But as fast they went, the spiders and the changeling warriors—"Berserkers," Snail said under her breath—went faster. For they were going running downhill now, and Blaze was laboring sideways and then uphill to meet them.

Laboring, Snail thought, remembering how women in labor sounded. The harsh breathing that quickened as the exhilaration of birth neared. The *Whoops!* some of the apprentices called it, when an overexcited birth mother—usually a first timer—actually threw up.

But Blaze was no laboring mare about to bring forth a foal. She was, as Alith had cautioned, breaking her heart for Snail.

In return, Snail's heart was breaking as well. Breaking for the valiant mare and all the brave folk—human and fey—who would die this day. Because in war, people and animals always died. Afterward, the still living felt the guilt.

They were going so quickly now, the rain was slanting sideways, stinging her eyes and mixing with her tears. *Tears, bah! Being a hero doesn't include blubbering.* And a hero was what they all needed this day.

Too bad I'm not one. She was too angry and too frightened and too slow to be a hero.

But Blaze was. She galloped without ceasing, seeming to take nourishment from the air. It was as if she read each leaf, pebble, stone as she ran. As if her hooves understood unseen paths, could find the perfect turning point, note the smoothest stretch of grass. As if she ran only for Snail's approval, and Snail's encouragement.

Until she dropped to her knees, and Snail fell over the mare's head, right into the path of a very large iron spider, three male changelings carrying sharp objects, and a woman dressed in a man's trews and shirt who wielded only a large milking stool.

Snail tucked and rolled and came up with only bruises—but then the woman swung the milking stool at her head.

Managing to raise her left arm to block the blow, Snail regretted it almost immediately, for she felt a jolt of hot pain and heard a crack as the stout wood hit her left forearm.

"*Vrest!*" she swore, remembering that it was what Dagmarra had said when they were on the bowser, an oath of great power and passion. Her arm went limp, and the woman reared back for a blow that was sure to cave her head in.

"Wait!" one of the men shouted, a tall, broad-shouldered fellow with a beard the color of oak bark. "It's the doctor."

But the warning came too late, for the stool—already in its downward arc—hardly hesitated.

Snail heard the crack of the stool breaking—or maybe it was her skull that broke. The woman gasped, saying, "I'm so sorry! I thought you was . . ."

Then Snail fell backward into a dark and lasting abyss.

It could have been hours, days later that she swam back to the surface, as if rising out of some murky pool. She was like a fish lured up into the light.

The light!

She heard something. Her name? A song?

> *Come to me, child, out of the night,*
> *Swim to the shore, take hold of the light . . .*

It *was* a song. At least she figured out that much. The notes of the tune cut through the pain, in her arm, in her head. It gave her courage. It made her . . . whole.

Whole?

> *Take my hand, my heart, my sight,*
> *Take my song, come into the light.*

She knew that voice, though she couldn't yet give it a name, but she swam as it directed, as it insisted, into a river of light, gulped air, becoming fully human and fully something else as well.

A memory?

A change?

A changeling?

Thinking was giving her a headache.

Or maybe the blow to her head had given her that.

The blow! Now she remembered. There had been a blow to her head, and a backward fall and something before that.

Her left arm seemed useless from the elbow down. *Broken for sure.*

She sat up, cleared her throat. "Give me something to wrap my arm." The words came out in a bubbly froth, as if she'd been underwater for real.

The milkmaid—now Snail remembered the milkmaid—ripped strips from her skirts, and Snail managed to direct her in fashioning a sling. With her left arm still throbbing and her vision hazy with the pain, she said, "Tell me . . ." Catching that frothy breath again, she finished the thought. "Tell me what happened."

The milkmaid bowed her head. "I'm sorry, Doctor." She paused, face reddening. "I'm a milkmaid, not a soldier, and I didn't think . . ."

"That's the problem with war," Snail said through gritted teeth. "No one takes the time to think."

The oak-bearded man frowned. "What do we do with her?" he asked, pointing behind Snail.

Snail turned, but slowly, the pain of arm and head making her dizzy with too much motion. She saw a figure clothed in a shimmer of light lying on her back, eyes staring up at the sky.

"When you fell, she was suddenly there," the man said.

"She lay down next to you, put a hand on either side of your head, began singing something."

The milkmaid interrupted. "Singing! In the middle of a battle! How *could* she?"

The man ignored her outburst and continued. "It could have been a prayer."

"Or a spell," the milkmaid interrupted. "I couldn't make it out. Was it a spell?"

"Shut it, Mollie," the man said, but Mollie was in full spate now, like a river, and couldn't stop. "You woke up soon after, even though I'd clocked you a good 'un, begging your pardon, m'lady doctor. Hope she brings down some of them berserking lords with her spells. I mean if we can wake her up." She'd said it all in one long rush and had to take a new breath.

In the moment between Mollie's breaths, the man broke through. "She's an odd one," he gestured to the woman on the ground. "Never mixing with the likes of us'ns."

"Maggie Light." Snail breathed the name, wondered why Maggie was just lying in the crushed and ruined grass. And while she was wondering, she suddenly realized that she felt better than she'd any reason to. Looked at her good right arm, then at the broken one, which seemed to be glowing with the same shimmer of light that now encased Maggie.

For a moment she recalled when the land had chosen Aspen as king. How he'd glowed gold all over. Maybe this was the same sort of magic. She got up slowly, walked over to Maggie, leaned down, and touched her cheek. It was cold and stiff. *But*, she wondered, *had it ever been otherwise?* She'd never actually touched Maggie's cheek before. Maggie often said she was a made thing, and maybe a made thing's cheeks were always cold and stiff.

Like the iron spiders?

"Oh, Maggie," she whispered under her breath, "what have you done? What have we all done?" She didn't expect an answer, nor did she get one. Aloud she said, "We can't just leave her here." She was thinking about the bogles and Red Caps, the ogres, the drows. She was trying to figure it all out. But now the sounds of battle suddenly burst over her, like a wave in a furious sea.

This isn't the time, she thought, *to consider what it all means. This is the time to be doing something about the war.*

The milkmaid said, "I'll keep a guard, m'lady." She sat down on her milking stool, which was, astonishingly, still intact.

"Thanks, Mollie. And you," Snail said, addressing Oak-beard.

"Casper," he said, "blacksmith by trade." Indeed, his hands had the worn look of an iron- and steelmaker. His fingernails were nearly black.

"Casper, you'd better take me to Odds," she said, the frothiness entirely gone now from her speech.

Casper turned away, looking out across the small valley. "I could do that, m'lady," he said, "but the professor looks a bit busy right now."

Snail followed his gaze and saw the changeling army was nearly into Jack Daw's camp, screaming their battle cries and waving their assortment of weapons wildly. Giant iron spiders were scattered amongst the horde, and the most giant of them all—piloted by Odds, of that Snail was certain—was pushing through to the front.

The Unseelie horde was ready, bows raised, arrows notched, lances held steady, hiding behind their barricade that bristled like a hedgehog, all spines out.

The two armies were almost joined in battle.

A battle we're sure to lose, Snail thought, her arm still aching but her head now totally clear.

29

ASPEN GOES TO WAR

*A*spen charged into the stream, his few warriors following behind. Screams of rage and pain, and the clack and clang of weapons clashing rolled down from the hill above: the sounds of battle being joined. *The changelings*, he thought. *That will be us soon.*

The rain had swollen the stream. It was now knee-deep and swift, and he had to slow to maneuver over the rocky bottom. It wouldn't do to trip and fall, hit his head on a rock, and drown in the shallow waters.

No, much better to die up there. He glanced uphill.

The changeling charge was quickly being repelled by the Border Lords that Old Jack Daw had chosen to man the initial defenses of wooden spikes and shallow ditches.

But even before Aspen was out of the stream and onto the grass, he could see that the first of the spiders had now reached the Border Lords and was tearing holes in their lines by simply grabbing both the sharpened logs and the plaid-clad soldiers, and throwing them off to the rear.

Aspen could hear the screams and curses as the Border Lords hit the ground. It seemed to make the others less than enthusiastic about filling the gap, especially with more iron spiders on the horizon. Aspen could see that the Border Lords were holding back, reforming, but not racing forward.

How many more spiders? he wondered, hoping that the answer was: *as many as are needed.* He was winded from the difficult river crossing, and for a moment he stopped to catch his breath.

Now he was close enough to see that though the changelings were not skilled, they were certainly enthusiastic, and a new wave of ill-equipped changeling infantry quickly flooded the hole in the enemy lines the first spider had made. They began flailing at everything in range with their odd mix of weaponry. Farmers wielded scythes and other reaping tools, workmen handled axes and mauls. Kitchen workers held long knives. But many of the changelings only had pointed sticks for weapons, or clubs that had more recently been chair legs or the spokes of a wagon wheel. Several held nothing more than rocks they had picked up in the stream. A few had actual swords, but they were very few, and Aspen had no idea whether the men flailing them about had any skill or training.

He caught his breath and watched as they hacked and

slashed, poked and pounded, and did some damage. But for every Border Lord they killed, it seemed that three or four changelings fell.

And he knew that the truly frightening members of the Unseelie army had yet to join the fray.

No longer winded, Aspen climbed out of the stream and began running uphill when suddenly someone shouted, "Sire!" and Snarl dragged him to the ground.

There was a whooshing in the air. Aspen looked back to see a dozen arrows clang off rocks and bury themselves in the ground ten yards past him. His troops were on the ground as well, all except Bite, who had been just a touch too slow. He stood tall, staring numbly at the three arrows that stuck out of his chest. Then he toppled wordlessly to the ground.

Aspen gasped and hesitated, caught between wanting to tend to the fallen soldier and the need to get up the hillside before more arrows arrived.

Croak didn't hesitate. He was the first one up. "Shields before the king!" he shouted, and sprang forward despite how badly his foot flopped around on his wounded ankle. He placed his shield before Aspen, and then Snarl was up as well, his shield at the ready in front of his liege. He didn't look back at his fallen clan brother. That would come later, if he was not slain himself.

If Snarl can go on, then I can, too. Aspen nodded at them

and got up into a crouch. "To me!" he shouted. "And to the top!"

The warriors rose first, and then the civilians, the latter ducking behind the soldiers and their shields until all were protected as well as they could be. They charged forward again, arrows coming steadily now, whistling past their ears or thumping into their shields.

Two more of Aspen's already small company were left on the hillside. Fortuna lay cursing the archer who had put an arrow through her other calf. She would live—at least till the battle was over.

Fal the woodsman was not so lucky. He had shared Alicanson's shield but was much taller than the boy and hadn't been able to crouch fully behind it. A foul arrow had taken him in the eye.

No tree, Aspen thought angrily, *will ever again feel the bite of his ax.*

But he had no time to mourn the friends he was leaving on the hillside or the ones who would certainly die soon, for before his mind and heart were ready for it, they had reached the Unseelie defenses.

"Now!" Aspen shouted, somehow certain that Croak and Snarl would know what he meant.

They did, shifting their shields aside to leave a gap for him to leap through. The Border Lords before him had wooden targets held high and broadswords at the ready, but those could not protect them from the gout of fire that Aspen shot at them. It was long and red as blood. Even Aspen felt the heat of it running from his fingers outward as well as up his wrists and racing up the blue rivers of veins, for he had put all his fear and anger into the flame. And all his hope, too.

With his sword, he cut the nearest archer down while he was still afire, and Croak and Snarl did the same to the ones on either side. Then the rest of Aspen's troop followed, and the real battle was joined.

For a moment—for many moments—it went well. The Border Lords scattered under this new assault of fire and steel, and both Aspen's group and the changelings pressed forward to the next level of defense, a short wooden palisade.

But this time, when Aspen let loose with his flame, there were no screams of pain and fear from behind the barricade. Instead, there was an angry hissing and then long lizardly shapes the size of ponies poured over the barricade, black and red and gold, with vestigial wings flapping though they could not fly, smoke curling from their nostrils.

"Dragonlings!" Aspen shouted. He knew his flames were useless against them. They fed on fire and were cloaked in their own armored scales. They were many. He was alone with his flame.

"Close ranks!" Croak shouted, but only the soldiers knew what that meant, and there weren't enough of them for the ranks to mean much. Still, they locked shields together, and Aspen found himself between Alincanson and Snarl, with Croak behind him shouting at the civilians to try to get them into some kind of order.

The dragonlings hit them like a battering ram, jaws snapping at their faces.

Alincanson and Snarl had obviously been trained for this kind of fight, because they fed the dragonlings their shields sideways to occupy them, then jabbed at the beast's eyes.

Aspen joined in, stabbing his long sword over the top of his companions' shields and scoring a hit on a red dragonling. The creature screeched in pain and spun wildly in the air, like a crocomorph taking prey in the water. It wrenched the shield from Snarl's grasp, almost taking his hand with it. The Wolf Clan soldier grimaced in pain but still finished the dragonling off with a thrust to its exposed belly. Then he was pulled back, and Croak stepped into his place, shield high.

The soldiers were holding against the dragonlings, but the sheer weight of the creatures was slowly forcing them backward. Aspen tried to lean into the shields, add his weight to that of his soldiers, but there simply were not enough of them to push the beasts back uphill.

The Seelie warriors took a step back, and then another, and it felt to Aspen as if the hill itself were fighting them as well, turning steeper as the battle began to go against them.

They had given up all the ground they'd gained, and still the dragonlings pressed them back. The warriors were no longer protecting the changelings' flank, and the Border Lords were creeping back into place for another assault.

Worse still, a group of Red Caps had flung grappling hooks around one spider's legs and dragged it to the ground, so now they knew the spiders were not invincible.

When Jack Daw commits more troops, Aspen thought desperately, *he's going to sweep us right off this hillside.* That gave him pause. *Why hasn't he committed more troops? He can plainly see . . .*

Aspen stopped and chuckled out loud, which earned him a confused look from Croak.

Mishrath protects us still. He glanced over his shoulder and saw Mishrath's soldiers arrayed on the hilltop under the queen's canopy, looking martial and fierce and more important, numerous. He thought smugly, *Daw thinks this is just a feint. He is waiting for* me *to commit* my *troops.*

They were forced back another step. *This can actually work to our advantage.*

"Stay together!" he shouted. "But fall back!"

Croak shot him a fierce glance. "Sire?"

"Fall back to the stream, Croak."

"If they charge us . . ." For the first time, there was fear in his eyes.

No soldier likes to go backward. Aspen almost changed his mind. But he looked over at the changelings and saw that the spiders were hesitating to move forward now as they saw the downed one get its carapace cracked open by Red Caps and its driver dragged out. He could not make out who the driver was. But now, without the spiders' support, the changelings' mad charge was faltering.

If they do not retreat calmly, he thought, *they will surely soon run off in a panic.*

"The Unseelie horde will not charge," he said to Croak. Then he shouted toward the changelings, not sure if they could hear him or if the professor was even there. "Odds! Pull your people back!"

If we can retreat in good order from the hill, we may yet live through the day.

Quickly they established a rhythm to their retreat.

Step back. Stab. Step again. Stab.

Falling back was easy with the dragonlings pushing on their shields.

Aspen's sword arm began to ache and his legs trembled with fatigue, but he kept up the rhythm. And so did his people.

Step back. Stab. Step again. Stab.

They were halfway down the hill when a horn blew from above, and suddenly the weight was off their shields. Everyone in the front line stumbled, and Aspen had a glimpse over their shields of the dragonlings slithering back up the hillside.

"They run," one of the kitchen maids said happily.

"No," Aspen said quickly, before she got it in her mind to chase them. "They regroup."

He glanced over at the changelings who were being herded downhill by several spiders. They had left too many of their number dead on the hilltop, but they were retreating in a far more organized manner than their charge.

There is hope, Aspen thought. But when he looked back to their own hilltop, he felt that hope shrivel and die.

It must have started as a single, small tear. Just a piece of canopy out toward the edge that perhaps was not as magic as the rest. Perhaps the queen had been exhausted when she spun that part, or perhaps after a long day and night of keeping the rain off, any canopy, no matter how magic, was going to sag a little.

It was just a small tear, but it was right underneath a big puddle of rainwater. And when the water started to flow, it was not going to be denied. The tear turned into a rent and the rent into a hole, and soon that whole section of canopy simply burst open and dumped water onto the fire below it.

And with that, two dozen of Mishrath's soldiers winked out of existence.

Aspen turned back to the Unseelie army. The sun was fully up now and breaking through the clouds, while a slight wind cleared away the smoke from the burning bodies and the dragonlings' lungs. A tall figure moved through the ranks and pushed to the front.

Old Jack Daw.

Aspen watched in horror as the old drow looked out across at Aspen's suddenly smaller army and then his gaze turned down the hillside searching for Aspen. Even at this distance, Aspen shivered when he met Jack Daw's eyes. A thin line of white split the grey of the old drow's face, and Aspen knew he was smiling.

Daw flung his arm forward, and his troops exploded from their positions, charging downhill on claws and hooves and booted feet.

Aspen turned to Croak. "Run!"

They ran. And behind them, the straggle of his army ran after.

SNAIL MAKES A DECISION

"*W*e must go, now," Snail said to Casper, the blacksmith. "If we are to catch him in time."

"Odds are—" Casper began, but Snail interrupted him.

"I am not interested in the odds. Only in the professor." She turned and miraculously saw her little mare up and cropping the few bits of grass that had managed to break through the trampled ground. *Not dead, then?* Blaze no longer even seemed winded. "Do you ride with me?"

"That's too small a beast for the two of us," Casper said. "You go, and I'll follow along as best I can."

Snail nodded, then went over to mare and breathed into her nostrils. "Just us two, again."

Blaze nodded as if she understood, and Casper helped Snail mount. Then with a slight tap of her heels, Snail encouraged Blaze to go toward the tag end of the charge of changelings up the hill. She turned for a moment in the saddle and saw the blacksmith laboring behind her.

He's fast enough, she thought. *Or else my pony has suddenly gone slow.* Then she turned back as they cantered along the broken ground, dodging the gouged-out places where the iron spiders had trod. There was a small wind, and the rain clouds seemed to be in retreat like a badly trained army.

Ahead of her the changeling men and women—a few on horses, most on foot—were shouting and screaming their challenges to the Unseelie folk who waited for them at the hill's top. Following the charge and towering above them all was the largest of the iron spiders. She knew that in its domed driving chamber would be Odds thinking himself safe, invincible. But she feared that—like Maggie Light—the spiders had some secret flaw and could be downed. Maybe by fire, maybe by a large ramming device, or maybe—she could see it clearly in her mind's eye—by something wrapped around their legs, which seemed to her the most vulnerable part of the spiders' bodies.

And if I've had that thought, surely some Unseelie drow—she refused to even think his name—*might have that thought, too.*

But as she got closer she heard a horn blowing, and coming closer still, saw the Unseelie unaccountably retreating back behind their defenses, when moments before they had clearly been pushing their opponents downhill.

She could hear a mumble and then a loud roar as the changelings and their Seelie companions cheered the victory. And then she watched without quite understanding as they turned and trudged back down the hill, their faces jubilant with the outcome of their charge.

Turn around! she shouted at them. *Don't turn your backs on them!* But few of them were soldiers, and even fewer had the belly for more hand-to-hand combat. She rode among the earliest retreaters now, trying to warn them, but they were laughing, and laughing at her as if she were a trickster spoiling their fun.

So, only she and Casper—both still going uphill to meet their compatriots, saw the danger. Snail watched in horror as above them the hilltop became alive once more with Unseelie warriors, cloaked and uncloaked, on claws and hooves and booted feet. They boiled down the mountainside, and the changelings had but a moment to try to wheel about and get set for the countercharge. And the ungainly iron spiders, their most potent weapon, had no room and little ability to turn quickly at all. In fact, one was already down, its legs buckled and entangled in some kind of snare.

It was a disaster. A rout. Snail watched in horror as changelings were cut down, ridden over, bitten, clawed, killed. She made a quick decision, and pulled so hard on the reins that she almost tore the bit from Blaze's mouth. She looked over the side, and there was red foam dripping from the mare's lower lip. She didn't yank again.

Still, she was able to get to the side of the hill by leaning over and urging her horse with a combination of voice and legs. They made a wide turn to follow the stream back toward where she'd left Aspen and his ragtag army. She didn't dare take the time to look over her shoulder to see what had happened to the changelings, spiders, Casper, Odds, or Milkmaid Mollie. She hoped she was making the right decision, though she suspected that no decision in war was the right one.

She shook her head at her stupidity. Or maybe at her innocence. *Of course there's a right decision.* Her lips were now set in a grim line. *It's the one that wins the battle. Only you don't know which one it is till long after.*

The stream seemed extremely dark and sluggish, though it had been clear when she'd last seen it. She wondered if this meant a battle she hadn't seen had been fought there. But she saw no bodies to indicate any such.

Perhaps, she thought, *just soldiers marching through it left the muddle.*

But she drew the mare away from the stream's edge, letting her thread through the trees, far enough to remain hidden, close enough to see what was going on.

She strained to hear any unexplained noises ahead or behind, besides the quiet *clip-clop* of the mare's feet through the underbrush. There was the *swee-swash* of wind across the tops of the trees, the gurgle of water over stones, and from far, far away, the battle cries of victors, the screams of the dying.

She was too focused on finding Aspen to be frightened, and too tired to weep.

Blaze plodded around a deep bend where the sound of the stream seemed stronger, almost as if it were singing to her. But there was another sound as well. She couldn't quite make it out.

Reining in Blaze by pulling on her mane, Snail turned the little horse into a darker, more concealing copse of trees. Touching one of the trees for luck as they passed, she remembered Mistress Softhands, her midwife mentor, saying that at night birch trees gleamed enough so you could find your way home through the woods. Funny she should think of that story now.

She and the horse slipped like ghosts through mist, heading toward the unknown sound. As they got closer, Snail realized the sound was voices. One quite a bit like Aspen's.

Because she wanted to be sure of what was happening before she rode headlong into it, and because she still held to the midwife's creed—*anticipate, alleviate, then await*—she went slowly, silently. She'd have to find out who the voices were before she could anticipate what to do next. Only then she could she figure out how to alleviate the situation. And after . . . if there was an after . . .

The ground was so soft, Blaze made hardly any sound. Snail was proud of that.

But Red Caps don't hunt by ear, they hunt by smell.

Neither Snail nor Blaze knew they were near until one laid a hand on her leg and grabbed the reins from her hands, and another pulled her off the horse, all the while giggling, his voice high-pitched and self-satisfied. The only good thing about the capture was that she landed on her feet and had not been pulled down by her broken arm. Though with her arm broken, she was unable to fight and was swiftly and firmly held by the biggest two of the little killers.

I'm so sorry, Aspen, she thought. She promised herself she wouldn't beg, she wouldn't weep. And she promised herself she wouldn't think of how the Red Caps would afterward dip their caps in her blood.

She lied. Of course she'd think about that. Had already thought it. Could not get it out of her head. But instinctively, she glared at the Unseelie blood-hunter giggling at her and spat between his eyes. That didn't make them let her go, but it certainly made her feel better, more in control.

"The drow will want to see you," he said. And giggled again.

Snail knew he meant Jack Daw.

"He will want to watch as we tear off your limbs."

"Well," she said, trying to sound brave and almost pulling it off, "he's the one I want to see as well. Take me to him."

"Yes, m'lady," another of the Red Caps said, as if her title was no more than a casual curse.

She looked around and counted. There were seven of

them. Of course. They always went about in seven, *a murder of Red Caps*, it was called. Like the dwarfs' *hule*, only much darker.

Someone else gave her a shove from behind. She bit her lip to keep from crying out. At least she was successful in that.

ASPEN AT THE RIVER

*A*spen made it down the hill with no arrows in his back, but he could tell by the yowls and yells behind him that his luck was about to run out.

Jack Daw's army was closing in and his own was on the run.

A quick glance to his left confirmed that the changelings weren't retreating in good order, either.

Add hundreds of dead humans to my butcher's bill, he thought.

He would have wept, but it seemed the Weeping Warrior had no more tears left in him. He charged into the stream instead.

The waters were even higher now, up to his thigh, and he struggled into the middle, his only consolation that the waters would slow his pursuers just as much.

It won't matter, though. The Border Lords will stomp through on their sturdy legs. The drow will ride around. The rest will swim or crawl or fly and catch us before we reach

*the far bank, let alone the palace. And with the changelings
routed, we cannot defend the palace, anyway.*

Aspen stopped, the rushing water making him sway a little as he held his balance against it.

There is really only one thing left to do.

"Sire?" Croak said, suddenly by his side.

"Keep running, Croak," he said wearily. "Get your men
and my mother. M'lady Snail if you can find her, and just
keep running."

Turning, Aspen saw that just as he had thought, the Border Lords were charging into the water. There were dragonlings and drows on horseback pacing the far bank, content
for now to let the Border Lords get wet. And get their due.

The Border Lords will want vengeance for their fallen.

"No, sire, I—"

"Croak," Aspen said, absently surprised that Croak was
trying for a sentence long enough for him to interrupt.
"That was my last order as your liege, and I expect it to be
obeyed."

He looked back at Croak. The old warrior nodded gravely
and wasted no more time. He splashed toward the far shore,
where the rest of Aspen's troop were just now realizing that
their monarch wasn't coming with them. Some of the civilians argued briefly, but Croak and his soldiers shouted them
down and kept them moving.

They think I am trying to fight to buy time. The Border
Lords were almost on him, and he drew his sword. *The*

sword of my father and his father and all our fathers back to before the worlds were separated and the courts split and mortal and fey lived as one under an endless sun.

He smiled grimly at the approaching men and dropped to one knee, balancing his sword sideways on the palms of his hands. "Sorry to disappoint, Lords," he said. Then he raised his voice so the drow on the far bank could hear him. "Daw! I surrender!"

I could have fought, he thought as the Border Lords approached, swords still upraised. *But fighting would only have bought a moment or two for my friends—my family—to escape.* Aspen could see that the Border Lords were weighing their desire to lop off his head against the danger of robbing Old Jack Daw of the opportunity to gloat before killing him.

Gloating can take a long time. Much longer than fighting.

Aspen bowed his head, not wanting to make eye contact with the Border Lords and possibly goad one of the wilder ones into striking him unwisely.

He will probably let you strike the blow that kills me anyway. Just let him gloat for a while.

"A long while," he whispered.

"Hold!" came the shout Aspen had hoped for. He looked up. The drow were kicking their horses reluctantly into the stream. At their head rode Old Jack Daw, grinning like a king who had just seen all his dreams of conquest come true.

As I suppose he has.

"Daw," Aspen said again, "I surrender. Call off your hounds."

Old Jack Daw nodded at the Border Lords, and they sheathed their swords but kept their hands on the pommels.

Well, that is one danger past, Aspen thought. Then added grimly, *I am still going to die, but at least it will take a while.*

"A long while," he whispered again. The sound of his own voice was not comforting.

The Border Lords waded around behind Aspen, cutting off any retreat.

Not that I was going anywhere.

The mounted drows moved forward slowly, the horses stepping gingerly along the rocky streambed.

Take your time, my lords, Aspen thought. *More time for my friends' escape.*

Aspen prayed that Croak had gotten his people safely away. He desperately wanted to turn around and see if they were over the hill yet and gone but was afraid Old Jack Daw would figure out what he was doing and send riders to run them down. To his right, the creatures that had been pursuing the changelings had stopped to watch what was now happening in the stream.

They can kill humans anytime. Watching a king die is a once in a lifetime experience, Aspen thought. Then he corrected himself. *I will be the third king to die in about as many weeks.* He wondered if they kept accounts of such things in the Wizard's Tower. *I may be about to set a record.*

It was almost funny.

Almost.

He comforted himself with the thought that with his death he could save a few lives that day. He began to make a list in his head: *Mother, Snail, Croak* . . . then stopped. He had to focus. Not dream.

"Aspen," Old Jack Daw was saying. "Prince Aspen." He sat his horse a few yards away at the center of a loose semi-circle of his mounted companions. "Drop your sword."

Aspen looked down at the sword of his fathers and hesitated. He realized that Jack had not addressed him as king. *That is a good thing. It puts him off guard, thinking of me as that weak boy he taught, the one he made a fool of.*

"Come now, boy. Do not try anything heroic and force me to kill you."

Aspen snorted. "You are going to kill me anyway." *Just keep him talking. The more time we spend in this stream, the more time for everyone else to escape.*

"Kill you?" Old Jack Daw said expansively. He put a hand over his heart. "I would not dream of it!"

"Dream of it?" Aspen scoffed. "You make a habit of it."

Old Jack Daw kicked his horse forward a single step. "If I kill you, the land would just pick another king. Another

Seelie king." He leaned forward, speaking softer, as if for Aspen's ears alone. "Perhaps one not so easily beaten."

I was not that easy, Aspen thought petulantly. *I got the best of you here. For a while.*

Old Jack Daw sat back up and looked pointedly at the fleeing changelings, then over Aspen's head to the hill behind him, where Mishrath's army was surely rapidly disappearing. "Though I do not know what any monarch can do with what I have left him. But still," he said, chuckling, "I am going to keep you alive for a long, long time to make sure no new king is chosen." He leaned forward again, sharing another secret with his defeated enemy. "It has been done before, you know."

Aspen dropped his father's sword. Not because Old Jack Daw had told him to, but out of shock.

It has been done before.

The sword sank to the bottom of the stream, carrying that piece of the sun within that only glowed for the true-born ruler of Faerie.

"That is better, *boy*. Now, I want you to . . ."

Old Jack Daw kept talking, but Aspen was no longer listening.

How do you keep the land from choosing a new king? he thought. *Why, you keep him alive. Forever.*

And suddenly Aspen knew the answer to all three of the Sticksman's questions.

If only I had figured this out before. I could have traveled to his shack below Wester Tower. Could have restored him there. But there is no way to reach him now.

Aspen stopped. Looked at the swift water bubbling past him. Heard his mother's voice telling him, *"All the rivers in Faerie are one, and so are its people."*

He leapt to his feet and heard the metallic hiss of the Border Lords drawing their swords. Old Jack Daw's horse skittered back a few steps, and the other drow closed in front of him.

"Sticksman!" Aspen shouted, knowing he had only seconds before he was cut into pieces. *If this doesn't work . . .* "Sticksman! I know the answers to your questions!" *If this doesn't work, at least my death will ruin part of his plan.*

Aspen saw a shadow on the water and heard a grunt behind him, and he threw himself forward, avoiding a sword stroke that should have chopped him in two. The world went dark and cold as he plunged into the waters, but he popped back out of them immediately.

"Sticksman!" he shouted again, then dove away from a Border Lord who was coming at him from his left. The water was waist high now, soaking the Border Lords' plaids and slowing them. He had not a moment to worry about carnivorous mer, only hoped that this being a side stream— and only newly deep enough for mer—they would not be here.

At least not yet. And a good thing, too, or I would already be dead twice over.

When he surfaced this time, the water was nearly to his chest, flowing fast and strong. The Border Lords were now more concerned with not getting swept away than with trying to kill him, and the drow were backing their horses to the shore.

"What trickery is this, Seelie?" Old Jack Daw shouted at him. "You have surrendered! I demand you stop this!"

Aspen knew he *had* surrendered, and honor demanded that he cease hostilities. But he also knew he was not taking any hostile actions.

Not really . . .

"My apologies, Jack," he shouted, not sorry at all, "but I have a favor to repay before I can go with you."

Any reply the drow might have made was drowned out by a crashing roar as a great waterspout bubbled out of the center of the stream. And atop the spout was a long, thin boat being poled by a long, thin creature in a black hooded robe.

"Sticksman!" Aspen shouted, and the Sticksman turned his wide bug eyes toward him. He shifted his grip on his steering pole ever so slightly, and the waterspout died. The boat rode the dying wave to Aspen, slowing to a stop before him.

"Your Majesty," the Sticksman said, extending a clawlike hand down and helping Aspen aboard.

Aspen flopped into the boat, bringing back memories of his escape from the Unseelie Court.

But this time I will not cower in the bottom of the boat. This is a thing I should face on my feet.

Tired and wet, and a little shaky, he stood.

"Sticksman."

The Sticksman sketched him a small bow. "You have my payment?"

Aspen nodded, looked briefly behind, where the Border Lords were dragging themselves onto shore.

There Old Jack Daw fumed at them, fist raised, urging them to charge again into the river where the boat floated, magically still against the increasingly swift and rising current. The drow's voice rose over the sound of the water. "You cowards, you faerie-fearful, plaid-wearing turncoats. Go back! Go back! Fetch him to me. Fetch me that boy, that quaking hostage, who would be king."

But the water was uncrossable, and possibly the Border Lords feared the mermen who even now might be swimming into the stream. So they ignored the Unseelie king and wrung out their plaids. But they said nothing, not a word of complaint. To do so would mean an instant battlefield execution.

The rest of the army—dragonlings, Red Caps, goblins, ogres, and more—ranged along the shore and simply watched the proceedings. Silent, every one of them.

Good, Aspen thought, *I want an audience for this next part. But I don't want them to hear what we say.*

"What is the Sticksman?" the Sticksman asked.

Aspen remembered what Mishrath had told him. "A creature both of and not of the Unseelie Court."

"How does one become the Sticksman?"

"By taking up his staff."

The Sticksman raised the bony shelf above one eye where a brow should have been. "How does the Sticksman come not to be once more?"

Three neugles dipped their hooves into the water upstream. Aspen saw them as they hastily stepped back out as if the water was too cold. Or too hot. Or bubbling with merman bile.

Before he could answer the Sticksman's third question, Aspen heard a commotion toward the back of the army, and a small group of Red Caps came through with a bound prisoner walking between them.

Snail!

She looked up as if he had spoken aloud. Their eyes met, and he read confusion and anger in them. She glared at him.

There must always be a Sticksman.

He lifted a hand to wave, then instead reached out, palm up, toward the Sticksman.

Goodbye, Snail.

"He gives his staff away."

The Sticksman blinked once but didn't hesitate more than that. He placed his poling staff in Aspen's hands.

There was a great shout from on shore and then a clash of arms. But Aspen paid it no mind. His staff was in his hand, and he could feel the waters pushing his boat, trying to send it downstream. Some of the black water splashed into the boat and draped itself around him, becoming a long, hooded robe.

He spoke to the river. *Quiet waters,* he said, slowing the current. *I have a passenger.*

He turned to his passenger, a tall, thin creature who was just beginning to glow with a golden light, and asked, "East shore or west? And I require two pennies for each passenger and a silver for the Sticksman."

The glowing creature took out a purse that had been hidden somewhere under his cloak and pulled out the requisite coins. He gave two pennies and a silver to Aspen. "Put me on shore here."

Aspen felt fuddled for only a moment, then he put his pole in the river and prepared to ply his trade.

SNAIL SINGS

*S*nail saw Aspen in the boat and couldn't understand what he was doing there or why the Sticksman had handed over his staff. Then she shook her head, wondering if she was losing her sight, because the Sticksman's head seemed to have a golden aura around it.

As she continued to watch, transfixed by the sight, the Sticksman took off his dark robe and stood there, unmoving, in the bow of the boat, like a great golden statue. The boat, making no sound at all, coasted majestically to shore.

Though Snail wanted to run to them, she couldn't move because the Red Caps had bound her hands, hobbled her feet, and held her tightly by a leash.

The minute the boat touched the grassy verge, the Sticksman stepped out, his long, golden insect legs bending at strange angles that the robe had always disguised. *Not alien,* Snail thought, *not awkward, just different. Noble. Even regal.*

For a moment, wherever the Sticksman set foot on the

grass, it turned gold as well, spreading a thin gold color ahead of him, like a carpet.

The Border Lords waited in the path of the golden figure, their wet plaids dripping river water, their swords raised. However, they didn't charge, for there was confusion in their midst, and they looked over at Jack Daw for orders.

But the other Unseelie folk—dragonlings, goblins, gremlins, ogres, hobs—suddenly bowed their heads or knees or both. They looked, Snail thought, not reluctant, but ecstatic.

"The king," ran a murmur though them, "the king has returned."

The Border Lords as one all turned suddenly and cried, "Up the Daw!" and raced in a single body to guard Jack Daw, though it was, Snail thought, more of an unruly mob than a trained troop.

They're shaken. I've never seen the Border Lords shaken.

The Sticksman raised his hands, and a shiver ran through the crowd. The drows' horses nickered and pawed at the ground. The Border Lords' knuckles were white on their sword grips. The Sticksman looked pointedly at the crown Old Jack Daw wore on his head. He had yet to say a word.

Dropping the leash holding Snail to them, the Red Caps scattered, mixing into the horde gathering around the Sticksman.

For a moment Snail stood forgotten, yet she didn't move because she had no idea what to do. And then, without willing it, indeed without knowing why, she began to sing. Her voice—never strong before—emerged, booming out with overwhelming power. At first she was terrified, then shocked.

The knee bends, but does not yield.
The sword's strong blade, the wooden shield,
The cry goes round, so turns the wheel.
The king comes home, the king comes home.

The book of eld we must now burn,
Our place in history we must now earn,
And celebrate the king's return.
The king comes home, the king comes home.

And now, as she sang, she recognized who was singing. It wasn't her own reedy voice but Maggie Light's singing some sort of spell. It wasn't one she'd heard Maggie sing before. So how could she know it? Yet the song poured from her, the two verses repeating and repeating.

As she sang, the Border Lords stood still, mouths open, transfixed the way the Seelie king's guard seeking Aspen had been transfixed so long ago. They could move neither forward nor back. It was as if they'd been bespelled into a deep sleep and were dreaming, though their eyes were wide open.

The song took moments, but the spell of it lingered long

enough for a group of goblins, gremlins, and hobs to rush forward and dispatch the ensorcelled Border Lords with large oaken cudgels and wicked little knives. Snail watched as the kilted company died, one after another, those difficult men who had chased her across two kingdoms. She felt nothing for them. Not hatred nor fear, not satisfaction at their deaths. Only a soft kind of relief.

At the same time, the dragonlings charged forward, singeing the hooves of the drow horses. When the drows were thrown off by their frightened steeds, this so startled the ogres that they lumbered forward, smashing every fallen drow in their paths with mammoth fists, every drow except Old Jack himself. Feathers flew up into the air before settling down into the pools of blood.

Then the three greatest ogres knelt, not to Jack Daw, the pretender, but to the golden one, the Unseelie king, come home at last.

The king comes home. The king comes home.

The song dwindled to its conclusion.

And Jack Daw stood alone.

The King Who Returned began to speak then, but Snail no longer cared. She was done with every toff who wanted to be king of this or duke of that and connived and killed to make it happen. There was only one toff she wanted to talk to, and he was poling the Sticksman's boat into the middle of the river that had been a stream just moments ago.

"Aspen!" she shouted.

He paid her no heed, though she was certain that he could hear her.

He's not that *far away.*

"Aspen!" But still, he poled on, ignoring her. Then a horrible knowledge hit her, and she shouted one last time, hoping that he would ignore her again. "Sticksman!"

Aspen turned and looked toward shore. Toward her.

Snail's heart sank into her shoes. "I require passage," she said, too softly for him to hear.

But the boat turned, and within moments ran smoothly aground. Aspen stepped off onto the slick rocks and picked his way to her using his long steering pole for balance. He wore a black robe, as the first Sticksman had, but it was smaller, just as he was.

"I require two pennies for each passenger," he said, his voice lifeless and dull, "and a silver for the Sticksman."

Snail didn't ask if he knew her; it was obvious he no longer did. Nor did she ask why he had taken the Sticksman's staff—as well as his curse.

He did the noble thing. He freed a cursed king and in doing so probably saved his own people. If she had to, she would remind the King Who Returned just what payment Aspen had made. She fought back against tears but knew she would lose. *And as a reward he gets an eternity of poling strangers back and forth across the river.*

"I require two pennies—" Aspen began again but stopped when Snail snapped at him.

"I know!" She shifted so he could see her bonds. "I can't pay you when my hands are tied."

"Oh," he said, and for a moment looked discomfited and a bit awkward. Like the old Aspen.

But noble for all that, Snail thought sadly.

He produced a dagger and sliced through the bonds holding her hands, then paused and freed her feet as well.

"I requi—" he tried again, but a glare from her stopped him.

What now? she thought to herself. *I have no silver. I have no plan.*

Poor Aspen ~~looked desperate~~ to speak, but afraid to as well, as uncomfortable in his new role as Sticksman as he'd been as king.

And soon I will have no friend, she thought.

Looking away from Aspen, she saw the Unseelie king pointing at Old Jack Daw.

"Bring me the pretender's crown," he said. "And his head as well."

Every creature in the Unseelie army produced something sharp and pointy and advanced on the old drow.

Suddenly she knew what to do.

"Give me your staff," she said.

It won't be so bad, she thought. *I won't even remember.*

Aspen cocked his head and stared at her oddly.

"Give me your staff," she said, louder this time.

And Aspen deserves better than this. His people deserve bet-

ter. He will be a good king. A great king. And who will miss a midwife's apprentice compared to that?

She knew the answer to that: *nobody.* Then she looked at Aspen. *Well, maybe one person will miss me.*

"Aspen," she said, then corrected herself. "Sticksman, give me your staff."

He straightened. Looked down at her. *When did he get taller than me?*

And then the Sticksman spoke; it was a single word. "No."

"What?" she exploded. "I made the best offer you will ever have, and you say no?"

He shrugged. "You do not want it."

He's right. I don't. I want it less than anything I've ever not wanted. But . . .

He stared at her.

"I need it." Tears were in her eyes now, and Aspen looked blurry. "I need to free you." She wiped at her eyes, looking away from him so the tears wouldn't fall. There were two bodies at Old Jack Daw's feet now and a dagger—probably poisoned—in his hand. It didn't matter; there was a whole horde of creatures ready to cut his head off. One of them would eventually succeed.

"It does not matter. You do not want to take it, and I cannot give it to you." Aspen pulled the sleeves of his robe down fussily. "Furthermore, I do not require freedom. I require two pennies for each passenger and a silver for the

Sticksman." He looked smug about getting his sentence out uninterrupted.

I'm losing him, Snail thought. *But who in their right mind would* want *to take on the Sticksman's curse?* She looked at Aspen. He'd always wanted to do something noble.

An ogre charged Jack Daw and got the drow's dagger in his eye for his troubles. But the dagger stayed there, and now Jack Daw was unarmed and doomed.

Who would want to live that desperately?

"Sire!" Snail shouted as loudly as she could to the new Unseelie king. "Hear me!"

The former Sticksman glanced over at her, then raised his hand. "Hold." His horde stopped in their tracks, weapons still at the ready. He peered closer at Snail, his big, blue eyes boring into her. "I know you, do I not?"

Do I not? she thought. *What a toff!*

She knew how to deal with toffs.

"Yes, Your Majesty," she said smoothly, and bowed low. Aspen tugged at the edge of her riding tunic.

"I require—"

"Shush!" she hissed back at him. "The king has your payment." She stepped out of the boat and called, "May I approach, Majesty?"

He waved a thin hand at her.

"Sire," she said in a normal tone of voice when she was close enough, "I am the boon companion of the prince who so recently saved you. And as such . . ." She paused and bowed low once more. *You can never bow too much to these toffs.* "I would ask a boon of you."

He didn't look convinced.

But what does a convinced bug-man look like anyway? "And," she added, before he could refuse her out of hand, "I can tell you where to find more of your kind. Possibly they're family of yours."

The Unseelie king leaned forward eagerly. "I have not seen my family for . . . for quite some time."

"They live with the changelings who have taken care of them for years, Majesty."

The Unseelie king straightened and went on, sounding toffy once again. "For the service your companion has done me and for information on my family, I will most certainly grant you a boon. What is it you ask of me?"

Snail pointed at Old Jack Daw. "I need you to spare that drow."

"Absolutely not," the Unseelie king spat. "I have had pretenders on my throne for far too long. I will make an example of this one."

"But, sire," she answered quickly. "I only require you to spare him for a short while so he may do one thing for me. If he refuses . . ." She smiled at Old Jack Daw. It wasn't a pleasant smile. "Then you can do what you like."

"And if he does not refuse?"

"I think you'll want to spare him anyway. Either way," she said, "I'll consider my boon granted."

The Unseelie stood considering for a few moments, then he nodded. "Your short while begins now. Do not make me wait overlong."

Yes, Your Toffiness, she thought, but wisely said nothing out loud. She marched toward Old Jack Daw, who frowned at her.

"So the little servant girl bargains with royalty for my life?" he rasped. He looked old and tired and grey.

But not defeated, she thought. *Not yet. Good.*

"Why would you do that?" he said.

Snail knew he wasn't actually curious. He was just buying time. His eyes traveled over her, looking for weapons he could grab, she assumed. Or considering her worth as a hostage, if he could get hold of her. But she answered him anyway.

"Not for you," she said.

"Oh," he said, looking back at Aspen in the boat. "For him."

"Yes, for him." She glared up at him. "You deserve to die. But I'm giving you a choice: die here and now, or perhaps live forever."

Jack Daw snorted, and the loose grey skin under his chin waggled. "Live forever as the Sticksman? With no memory of who I was? I'd rather die right—"

"Don't say it!" Snail said. "Or it will be so. But think, old drow—a lot can happen in a thousand years or more. Maybe someone will do for you what Aspen did for the king"

She waited for his answer thinking: *Though not if I can help it.* "So choose, drow. Life or death."

It was no choice at all, really. Drows came out of the egg clawing and fighting for life, and Old Jack Daw was the greatest fighter and clawer of them all. He gave Snail a defeated nod.

"Call him."

"I will," she said, turning back toward Aspen and the king. But then she stopped. "But you have to want to live. *Want* to take the Sticksman's place."

"Call him," he growled at her, and for a moment she heard the voice of a creature who had upended two kingdoms and been a hairbreadth from ruling over all of Faerie. "I want to live."

Maybe this isn't such a great idea. Maybe I should just let the Unseelie king kill him.

But then she thought of Aspen poling the river in a long black cloak for all eternity and knew that she couldn't leave him to that fate.

"Sticksman," she called again, as she and Jack Daw walked to the shore. The Unseelie king waved his arm, and the horde parted to allow them through. "I have someone who requires passage."

Aspen watched them approach stonily, then grumbled at Snail when she was close enough to hear. "It is dangerous to toy with the Sticksman. You said you required passage, and yet you have no pennies nor silver. And this one," he said, looking at Old Jack Daw, "does not require passage and will not for—" He stopped, eyes widening. "For as long as I can tell."

Old Jack Daw looked down at Aspen, and Snail could see him scheming and straining to find another way out. But he was surrounded by a suddenly hostile army and knew the only escape was the one Snail had given him.

"Sticksman," he said reluctantly, "give me your staff."

Aspen cocked his head. "Do you really want it?"

"Yes," Old Jack Daw said, snarling. "I want it. I want to take up the Sticksman's staff and forget all that has befallen me. I want to forget you and your changeling girlfriend. I want to forget the years I had to spend listening to your whining and pining. I want to forget this ignominious defeat and the horror of—"

He stopped cold as Aspen placed the staff in his hands. He looked down at it, then back at Aspen, who was once again bathed in a golden glow.

"Neither of you," the new Sticksman said, looking at Snail then back at Aspen, "requires passage." His voice was bland and biteless, the total opposite of his tirade of just moments before. "And you will not require it for a goodly long time."

Then the newest Sticksman turned and stepped onto the

rough decking of his boat, gathering his blackwater cloak about him.

Aspen leaped to the shore.

"Sire," Snail heard someone say, perhaps one of the Red Caps, "are you just going to let him go?"

"There must always be a Sticksman," the Unseelie king replied. "Better him than me."

Snail let herself smile then and beamed at Aspen. "We did it!"

He looked at her strangely, his ears red, his face squinched. She frowned. "What?"

He was mute for a moment, then squinched his face up even more before speaking. "He called you my girlfriend."

She glared at him, her face now hot, too. But maybe not with anger. Well, not completely, anyway.

AFTERWARDS

cAs it is written in *The Great Book of the Two Kingdoms*, penned by the chief archivist of the Seelie Wars himself, one of many books published by his own imprint, Odd Books:

Thus the two kingdoms were united under two co-rulers, and there was a true peace. The practice of taking changelings was forbidden, and every human survivor of the Seelie Wars was given land in whichever faerie land they chose. Those who wished to return to their own world were shown to the Door and allowed through, where, it is presumed, they crumbled into dust.

The Seelie king—or more likely, the new Seelie queen—showed great mercy as the runaways, malingerers, cowards, and others who had hidden themselves away rather than fight were welcomed back regardless. And the Order of Midwives achieved the highest status in the kingdom, elevated by the Seelie queen, whose mother-in-law, the Dowager, became their most active supporter for the rest of her long life.

The moat troll raised his adopted child Og and many halflings with the great warrior and leader of the armies, Dagmarra, honorary member of the Poppy Clan.

The dead simulacrum, Maggie Light, was set up in a glass casket that stood in the front hall of the Seelie castle to await the birth of someone who might know a way to make her live again.

And though there must always be a Sticksman, no one—no living Seelie nor Unseelie, not man, woman, nor child—has ever seen him since the final battle of the Seelie Wars, for it is forbidden upon pain of death to call on the Sticksman for passage.

All the seers agreed that the peace that descended on the Seelie and Unseelie lands would last for a thousand years or more.

But a lot can happen in a thousand years.

Or more.

JANE YOLEN, called "the Hans Christian Andersen of America" (*Newsweek*) and the "Aesop of the Twentieth Century" (*The New York Times*) is the author of well over three hundred and fifty books, including *Owl Moon*, *The Devil's Arithmetic*, and the How Do Dinosaurs . . . series. Her work ranges from rhymed picture books and baby board books through middle grade fiction, poetry collections, and nonfiction, and up to novels and story collections for young adults and adults. She has also written lyrics for folk-rock singers and groups and done voice-overs for several animated shorts. Her books and stories have won an assortment of awards—two Nebulas, a World Fantasy Award, a Caldecott Medal, the Golden Kite Award, three Mythopoeic Awards, two Christopher Medals, a nomination for the National Book Award, and the Jewish Book Award, among others. She is also the winner of the World Fantasy Association's Lifetime Achievement Award, the Science Fiction Poetry Association's Grand Master Award, the Catholic Library's Regina Medal, the Kerlan Award from the University of Minnesota, the 2012 de Grummond Medal, and the Smith College Alumnae Medal.

Also worthy of note, she lost her fencing foil in Grand Central Station on a date, fell overboard while white-water rafting in the Colorado River, and her Skylark Award—given to her by NESFA, the New England Science Fiction Association—set her good coat on fire. If you need to know more about her, visit her website at www.janeyolen.com.

ADAM STEMPLE is an author, musician, web designer, maker of book trailers, and professional card player. He has published many short stories, and CDs and tapes of his music, as well as seven fantasy novels—five for middle graders and two for adults. One of his middle grade novels, *Pay the Piper* (also written with Jane Yolen), won the 2006 Locus Award for Best Young Adult Book. The Locus plaque sits on his shelf next to two Minnesota Music Awards and trophies from his Fall Poker Classic and All Series wins. His first adult novel, *Singer of Souls*, was described by Anne McCaffrey as "one of the best first novels I've ever read." For musings, music downloads, code snippets, and writing advice, visit him at www.adamstemple.com.

For more on this series, go to
www.theseeliewars.com